A SHADOWED LIVERY

Inspector James Given
Book One

Charlie Garratt

SAPERE
BOOKS

A SHADOWED
LIVERY

Published by Sapere Books.

20 Windermere Drive, Leeds, England, LS17 7UZ,
United Kingdom

saperebooks.com

ISBN: 978-1-913028-63-3

Prologue

At precisely twelve o'clock on Thursday, 29th September 1938, Peter Bishop fell five feet ten inches to his carefully calculated demise. Beneath the hood, his blood vessels burst as the rope choked the murderous life out of him. His neck snapped.

There had been six of us in the small observation room. I'd arrested the man and was trying to push out of my mind the horror I imagined on his concealed face. The prison governor was scrutinising the hangman's preparations, the chaplain was leafing through his Bible and the newspaperman stared fixedly at Bishop, probably wondering how he might write this up for the late edition. Alongside us was the doctor, fidgeting all the while, repeatedly pulling his watch from his pocket as if he was late for the theatre. Our final companion was a young warder, who had been given the job of recording the events for posterity. He stood apart from the rest and made copious notes on a pad. His scribbling and the doctor's shuffling feet were the only sounds to be heard above the ticking of the clock.

Bishop's knees had failed him briefly when the noose was put in place but his composure soon returned after Mr Markham made the final adjustments and whispered a few concluding words in his ear. The executioner knew Bishop's weight to the last ounce and the exact length of drop it would take to kill him quickly and with minimal suffering. But it wouldn't be painless.

One minute before noon, Mr Markham placed his hands on Bishop's shoulders a final time, stepped clear of the trapdoor and took hold of the metal lever which rose from the floor beside it. The condemned man stiffened. Governor Jackson lifted a telephone receiver, spoke a few short words, then nodded to his colleague on the other side of the glass. In the remaining seconds, as the clock moved to the appointed hour, I envisioned the same scene a hundred miles further north at Strangeways Prison, where the murderer's accomplice, Harold Stack, was facing an identical fate.

It might be ten minutes before Bishop's heart would stop beating, even though the life had already gone from him. This allowed sufficient time for the doctor, Governor Jackson, the note-taker and the hangman to descend to the silent chamber where Bishop's still-warm body now waited.

The prison chaplain, the editor of the *Birmingham Post* and I tried to share a few words but we were all affected by what we'd witnessed. I believed the man had been treated justly, much more so than the poor shopkeeper he and his mate had kicked to death on the street. Even so, I couldn't help feeling some compassion. I'd seen death many times and in many forms over the years and I'd never get used to it. Perhaps I was in the wrong job.

After a short while the Governor and doctor returned, telling us that Bishop had been formally declared dead. Hands were shaken and the cheerless party took tea in Governor Jackson's private rooms; it was an awful affair. I was thankful when, after a decent interval had elapsed, I was able to leave. The young warder accompanied me down the dark corridors until I exited through the lodge gate into the daylight on Winson Green Road. I was never happier in my life to feel the sun on my face and the clean air in my lungs.

Superintendent Dyer's office was on the third floor of the squat red-brick building in Warwick, which had been home to police headquarters in the county for the last half century. I'd been sitting in the canteen, drinking strong tea and playing a hand or two of crib, when a message arrived for me to go up to see him.

Henry Dyer rose from his seat as soon as I entered his room, stepped around his massive desk and offered me his hand. He was a great bear of a man, barrel-chested and six or seven inches taller than me. We looked like two different species. He was smiling, which was a relief. You only needed to be wary when the smile wasn't there.

'Come in, James, take a seat. You're well, I hope?'

I nodded, though I felt far from well. This case had been taking it out of me and the pointlessness of the hanging had made me feel sick, despite knowing Bishop would have carried on his vendetta if I hadn't caught him. Hopefully it would serve as some kind of deterrent to his pals, but I doubted it.

Dyer's office was as expansive as the man. The oak-panelled walls were decorated with certificates and photographs of him with local dignitaries, and I wondered if he changed them around depending on who might be invited in. The desk-top held only a single file and a framed photograph of his wife and daughter. They both looked happy, but that was before the girl, Sarah, had been knocked down and killed by a drunken driver. Seventeen years of age and her whole life taken away. Dyer never talked about it, yet, on occasions, I'd see the sadness cloud his eyes.

Our paths hadn't crossed much in my early days, when I was a lowly copper plodding the streets of Kenilworth. I'd worked hard and shown my aptitude for investigating beyond the obvious, so made Detective Sergeant in a little over five years.

Dyer and I then met more often, as he preferred to be kept updated directly on cases which interested him, receiving information "from the horse's mouth", as he liked to put it. We got on well and I'm convinced it was on his insistence I was promoted to Inspector a couple of years ago. When my Chief Inspector, Mark Blackwell, decided to take some time off to look after his sick wife, Dyer pulled me in to his team.

'Thanks for coming over to see me. I'd have called in to Kenilworth but I've been up to my eyes in it here since you finished up with Bishop and Stack. How did it go?'

'Unpleasant, sir. I wouldn't want to see that too many times. The case itself was nasty enough and having to go to the hanging put the lid on it.'

'Something I've never had to do myself, I'm glad to say.'

'Unfortunately, those two are only the tip of the iceberg, the foot-soldiers. There are some very nasty individuals tied up with that lot, and clever with it. Too clever to leave a trail from the likes of Peter Bishop, and I think it's going to get worse. They hate Jews and, sadly, shopkeepers like Shapiro make it too easy for them. I don't know why he couldn't just try to fit in more, be less obvious.'

'Easier said than done, James, don't you think? They look different from us and most of them seem to have some kind of foreign accent. Even if they changed their names and dressed as we do, we'd be able to spot them a mile off.'

'It doesn't mean they should be beaten up by mindless thugs, though, does it, sir?'

'No, of course not. Are you any nearer to finding who's behind it?'

I ran through the main possibilities with him but had to admit I was no closer to a breakthrough. Bishop and Stack hadn't revealed who was giving the orders and I doubted they even knew. A message would be passed down the line and the fools would willingly do as they were told. Dyer nodded and probed as I went through my explanation, but I could see he had something else on his mind.

'So how can I help you, sir?'

'Always to the point, James. How do you know I didn't invite you in for a cup of tea and a friendly chat?'

Now I was embarrassed. He was right though, why didn't I just wait for him to act out being a good boss?

'Sorry, sir. I thought you'd be busy and would want to be getting on.'

He leaned back in his chair, stretched and laughed; a terrifying, booming sound.

'You're right there. As you've guessed, I do have something I'd like you to take a look at. With any luck it won't be as harrowing as what you've just been through.'

One

The taxi swung out of the avenue and I got my first view of Grovestock House, its blindingly white stucco frontage gleaming in the autumn sunlight. The drive curved gently round a neatly manicured lawn and our wheels crunched on the gravel as we pulled up outside the front door.

As I stood outside waiting for the doorbell to be answered, I wasn't sure if there would be anything challenging in this case.

'Just go through the motions,' Dyer had said to me. 'There needs to be the appearance of a complete investigation, but we already know what happened. And remember, it's not me wanting another look at it, it's the Chief Constable. He's getting pressure from the press, who think we should have investigated the deaths more thoroughly. They're suggesting the case wouldn't have been tied up quite so quickly if the family wasn't so well connected.'

Briefly, we went through the file together. I recognised the outlines of the case from the newspaper coverage. "Warwickshire House of Death" had screamed one headline, followed by every grim detail of the tragedy. Lady Isabelle Barleigh had killed her wheelchair-bound son with a shotgun before turning the gun on herself. This had been quickly followed by the suicide of the young man's fiancée. What made the whole affair more chilling was that the couple were to have been married two days later. Instead, they were now sharing a graveyard. I'd felt ill reading the article but, on the face of it, the facts had looked clear. Nevertheless, I was hardly surprised when questions started to be asked about why the whole matter was despatched so quickly. The deaths had only occurred a few days earlier and, somehow, strings had been pulled to convene a quick inquest and then a funeral to replace the wedding celebrations.

Now I was wishing I'd argued more against being assigned to this one, especially as Dyer had taken me off the Jewish beatings investigation and passed it to that idiot Terry Gleeson. If what happened at Grovestock House was as clear-cut as the preliminary work suggested then why give it to me? I'd told him that there were plenty of other good coppers around who'd adequately tie up the loose ends. I think Dyer knew the Bishop and Stack case had given me a good deal of pain and he was trying to do me a favour. Or perhaps his instincts told him that the initial enquiry had been a bit cursory and, perhaps, unreliable.

Anyway, I hadn't resisted much so I'd left, briefly calling in to my station in Kenilworth, then home to collect a few things, arriving at Grovestock House before lunch. On the way I'd re-read the file and acquainted myself with the facts as they'd been recorded so far. It was unfortunate that a few days had passed and allowed the trail to cool but it couldn't be avoided in the circumstances.

The local constable, Sawyer, had been pretty thorough in his approach. He'd been telephoned about the deaths around midday, cycled over as soon as he could, arriving an hour later. By then, the body of the fiancée had been discovered; she had shot herself with the dead man's revolver. First thing he did was make sure the gates were guarded. Nothing to be done for Tom Barleigh, his mother or girlfriend, so he set about photographing the scenes and interviewing witnesses, several of whom told Sawyer that Lady Isabelle had been increasingly set against the marriage, though none knew why. He'd written his notes up swiftly and gone through them with Gleeson, who hadn't bothered to interview anyone himself. Just like him, idle bugger.

The local doctor decided there was no need for a post-mortem and Sawyer presented his evidence to the inquest, which made the same conclusions he had. It was starting to bother me that everything had been despatched so quickly, so neatly.

I had done my research on the family prior to my visit. Grovestock House had been built sometime in the middle of the eighteenth century when Thomas Barleigh had wanted a new home to reflect his recently acquired status as a Privy Councillor to King George III. He'd been appointed following his generous support to the monarch in a series of conflicts with France, particularly in the Americas. Thomas was no soldier though, he was one of the new breed of industrialists, building up a fortune manufacturing muskets and pistols. Items put to good use by George's army in its attempts to suppress uprisings across the empire.

Thomas's grandson, having become a regular drinking partner to the Prince Regent, was raised to a baronetcy when the prince ascended the throne in the early eighteen hundreds and the house had been refurbished and extended to celebrate. Shifts in political allegiance over the next two centuries meant Sir Arthur Barleigh, the present incumbent, no longer had the power and influence his ancestors enjoyed. Nevertheless, the family was still important in the social merry-go-round of the county, hence the newspapers' interest and the Chief Constable's newly-found desire to make sure the job was done thoroughly.

A man in his late forties swung open the door. He wore a dark jacket and pin-stripe trousers, and his hair was greying at the temples. He gave off the unmistakeable smell of brilliantine as he looked at me enquiringly over the rim of his glasses. He was beyond question a butler and I remembered from Sawyer's report that his name was Jervis.

'Inspector James Given, Warwickshire Constabulary. I believe you've been expecting me.'

'We have, sir. Sir Arthur asked me to prepare a room for you so I'll take you up if you'll follow me.'

'There'll be no need, thank you, Mr Jervis, I won't be staying here tonight. I've already booked a room in the village. However, you can look after my overnight bag for now if it's not too much trouble.'

He took it and asked if there was anything else I needed. I told him I'd like to have a look at where the deaths took place.

'Very good, sir, would you like me to accompany you?'

'No thank you, that won't be necessary, just show me where Lady Isabelle and her son died.'

He pointed to the left of the house. 'The shootings took place down there, sir, on the side lawn.'

I let the butler go about his business, instructing him to tell everyone in the house I'd arrived and would be conducting interviews later in the day. I didn't think for a moment I'd get through many but it would do no harm to put them under a little pressure.

Before heading to the side of the house I turned on the step and surveyed the grounds. It wasn't a grand estate by any means and I suspected it had once been much grander. Perhaps a profligate ancestor had squandered too much of the family fortune on high living. It still remained a couple of hundred acres at least, judging by the distance from the gate to the main house. A lawn, directly in front of the main door, was circled by the drive and bordered by several dozen rose bushes, whose scent would have been breath-taking in the height of summer. At its centre stood a magnificent cedar, fully thirty feet across and towering well above the roof top. The whole garden was walled or hedged on the two sides, with openings to further gardens, woods or fields beyond. The entire landscape sloped down to a lake sculpted into the fields below.

When I turned again and stepped back, I was able to take in the full grandeur of the house. There were two enormous bays rising to the roof and there were roughly twenty windows, all in the Georgian style. Ruefully, I compared this with the single window on each floor of my own little cottage in Kenilworth. The gravel crunched beneath my feet as I walked to the side lawn and through the gate. High walls and hedges surrounded the area and it was obvious that whatever had taken place here wouldn't have been seen from anywhere in front of the building. Not unless someone was close enough to the gate. I noted there was no other access, or exit, apart from a side door into the house. The side walls were of much plainer red-brick and of a much earlier period, the grand frontage being merely a façade. I wondered what else in this case might be not what it seemed on the surface.

'Good afternoon, constable.' I looked at my notes. 'Sawyer, isn't it?'

'Yes sir, John Sawyer.'

'I've had a chance to have a look at your report but there are a few things I need to go over with you, to get them clear. Well done with the photographs, by the way, a very thorough touch.'

'Thank you, sir.'

He'd joined me at Grovestock a few minutes after my inspection of the front gardens. He was tall even for a copper, towering over me when I stood to shake his hand. His blond hair and fresh features, accompanied by the flushed cheeks when I praised his work, gave the impression of an overgrown schoolboy in a policeman's uniform.

'I had my Brownie with me, sir; I tend to put it in my saddlebag when I'm out in case I see anything interesting to photograph on the way. There's not usually much use for it in my work round here, though. Lost cats, neighbour disputes, that kind of thing. I'm lucky enough to have a darkroom at home so was able to develop them myself as well.'

Sawyer's boyish enthusiasm was naive, but clearly he was smart and not afraid of using his own initiative. I was certain it would have been the first murder he'd looked at so he'd done well to keep calm and record everything as fully as he had.

'Why did you conclude Isabelle Barleigh had shot Tom and then herself?'

'Well, it all looked very obvious on the day, sir. The two of them were lying on the ground with the weapon between them. He'd been shot in the chest from close range, toppling him out of his wheelchair, and she'd shot herself under the chin, really the only way she could have done it with a shotgun.' Sawyer turned green as he remembered. 'Also, people from the house and the estate were there in minutes, so it seemed unlikely that anyone could have carried out a murder then disappeared down the road without being noticed.'

'Not likely, or not possible?'

He now hung his head slightly at the thought he might have missed something.

'I suppose it might barely have been possible, sir, for someone who knew the place well enough.'

I asked him if there was anything else at the scene, anything at all which might suggest a different set of circumstances.

'Nothing really, sir. The only slightly odd thing was that Lady Isabelle had a scrap of paper clutched in her left hand.'

'Paper?'

'It appeared to be a bit of a letter, judging by the partial address in one corner. It turned out to be that of Miss Bamford's father, Gerald Bamford. I searched the garden thoroughly but didn't find any more of it and presumed the scrap was all she had.'

'And what about Jenny Bamford? You concluded she'd committed suicide as well. Did she leave a note?'

'There was no note, at least none that I found. When I was let into Tom's room by Jervis, Miss Bamford was lying on the bed with the revolver on the floor below her hand. It seems that the gun belonged to Tom Barleigh and everyone knew he kept it in a drawer in his bedroom. She had a single bullet hole to the side of her head and the pillow was covered with blood, so it was clear she'd died where she lay.'

He looked queasy again so I let him settle before continuing.

'Did you interview everyone when you arrived?'

'I took statements from everyone there. You'll know from the file that Billy Sharp and Tom Barleigh's nurse, Trudi Collinge, disappeared before I could interview them. I would have liked to speak to Jenny's family as well, to see if she'd been unhappy and so on.'

'But you didn't manage it?'

'No, it wasn't possible. Parents are divorced, she's in Australia and remarried. We sent a telegram to the local police so they could let her know her daughter was dead. Her father showed up briefly at the funeral but then left part way through before I could speak to him. I asked one of the other lads to call round to see him but apparently the house looks like it's been empty for a few days.'

16

'What about Sir Arthur? Did you get a full statement out of him?'

'That wasn't easy, sir, but I did get something. I was told by the butler that Sir Arthur had some urgent business which he needed to attend to and it would be really helpful if I could interview one or two of the others first. It made no real difference to me so I just got on with seeing everyone else that I could. When I'd finished, Jervis came to fetch me to go to Sir Arthur's study. He seemed a bit surprised to see me still there but did agree to be interviewed. Apart from telling me where he was when each of the shootings happened he wasn't able to add anything to what everyone else had said.'

'Did he suggest any reason why his wife might have done such a thing?'

'He said he was at a complete loss about it. To be honest, he seemed ... overcome, if you understand me. Like he didn't really know what was happening. I thought I'd best leave it alone until I was told to do otherwise by someone more senior. I did telephone next day in case he was feeling any better but was told he'd been given sedatives and was sleeping.'

'Tell me about him. How is it that he's "Sir" Arthur?'

'He's a baronet and inherited the title. It's come down through about eight generations until he took it over when his father died at the end of the Great War. That was about the same time he married Lady Isabelle.'

'"Lady" Isabelle? She was a proper toff then, was she?'

'No, I don't think so. I'd be fairly sure she picked up the title from him. I don't know much about her but I've an idea she was just a local girl who got lucky.' Sawyer then came up with a question he must have been dying to ask since we met. 'Excuse me, Inspector, and I know it's perhaps none of my business, but why has it taken so long for someone to follow up the

17

case? I mean, I know Inspector Gleeson went through the file but he didn't even come down to the house, just met me at the station. Said there was no need. But now you've turned up.'

'You're right, it would have been much better if I'd have been able to make it straight away but I wasn't available. On the day I was still tied up with the Peter Bishop hanging.'

'I read about that case. Didn't they kick a Jewish butcher to death in Birmingham?'

'They did. Bishop and Stack scarpered but I got lucky when they were heard bragging about it in a pub. They were both members of a Blackshirt gang, followers of that idiot Mosley, and had been planning the attack for weeks. Anyway, by the time it was over, you and Inspector Gleeson had finished the investigation.'

I told him Gleeson had forwarded the file to the Chief Constable with a recommendation for no further action.

'If you hadn't made such a convincing case for a murder and two suicides it might have been chased up sooner.'

'I'm sorry, sir, it all seemed so clear cut.'

'Don't worry about it, you did a good job. I can think of half a dozen officers, with much more experience than you, who would have come to the same conclusion. It was only after the inquest, when the big boss started getting pressure from the newspapers, that he asked Superintendent Dyer to have another look.'

'And you think there's more to the case than meets the eye, sir?'

'I don't know, but it's all a bit too neat and tidy for my liking. Let's just sniff around a bit longer and see what turns up. If it's nothing more than me being overly cautious, then you'll gain more respect from your colleagues and I'll have had a nice day or two in the Warwickshire countryside.'

Sawyer filled me in on the other interviews he'd carried out with the household staff and the gardeners. No-one had witnessed anything and all except the butler were able to account for where they were when the shootings happened. Sawyer had also spoken to a friend of Tom's, Alan Haleson, who was staying at Grovestock House and would have been his best man at the forthcoming wedding. Haleson had reported his version of the events but was on his own when each of the shootings took place.

'So what would you like me to do now, Inspector?'

'It's imperative we find the young gardener, Tom's nurse, and Jenny Bamford's father. And I've to get a full interview with Sir Arthur. You follow up the first three as best you can. I'm going to finish reading the file and then go back to the bereaved husband and a few of his staff. Let's see how we get on and we'll meet up again tomorrow.'

I found Jervis in his pantry, a small room between the kitchen and main part of the house. This was the nerve centre of his fiefdom. There was all the paraphernalia associated with ensuring the life of his master was well run and comfortable: the wine coolers, ice buckets, silver trays, cutlery boxes and so on. The room also contained a small table and two chairs; an old one seemingly from the kitchen, and a slightly more welcoming one placed in the corner. Jervis had an open ledger on the table when I popped my head round the door. A number of others were neatly stacked on the shelf above him.

'You look busy, Mr Jervis.'

'Not really, Inspector, just catching up on some paperwork.' He smiled sorrowfully as he got up to beckon me inside. 'Much less to do now with fewer people in the house. We were expecting this to be such a happy time. How can I help you?'

The man looked upset and seemed to be putting on a brave face for the sake of the other servants. He must have felt the tragedy as heavily as everyone else.

'I need to see Sir Arthur. Could you go up and tell him I'm here and want to interview him?'

'I'm afraid I can't, sir, he's not here.'

'Not here? A moment ago you said he was in his room most of the time. I thought I asked you to tell everyone I'd like to see them today.'

'I'm sorry, sir, I should have said when you arrived. He decided this morning he needed to get out of the house so left quite early for a ride.'

'Does he often do this?'

'Before all of this happened he'd go out several times a week and could be away for hours. On more than one occasion he'd travel as far as Banbury and back in the day; a good three hours' journey in each direction. I believe he thought you wouldn't be here until the evening. I couldn't say when he'll come home but I'll let him know you want to see him if you're still here. He's said we need to give the police as much assistance as we can and I should put the house at your disposal if you need somewhere to stay or work.'

I was annoyed at Sir Arthur's absence but all I could do was interview the butler and hope his employer would return soon. I thanked Jervis for the offer of a room to work in, took a seat and checked some of the details from the file with him.

'So where were you at the time of the first shootings, Mr Jervis?'

'It's as I told the Constable, sir. I'd just entered the lift upstairs and pressed the button to come down. I wouldn't normally use it, of course; the servants aren't really allowed. We're supposed to use the side stairs, but I was bringing down a large basket of bed linen that needed to be aired for the guests due to arrive.'

'Surely that isn't your job?'

'It's usually one of the maid's jobs to fetch the linen but there was so much it needed someone stronger. I thought the first bang was something to do with the lift machinery starting up. Then, when I'd travelled a few more feet, I heard the second bang and was certain it was a gunshot fairly close by, much closer to the house than would be usual. I got out as soon as the lift arrived on the ground floor then saw Miss Parry at the bottom of the stairs, about to run out of the front door.'

There was a silence.

'And who is Miss Parry?'

I think I knew the answer before he gave it. It would be too much of a coincidence for it not to be her.

'Miss Elizabeth Parry is the housekeeper, Inspector.'

I hadn't expected to hear her name ever again. It made my stomach churn and my head spin.

'So what did you do?'

'I knew something must be wrong so I joined her. Mr Haleson, Mr Barleigh's friend, also appeared at that point and came with us. I wasn't sure which direction to go but she said it was on the side lawn so we went that way. I shouted for her to stay behind me in case there was still any danger.'

'That was very brave of you, Mr Jervis.'

'I don't know about brave, sir; I was doing my duty.'

I went on to question him about what he'd seen when he arrived at the side lawn and he repeated what he'd told Sawyer. He also confirmed he'd gone inside to find Sir Arthur straight after the bodies were discovered. He had asked Elizabeth Parry to tell the rest of the staff what had happened.

'You let Miss Bamford into the house when she returned?'

'I did.'

'And you told her what had happened?'

'Oh no, Inspector. I was under strict instructions from Sir Arthur not to say anything, that I should simply inform her he wanted to see her upstairs in his room.'

Jenny left him in the hallway and climbed the main stairs to the upper landing. Shortly afterwards he was making his way to the kitchen to join the other staff when he heard a shot from upstairs. He ran back through the house and up the central staircase then searched from room to room to try to find where the shot had been fired. He arrived at Tom Barleigh's room last of all and saw Sir Arthur and Alan Haleson standing over Jenny Bamford. A revolver was on the floor beside the bed.

His voice caught in his throat when he recalled seeing the dead young woman, though his face gave nothing away. I couldn't help wondering if he was perhaps fonder of her than of the others. There was nothing else he could tell me so I asked him to contact me straight away if he thought of anything important he'd missed. I didn't really expect he would. Jervis had a butler's loyalty so family secrets would remain secret.

Sir Arthur still hadn't returned when I'd finished with the butler. I decided to move on to the maid who had witnessed the first two deaths on the side lawn. I asked for her to be sent to the room which had now been put at my disposal, the "morning room". I'd spent several years at sea, often with four to a cabin, and it amused me to think the aristocracy have special rooms they only utilise at particular times of the day. I even think my own little cottage is spacious, having the luxury

22

of an extra bedroom for me to use as an office.

Marion Clark stood before me, looking nervous, and confirmed she was upper housemaid to Sir Arthur and Lady Isabelle Barleigh. She'd been in their employment for about two years. There was something about the girl's face that hinted at a touch of stupidity and though she was twenty years old or thereabouts, she looked much younger.

'You were interviewed by Constable Sawyer on Tuesday, weren't you, Marion?'

'Yes sir, I was, sir.'

'Well, I'm a detective and an Inspector, so much more senior than he is and there can be no lies from you. Do you understand me, Marion?'

If the girl had been nervous before, she now looked like she'd faint away any moment, her eyes darting this way and that, and her hands wringing her apron front.

'I understand, sir. I wouldn't lie.'

I told her to take a seat.

'You've known the family for a good while now, so what do you make of them?'

She appeared to struggle for words.

'They've always treated me well, sir.'

'I wasn't asking how they treat you, Marion. Were Sir Arthur and Lady Isabelle a happy couple?'

'That wouldn't be for me to say, Inspector Given, I'm not one for telling tales.'

'But that's exactly what I want you to do, Marion. In fact, I'm actually *expecting* you to tell tales. We have three deaths here and I dearly want to get to the truth of what happened. But we'll perhaps come back to what you think of the family a little later. For now you can tell me what you saw on Tuesday.'

'Tuesday? Well, sir, Tuesday is my day for cleaning Mr Tom's room. His nurse, Miss Collinge, sees to it most days but once or twice a week the other staff take a turn and on Tuesday it's me. I start with the beds, then brush the carpet and finish up by tidying his desk.'

For some reason this turned on the waterworks and we had to pause for a minute or two.

'I'm sorry sir, it's just the thought of it... Mr Tom is — was — very fussy, you know and didn't want us messing about with his papers, only to put them neatly into piles where he left them. I was at the desk, and I could see out of the window and across the side lawn. It was such a lovely day I couldn't stop myself from looking out for a few minutes. I wasn't slacking sir, honest I wasn't. If only it had been raining then none of this might have come about. Mr Tom wouldn't have been outside and his mother wouldn't...' She sniffled and I was certain she'd open the sluice gates again.

'Hold on, Marion, let's stay with what you saw out of the window.'

There was more sniffling and a blow of her nose before we could resume.

'As I said, sir, I was by the desk, and looking out of the window at Mr Barleigh out on the lawn. He sat in his wheelchair reading most days when the weather was good enough. Always very fond of his books he was, sir, even before his accident.'

'You were here before that happened?'

'Oh yes, sir, though I hadn't been here long then, a great shock to us all it was, especially to Lady Isabelle. She seemed to worry about him all the time after he came back from the hospital.' The maid looked like she was going to tell me more but caught herself and returned to my earlier question. 'Sorry, sir, I was telling you what I saw. Suddenly the blackbirds pecking for worms took off and Lady Isabelle came into view, from the front gate I think, though I couldn't be sure. I straight away thought something must be wrong, 'cos her ladyship seemed to be shouting and waving her hand about like she's half mad.'

'What about the other hand?'

'The other hand? Well, I think she must have had the shotgun under her arm because she was holding something close to her side.'

'Did you see the shotgun, Marion?'

'No, I didn't. But that's what it must have been, mustn't it, otherwise where would she have got it from?'

'That is something quite else. You remember what I said, and tell me what you actually saw, no more and no less. Understand? So what happened next?'

'Mr Tom looked up at her — I didn't see no more, sir, because Miss Parry, the housekeeper, had been watching me from inside the doorway and shouted for me to get on with my work.'

'So you didn't see the actual shooting take place?'

'No sir, can't say as I did. I heard the shotgun go off right outside, and Miss Parry and I both looked at each other but before we can do or say anything, there's a second shot. We were then so terrified, sir, honest sir. Miss Parry tells me to go back up to my room, quick as I can, and she heads off down the stairs to look for Mr Jervis. I...' She stopped, blushing.

'What is it, Marion? Remember, this is a police matter, we need the complete truth.'

'Yes, sir, Mr ... Inspector. Well ... truth is I didn't go straight back upstairs. I crept back across the bedroom and peeked out of the window. It was only for a second, 'cos I couldn't face it no longer, but what I saw was the two of them, Mr Tom and his mother, lying on the ground with the shotgun beside Lady Isabelle.' She stared sightlessly ahead, remembering. 'There was just the wheels of his chair going round and round...'

'Did you see anyone else there, Marion?'

'No, sir. All I could do was stare at those bodies. The blood and the stillness all around. There was no-one else there that I saw.'

The maid seemed transfixed by the memory and I had to prompt her to continue.

'It's all I know really, sir. I ran up to my room and stayed there until Miss Parry called all the staff together to tell them what had happened.' Suddenly she looked at me, her eyes focusing. 'Why'd she do it, sir? They were so close, the two of them.'

'Well, that's what I'm here to find out. Where were you when the third shooting occurred, that of Miss Bamford?'

'Just where I said, sir. Miss Parry had called all the servants together in the kitchen to tell them what had happened. She was shaking like a leaf and said there'd been a terrible accident. A minute after she told us Mr Jervis had phoned the police there was another shot, from upstairs.'

'Who was in the kitchen at the time, Marion?'

'Well, sir, apart from me and Miss Parry, there was Mrs Veasey, she's the cook, Peggy Shaw, the other maid, and Mr Perkins, the head gardener.'

'So there were five of you, is that correct?'

Clark slowly counted the names in her head and on her fingers to confirm the number. 'Yes, sir, that's it.'

'Mr Jervis and Nurse Collinge weren't there with you?'

'No, sir, they weren't. Mr Jervis had been waiting for Miss Bamford to come back and someone said Nurse Collinge was too upset to come down. She was very fond of Mr Barleigh, you know.'

'Had you seen Jenny Bamford arrive back at the house?'

'I hadn't, sir. As I told you, I went to my room like Miss Parry had told me and stayed there until she called for us to the kitchen. I don't know when Miss Bamford came back, sir.'

I spent another few minutes clarifying some of the points she'd made and I underlined a couple of items in my notebook, then told her she could go. There was still something niggling me about what she'd seen that didn't seem right.

Two

Tom Barleigh's bedroom was off a side passage which had the passenger lift on the opposite side, a little further down. I assumed the lift had been installed after Tom became confined to a wheelchair. It was a large room, occupying the upstairs rear corner of the house. I intended to return later for a more detailed examination but for now was trying to get the general layout and the key events straight. I checked what Marion Clark could have seen from her vantage point by the window and, as importantly, what she couldn't have seen.

The room was much as the maid had described it, particularly the general disarray of documents and photographs on the desk. I was pleased to see nothing much appeared to have been disturbed, with the exception of the bed covers. I was taking a last look from the window when I heard the lift come to a halt, closely followed by a tap at the open door. The woman stepping guardedly inside was two or three years younger than me and her pretty face was framed by long auburn hair. Her lips formed a cautious smile as I peered over my spectacles at her. I had never expected to see her again, yet here she was before me.

'Is it really you, James?'

'Hello, Elizabeth.'

Elizabeth Parry was tall for a woman, almost my height. We'd met at the wedding of a mutual friend when she was keeping house for a clergyman. Six months later, I wished I'd never laid eyes on her.

She and I hit it off straight away and soon were going out as often as we could, and the last time I saw her I'd asked her to marry me. She'd squeezed my hand and asked for time to think about it. I didn't hear from her for a few days so called at the vicarage. I was told she'd left her job and moved away. That was three years ago, before my promotion, and I'd never heard a word from her since.

'I'm working here as Sir Arthur's housekeeper, I came here after I left Reverend Gardner.'

Both of us knew she owed me more explanation than that.

'I-I'm sorry I never wrote to you, James, but everything happened so suddenly and my world was ... turned upside down. I just needed to get away. I did intend to get in touch but by the time it was all over I didn't know how to go about it without hurting you all over again.'

'What was it that was so serious you needed to run away? Was it me?'

'No, James, no. Don't think that. It was something personal and I wasn't sure you'd understand. I can't tell you about it now, but I will, I promise. If...' Suddenly she threw her arms round me, hugging me close. 'Oh James, it really is so wonderful to see you. I've missed you so much.'

Her embrace was as I remembered it and, despite all the hurt she'd caused, I found myself wanting to forgive her. But I'd almost fallen off the wagon when she left and now here she was again in my life. I pushed her gently away.

'I can't do this, Elizabeth. I'm here to investigate a murder and you're involved. A witness.'

Elizabeth's face fell, and for a moment I weakened. Then she nodded and we sat down, she in an armchair and me on the edge of Tom Barleigh's bed. She told me that when her life settled down she'd gone back to see Reverend Gardner but he'd died. An old friend of the Reverend's knew of the opportunity coming up at Grovestock House and recommended her to Lady Isabelle.

I found it difficult to concentrate and brought the conversation to an abrupt end, saying I would need to interview her more fully later.

'Of course, James, I hadn't planned on going out again today. If you're free later we may be able to take a cup of tea in the kitchen, I'm usually down there at about three o'clock.'

Despite the pain she had caused, Elizabeth Parry reminded me of better days, when the air was filled with the scent of fruit fields instead of the stench of death now cloying my nostrils. The life of a police officer leaves very little room for contact with pretty young women, unless they're colleagues, suspects or victims. As she left, I couldn't help thinking that taking tea with her again would be a very pleasant prospect indeed.

The room Jenny Bamford had been using revealed nothing other than the clutter of a young woman preparing for her wedding day. She'd worked in Leamington and lived in a small flat in the town, so this guest room had few personal touches in it. Her coat was hanging on the back of a chair and her gloves lay on the dressing table. It struck me Jervis must have been convincingly calm if Jenny Bamford took the time to remove her outdoor clothes before going in to see Sir Arthur.

I located the servants' stairs, which were behind a door at the end of the main corridor, safely hidden from the family and any of their guests. I made my way down, pausing for a minute on the landing to take in the view from a large window overlooking the side of the house. I could see most of the side lawn, the point where Tom and his mother had died, and a substantial area beyond it across to the boundary wall of the estate and the woods on the other side. Anyone standing here at the time of the deaths would have had a good view of events and might even have seen the escape route of any third party, if one was involved. Having made a note of this, I continued down the stairs, and through the kitchen, stopping off there to make my introductions to Mrs Veasey, the cook, before going out onto the side lawn.

Referring to my notes, and glancing frequently up at Tom Barleigh's window, I marked the limits of the area of the lawn which could have been seen from that vantage point. I also took account of any obstacles to what Marion Clark observed, noting in particular a substantial, mature rhododendron around ten feet or so from the side of the house.

I'd already seen, when I first arrived, that this area was screened from the front by a high brick wall, which continued all the way around two more sides, ending at the rear corner of the house. The side of the building itself completed the enclosure. From the little I knew of country houses I guessed this was once a productive vegetable garden. Now, where there would have been espaliers of apples, pears and figs, the wall was covered with a fine variety of climbing roses, still filling the air with a delightful scent even this late in the year. The only access was either from the kitchen or through the gate in the front wall. It would barely be possible to force a way through the laurel hedge connecting the gateway to the front of the house, and not without considerable damage to the hedge itself. The area was mainly laid to lawn, with one small flower bed and a few well-established shrubs. Only three windows overlooked the lawn, one being Tom Barleigh's bedroom, another was the kitchen and the third was the one I'd looked through on the servants' stairs.

On the day of the deaths, Sawyer, after taking the photographs, had produced his own plans of the places where the deaths had occurred. I could see his drawings of the boundaries corresponded very closely to my own. This suggested the location of the bodies he'd marked would be similarly accurate. Consequently, I took the photographs of Lady Isabelle and Tom Barleigh and laid them on the ground in their appropriate positions as indicated on Sawyer's sketch.

Firstly, I confirmed both bodies would have been visible from Tom's bedroom window and the kitchen window. Then I put down my coat and jacket with the photographs on and tried to view them from several vantage points in the garden, including each of the corners, the kitchen door and the gateway from the front of the house. With the exception of the area behind the rhododendron, which seemed to be well trodden, it was clear the bodies wouldn't have been hidden from the view of anyone on the side lawn itself. Now I realised what had been bothering me about Marion Clark's account.

I stepped out of the enclosed area and looked back through the gate from a number of angles, noting the bodies could only be seen when I was within a couple of feet of the opening. As I turned back I caught a glimpse of something shiny under the border plants. It was a small trowel. There was a letter 'B' carved crudely into the handle.

I lifted the tool and made a note of exactly where I found it. Once more I was turning to go back through the gate when I spied someone in workman's clothes coming towards me from the direction of the kitchen garden.

'What are you doing?' he demanded.

'I am Detective Inspector Given, and I'm here to investigate the deaths. And who might you be?'

'Begging your pardon, Mr Given, I'm George Perkins and it's just that we've had no end of busybodies prowling around the place, newspapermen and the like, since it all happened. I'm the head gardener here, sir, and it was my gun the mistress used to shoot Mr Barleigh.'

I asked him to say no more until I'd finished clearing up and made my final notes. We then went inside to the morning room so I could take down a statement. He'd been in the employment of Sir Arthur and Lady Isabelle for almost twenty years, since they first came to live in the house at the end of the Great War. I asked him how he got on with them.

'They were good enough employers. Lady Isabelle herself usually had a kind word and would send small presents for the children at Christmas. She'd often visit the tenants' and workers' families if they were unwell or on hard times. The Master was, naturally, always a bit more distant but pleasant enough when we met. I only once saw him raise his voice except when I could see it was deserved, like if the staff were lazy or something wasn't done exactly to his liking.'

'When was the "once"?'

He sniffed, and looked at me cautiously. 'Day before the shootings took place. I was coming through the orchard on my way back from the bottom field and saw Sir Arthur and her ladyship talking, walking away from the house. I don't think either of them saw me because they kept on arguing fierce until he noticed I was nearby. Then he stopped sharp. He greeted me in a friendly enough manner but her Ladyship didn't speak.'

Perkins had then gone about his business and Sir Arthur and Lady Isabelle parted in different directions, he further into the garden and she back towards the house. I asked him to take me through what had happened on the day of the deaths.

'In the morning I'd been up early enough, 'cos it was a fine day, and I went down to the woods for an hour to try to bag a pigeon or woodcock. I'm partial to a little pigeon pie and the Master is good enough to allow staff to take game so long as they don't abuse the privilege. I'd not had much luck, only taking one small bird which ended up being cooked up for the dog, 'cos it wasn't sufficient for my dinner. As usual, I left my gun in the corner of the potting shed when I'd finished and went to deal with a problem young Herbert, one of the under-gardeners, was having with a tree round the back.'

'What time was this?'

'Well, I'd heard the church bell ring as I entered the yard shortly before Herbert found me. It's a fine clock they have Inspector, rings the quarters as well as the full hours. Would have been just about eight o'clock.'

'So how long were you away from the gun?'

'It were about twenty minutes. I'd heard the bell ring again for the quarter hour when I was finishing off with the lad.'

'And when you got there the shotgun was gone?'

'Yes, it was. First off I scrambled round the shed searching for it and asked a couple of the men if they'd seen it but as soon as it became clear it really was missing I hurried over to let Sir Arthur know. I thought we should inform the police but he seemed in extra good humour and suggested it might be a prank.'

'He didn't do anything about it, then?'

'He said I should search around a bit more and have a word with the young boys working on the estate. But the gun didn't turn up. Leastways, not until later in the day...'

He was evidently upset and said he'd hardly slept a wink since the whole episode occurred.

'Perkins, you should have locked it up perhaps, but you can't blame yourself too much. Another gun would have been found.'

'Regardless of that, Mr Given, this was mine, and I'll never be able to forget it.'

'You've no idea who might have taken the weapon? Any of the boys in the garden?'

'Could have been anyone, s'pose, no-one would think twice if they saw someone in the yard, there's so much coming and going at that time of the day. The only one who keeps popping into my head is Billy Sharp.'

'Billy? Why him?'

'He was always messing about with the shotgun when he could get his hands on it. He thought I didn't know but you have to keep your eyes open when you're managing a bunch of men like we have here. Most are good enough, but some'll be sloping off for a smoke or a sleep given half a chance.'

'So Billy is one you'd have to keep an eye on?'

'Oh, not really, he's a hard worker and loves to be outside in all weathers. But he did seem to have a liking for my gun. I'd see him pretending to take aim at birds and cats in the yard when he thought I wasn't around. He always put it back where he found it though, and there was never a mark on it. I think he must have wiped it down on his scarf or something.' Perkins paused for a few seconds as if struggling to find his words. 'It's hard to say this, Inspector, because I like Billy and can't see how he'd do anyone any harm.'

'Go on, Mr Perkins, I have to know the truth, no matter how difficult it might be.'

'It's just — I'd caught him playing with my shotgun before I went out shooting. As I said earlier, Billy seems to love his work and will often be up and about very early. I don't think he can have been expecting me to be down in the yard by seven and was surprised when I came up behind and grabbed him by the shoulder. Nearly jumped out of his skin he did.'

'And he had the gun with him then?'

'Up to his usual trick of acting the brave hunter. I took it off him straight away and tore him off a strip. Told him he'd be for it if I caught him messing with guns again. He said he was sorry and wouldn't touch it any more. I left him in the yard to get on with his work. I can't believe he'd have taken it later and done these things, but I also can't get it out of my head that he might have. Especially now he's missing as well.'

Following Sir Arthur's reluctance to do anything about the missing shotgun, Perkins had gone about his business as normal, taking several of the men down to the orchard to do the final harvesting and tidying up.

'We were working at this when I heard the first shot. We've plenty of shooting around the place but most of the men who'd normally be doing it were with me at the time.'

'Did you go to investigate?'

'We all dropped our tools and ran towards the house but before we'd gone a few yards we heard a second shot. We stopped, scared for our own lives to tell the truth. I ordered the rest to stay in the vegetable garden and I carried on but a bit more cautious-like. When I reached halfway across the garden I saw three people run from the house and then to the side lawn. It was Mr Jervis, Miss Parry and Mr Haleson. They ran to the gate and suddenly stopped. I could see why when I joined them a few seconds later.'

'What did you see when you finally got there?'

'There were two bodies with Mr Barleigh's wheelchair lying on its side between them. I could see it was her Ladyship and Mr Barleigh, both covered in blood. I didn't know it straight away, but it was my shotgun lay close by Lady Isabelle.'

'Was anyone else there?'

'If you mean anyone who could have fired the shots other than Mister Tom or her Ladyship, then there wasn't, only the three from the house. Mr Jervis was more flustered than ever I've seen him. He's normally such a settled sort of a man, taking everything in his stride. He was out of breath. Miss Parry, for her part, seemed to go into shock and I thought she was going to faint clean away.'

'Mr Haleson was a friend of Tom Barleigh's, I understand?'

'He was to be best man at his wedding.'

'And Sir Arthur wasn't with them?'

'Sir Arthur? No, sir, he didn't come out of the house at once. He only arrived when Mr Jervis went back into the house to fetch him.'

Most of this matched with what Sawyer had included in his account of the interviews he'd carried out, though I'd gained a little more clarity on who was where at the time. Perkins, the actual owner of the shotgun, was lucky he had witnesses to where he was when the first shootings took place.

'You didn't see anyone running away when you were coming up from the vegetable garden?'

'No-one at all, Inspector, and it would only be a couple of minutes from where I and the other gardeners heard the shots to me having a full view of the house.'

This seemed to confirm Sawyer's conclusions were as reasonable as might have been expected. Perkins also corroborated Marion Clark's recollection, that several of the staff, himself included, were in the kitchen at the time of the third death. I double checked who was present and so was able to exclude a number of the household from any involvement.

Then I showed him the trowel I'd found and he immediately pointed out the carved initial.

'That's Billy Sharp's. Definitely.'

I found Elizabeth Parry in the kitchen at a little after three. I didn't want to talk to her with the cook listening in the background so we had a cup of tea then went through to the morning room.

The interview began routinely enough, although I had to remind her we needed to put our previous relationship to one side.

She gave me satisfactory answers to my questions, adding little to what I already knew and corroborating the maid's account of the first deaths. Elizabeth hadn't seen anything from the window, being only a step inside the doorway when Lady Isabelle crossed the lawn. She also confirmed what happened when she joined the butler and Alan Haleson outside the front door. Half a dozen witnesses had been with her in the kitchen when Jenny Bamford died but when I asked her where she was after this she pulled me up short.

'Shall we go out into the garden, James? It seems such a waste of a lovely day to be cooped up in the house.'

She looked slightly distracted so I thought she might have something to tell me which she didn't want overheard. Despite my better judgement I couldn't help enjoying the prospect of a walk in the pleasant late autumn sunshine with her. As we made our way through the main hall she took a quick glance at herself in the large gilded mirror hanging there. I caught a brief primping of her hair and an even briefer smile before she continued on her way. This made my head spin. Here was a woman who had deserted me without a word of explanation and now here she was, throwing her arms round me as soon as we met, then preening herself as if going in for the kill. I needed to ignore this and get back to the question I'd asked her earlier.

'In the morning room you were about to tell me where you were when Jenny died.'

There was an almost imperceptible intake of breath, and the slightest of blushes flushed her cheeks. So was she going to lie to me? Or was she simply embarrassed by my persistence? Elizabeth sighed and spread her arms, turning and drawing in our surroundings.

'Look at all this, James, sunshine, a beautiful house, idyllic gardens and yet such a tragedy. Who would believe three people died here less than a week ago? I can barely think about it without shuddering.'

'Murder and suicide are terrible things, Elizabeth, and it's why we need to get to the bottom of what happened. Why I have to ask everybody, including you, these questions.'

'I know, James, but you mustn't blame me for not wanting to talk about it. I can't say I know anything about Miss Bamford's death, really. I was in the kitchen at the time and still terribly shaken by what I'd seen. Most of the other staff were there with me when we heard the shot from somewhere in the house. I think we'd have all escaped through the side door but for the two bodies still lying outside.'

'And no-one entered or left the kitchen between you calling everyone together and Jervis arriving?'

'No, I'm certain of that. There were only a few of us so I'd have noticed.'

'What happened when Mr Jervis came in?'

'He told us Miss Bamford had taken her own life. We were all horribly shocked. Mr Jervis himself looked really upset and young Marion was almost hysterical. Mr Jervis said the police would be arriving soon and we should all stay in our rooms until called for, so that's what I did. I'm afraid there's not much more I can tell you.'

'And you stayed in your room until Constable Sawyer called for you?'

'Yes.'

'Thank you, Elizabeth. I'm sorry I've had to put you through this again but I'm sure you understand it's necessary.'

'I do, James, you're only doing your job, after all. May I go now?'

As she walked away I wondered why she'd left so abruptly when I asked about her whereabouts after Jenny's death.

Peggy Shaw was small, pretty and lively, completely different to Marion Clarke. She was the kind of girl you felt you'd be friends with straight away and I was certain she'd have at least one young man from the village in tow at all times.

We were back in the morning room and the second maid was sitting across the table from me, her hands folded demurely in her lap. She didn't seem to be at all nervous in the situation.

'Tell me, Peggy, where were you when Mr Barleigh was shot?'

'Well, sir, I was just going up the back stairs from the kitchen. I remember I was only two or three steps up when I heard the first shot outside.'

'You knew it was a shot then?'

'Not at the time. I didn't know what it was, just a big bang, it was only later I found out, when we were all in the kitchen.'

'Why were you going upstairs?'

'I knew Mr Jervis had gone up to collect the linen and though he said he'd do it I thought he might need a hand. It was my job after all. I didn't get there though.'

'What happened next, Peggy?'

'Well, sir, I took another couple of steps then the second shot went off. I still didn't know what it was for sure but was now a bit frightened. I stood on the stairs with my back to the wall for a minute, trying to decide what I should do. Then I slowly went to the landing and looked out of the window. I couldn't believe it when I saw Mr Barleigh and her Ladyship sprawled out on the grass. There was lots of blood, I've never seen anything like it.'

Something in the girl's story suggested it wasn't the first time she'd told it and I guessed it had resulted in her being bought a drink or two over the past few days.

'You had a good vantage point up there, Peggy; did you see anyone else?'

'Actually, sir ... yes, I did. I saw Billy Sharp.'

Three

As the day drew to a close Sir Arthur still wasn't back from his ride, so there was nothing else to be achieved at the house. I went into the village, where I'd arranged to stay at the Victory public house. It was less than twenty miles to my home in Kenilworth but I'd probably be at Grovestock House for a couple of days so the journey back and forth hardly seemed worthwhile.

It was almost dark when I arrived outside the Victory. There was now a coldness in the air which often follows a bright autumn day, the gods telling us we shouldn't be fooled by the sunshine because winter isn't far off. I went inside, where I was greeted by a roaring fire and the friendly landlord, who introduced himself as Mr Terence Cudlip. We chatted for a few minutes before he took me up to my room and I was pleasantly surprised at its decor and spaciousness, even though it was a simple country pub.

Before dinner I phoned Sawyer to pass on the news that Peggy Shaw had seen Billy Sharp climbing over the wall into the woods beyond the house shortly after the first two shots. I told him to ask around if anyone had seen Sharp in the village. Afterwards I made my way down to the bar and ordered a glass of Vimto. I hadn't been in a pub for a while and the smell of the hops and yeast almost sucked me in but I stuck with the soft drink.

The landlord offered me an evening newspaper which I read for a little while but the pages were full of news of Mr Chamberlain's triumphant return from Munich. Like everyone else, I was pleased a war seemed to have been averted.

Nevertheless, I couldn't help thinking that if the price was gifting part of a country to Herr Hitler, the postponement of the conflict would only be temporary. Sudetenland may not mean a fig to most people in England but the same might have been said of Sarajevo twenty-five years ago, when events there soon led to the deaths of millions of young men across Europe.

I remembered my time in Germany when Hitler was released from prison and was idolised by his followers, ready to do anything he asked of them for the glory of 'the Fatherland'. I found it hard to understand how the Prime Minister could be taken in by him.

As ever, the papers reflected the inability of people to see what was in front of their noses. Whilst an article on the front page related measures being taken against Jews in Germany and another discussed the sorry conditions of Czech refugees, correspondents on the inside pages were praising the Prime Minister to the hilt, with one person proposing a national collection to buy him a country estate so he could enjoy his treasured hobby of salmon fishing.

I turned my thoughts back to the case. I couldn't shake from my head the sense that something wasn't right. With three tragic deaths, how could it be? But there was something beyond this, something I couldn't quite reach. And it was sitting on my shoulder, casting a shadow over the entire scene. For some reason I couldn't accept the version of events which had been taken to the coroner. There was something I wasn't seeing and I felt in my bones I was missing something vital. All I could do for now was to examine the evidence, carry out the interviews and hope it would all become clear.

Dinner was plain enough fare. It was clear the proprietor had been hoarding food with a view to a more negative outcome from the Prime Minister's Germany trip. I decided to spend another hour in the bar before going to bed. I was dealing a few hands of patience and watching some locals playing darts when a young man came in and sat down on a barstool beside me. He ordered himself a drink and exchanged a few pleasantries with the landlord before turning to me.

'It's Mr Given, isn't it?'

I was surprised, but confirmed he was right.

'I'm Alan Haleson, a friend of Tom Barleigh's. I was told at the house I might find you here.'

'Ah, Mr Haleson, I tried to speak to you earlier but was told you'd gone out for the day.'

'Yes, I had to go into Birmingham urgently with everything that has been happening over the last couple of days.'

'Sorry? I'm not sure I understand you.'

'Oh, I assumed you knew that I'm a civil servant. I'm attached to the Foreign Office and part of the team involved in the Munich discussions. I should have been in Germany with them but for all that's gone on here. The Prime Minister keeps an office in his constituency in Birmingham so I was able to make contact with my colleagues through there. There's a mass of things to do now Mr Chamberlain is back so I have to leave for London first thing in the morning. Jervis said you'd been looking for me so thought I should try to catch up with you before I go.'

Haleson went on to tell me he'd known Tom Barleigh since their first schooldays together and though after leaving school they lived some distance apart, they'd always kept in touch and visited each other regularly. So close was their friendship that he was to have been Mr Barleigh's best man and had travelled up to Grovestock House for that reason. Following the tragedy he'd stayed on to help as best he could. I asked him to go through a few things whilst he was with me and he agreed but was adamant he had to get back to London the next day.

'Was there any hint something was wrong in the household?'

'Not in the household generally, although Lady Isabelle was still trying to put Tom off the marriage, so he was a bit out of sorts.'

'Oh?'

'He seemed quite ... morose in the two or three days before the wedding, something not normally in his nature. Even in the days following his terrible accident he had never lost his cheerfulness. So it was a surprise to see him so fed up, but I initially put this down to the normal bridegroom jitters.'

'Why was his mother opposed to him getting married?'

'She was over-protective. She believed she was the only one who could look after him and that Jenny was only marrying him because she felt sorry for him. Lady Isabelle had been on about it for weeks but Tom was having none of it.'

'What made you change your mind?'

He was silent for a moment. Then he said, 'It was something that happened on Monday night. I'd been out for quite a long walk after dinner so decided to use the lift rather than stagger up the stairs. I'm not usually quite so lazy but on this occasion I was suddenly very tired. As a result I came out in the corridor by Tom's room and heard him choking and cursing from the other side of his door. I called to ask if he was all right but he shouted: "Get out of the house now, Alan! I don't know how this whole affair will end but you don't want to be here when it does!" I tried the door but it was locked and no amount of argument would get Tom to let me in.'

'So what did you do?'

'What could I do? I had no alternative than to leave him to it. I was worried he'd finally realised Jenny might be marrying him for the wrong reasons.'

'How do you mean, the wrong reasons?'

'Well — I don't know, just not simply for love. I'm sorry, Inspector, I really don't have time to go into it more now, and I'm not sure I could explain it properly. I have to leave early in the morning and there are papers to prepare before I go to bed. Suffice it to say it wasn't a match made in heaven.'

I pressed him but he stayed firm. He promised that he'd write to me as soon as possible, providing a full account of the day the shootings occurred.

Haleson had pressing business for the Prime Minister, so I doubted I'd be able to prevent him leaving even if I tried. I'd have to trust he'd be easy enough to find if he didn't honour his word.

I didn't sleep much that night. The discussion with Alan Haleson had left me disturbed and I was uncomfortable that I had let him go off without providing a full statement.

The story of an otherwise loving mother suddenly turning on her son and killing him was troubling me. It seemed impossible that her unhappiness with his planned marriage would be enough to turn Lady Isabelle into a murderer, no matter how much Tom Barleigh was out of favour; it was paradoxical. I decided to proceed on the basis someone else was involved until I had clear evidence to the contrary.

This early in an investigation everyone has to be treated as a possible suspect, regardless of rank or station, unless they have a cast iron alibi. I understood from the gardener that Haleson had arrived on the side lawn along with the butler and Elizabeth. It was obvious that any of them could easily have dashed from the scene of the killings and through the kitchen into the main part of the house before leaving again via the front door. I couldn't believe Elizabeth might be involved but she needed to be considered along with the others. As for Haleson, I'd not even asked him to account for his whereabouts and now had to hope he'd tell the truth if, and when, he wrote to me.

I was also out of sorts by being in new surroundings. The room in the Victory was comfortable enough and, God knows, I'd slept in far worse accommodation in my time. Years at sea in cramped, shared cabins, constantly rolling and echoing with engine sounds, or months on end sleeping in fruit pickers' sheds, should have meant I could sleep anywhere, but the first night in any bed other than my own always brings on a bout of insomnia.

About two in the morning I got up and tried to make more sense of the files Sawyer had prepared. I went through the photographs of Lady Isabelle, young Barleigh and his fiancée, examining them from every angle but, even though I was awake, my mind wasn't functioning efficiently enough to generate any flashes of insight. So I went back to bed and continued to toss and turn throughout the night. I must have finally drifted off because I woke up with a start when Cudlip rapped on my door to let me know breakfast was almost ready. I slipped on my glasses to read the time on the bedside alarm clock and saw it was a little after eight.

The night had left me tired and sullen, and certainly not in any mood for Cudlip's heartiness as he served me a mountain of bacon, sausages and eggs. I tried hiding behind the newspaper I'd saved from the previous day but the landlord wasn't going to leave me in peace.

'What's the plan today, Inspector?'

'I have to go up to Grovestock House again later but thought I'd take a stroll around the village first. Buy a newspaper and suchlike.'

Cudlip laughed. 'That's the first ten minutes gone then. Not much to see around here.'

'Perhaps you're right. Still, it's not a bad morning and the fresh air might wake me up.'

Seemingly satisfied he'd done his duty for the time being, he left me to finish my breakfast, returning when I was halfway through my second cup of tea.

'Anything else I can get you, sir? More tea? Another slice of toast perhaps?'

I patted my increasingly tight waistcoat, protesting I was too full to touch another thing and he started to clear away the dishes. 'Actually, Mr Cudlip, there is another thing you can help me with. I was wondering if there'd be anyone in the village who'd know anything about the Barleighs or Miss Bamford. Any thoughts?'

'Well, I can't think of any particular friends, the family kept pretty much to their own kind, if you get my drift, and Miss Bamford wasn't actually from the village herself. I do know the son had spent a bit of time recently with Miss Leeming.'

'And she is?'

'She'd have been the schoolmistress, retired now. She taught my boys and they always thought very highly of her.'

'Did she teach Tom then?'

'Oh no, he was boarded out to a place up in Henley-in-Arden. A "prep school" do they call it? That's where he'd have met the young man you were talking to last night — Mr Haleson. I can't say why Tom Barleigh and Miss Leeming had struck up a friendship, it's only something I picked up in the bar.'

It was chillier outside than I'd expected and I shivered as I stepped into the morning air. I buttoned my overcoat, pulled on my leather gloves, and looked around me. It had been dark when I arrived the previous evening and I'd not seen anything of the village, there being nothing as civilised as streetlamps in this part of the world.

The street was deserted except for one or two parked cars and a postman making his way from letterbox to letterbox. His bicycle leant against the wall of a house, suggesting he had a much larger area than Priors Allenford to cover on his daily round. He looked briefly across at me and tipped his cap before continuing with his morning's work.

The Victory was part of a jumbled terrace of buildings, a number half-timbered, the remainder stone built, their roofs at varying heights and a similar mix of slate, tile and thatch. Priors Allenford had been built over many centuries and its builders demonstrated no commitment to maintaining any sense of uniformity. The terrace was perhaps a hundred yards long, though I could still smell the bakery on the distant corner. I would certainly have headed towards it if I hadn't been so full from the feast Cudlip had forced on me.

Another higgledy-piggledy, but shorter, terrace lined the opposite side of the road, punctuated at each end by a narrow lane. At the side of one of these lanes stood the church, its square clock-tower dominating the skyline. At the other end, a series of individual cottages, each with its own hedge or picket fence, seemed to smudge the view until the road turned away towards the west. The church bell tolled out for half past nine.

I followed Cudlip's directions to Miss Leeming's cottage, which lay slightly off the main road, only a few minutes' walk from the Victory. Even though it was still quite early, and the sunlight was barely breaking through the clouds, I could see the lady I assumed to be the ex-schoolmistress already at work in her garden. I'd imagined her to be fairly elderly, frail, silver hair, walking stick and all of that. Instead, she appeared to be only recently retired, her hair still dark and with the bright complexion of one used to lots of time spent outdoors. Her spectacles were perched on the tip of her nose, as if she only needed them for close work, and she peered over them as I came into view. She raised her secateurs in greeting and gave me a wide smile.

'Lovely morning.'

'It certainly is, but a bit cooler than I'd like. Beautiful garden.'

'Why, thank you. I do my best, you know, but it's getting to be more of a struggle. Not as young as I used to be. Are you out for a walk? I don't think you're from the village, are you?' She pointed at my shiny leather shoes. 'This lane doesn't really go anywhere, fizzles out into a farm track beyond the trees, so I think you might need something tougher than those if you plan walking in that direction.'

'Actually, I believe it's you I'm looking for. Miss Leeming, is it?'

She now looked at me with a hint of suspicion.

'That's correct. Barbara Leeming. And who might you be?'

I explained who I was and told her I was investigating the deaths at Grovestock House. At this she cast her eyes down and shook her head.

'Such a sad, sad loss. I didn't really know any of them well, apart from the boy, but it's still an awful waste of life. Everyone in the village is so shocked.' She placed the secateurs in her basket and stretched her back. 'You'd best come inside if we're to talk. I'm about ready for a cup of tea anyway.'

Her sitting room was, unlike the woman herself, as I'd imagined it might be, with its low ceiling, dark beams, oak furniture and a small drop leaf table pushed against one wall. Miss Leeming added a couple of blooms to the already full copper rose-bowl on a white lace doily on the sideboard. Next to it was a silver tray with a china teapot and matching pair of cups and saucers. Reinforcing the image of learned elegance was a bookcase packed with novels and school books. She asked me to sit in one of the two armchairs looking out onto the rear vegetable garden whilst she brewed the tea and brought over the tray, placing it on a small table in front of the window.

'Now, how can I help you, Inspector?'

'I understand Tom Barleigh visited you on a fairly regular basis. Why was that?'

'He came first to ask for my assistance in researching his family. He'd heard I had a keen interest in local history and hoped I might have some records which would shed light on issues he'd encountered. I'm afraid that apart from a few papers relating to Grovestock House and to local people who'd served in the Great War I wasn't able to help him much.'

'But he still came to see you?'

'He did, probably once a week, sometimes more. His driver would bring him into the village, wheel him down the lane to the cottage and if the weather was good we'd sit in the garden, otherwise we'd sit here looking out. I think he was quite lonely. I was too, since I had finished teaching, so it was nice to have his company.'

They'd chatted about this and that, she said. He'd keep her up to date with his research and she would tell him what she'd been doing in the garden. Sometimes they would play chess or discuss stories she had seen in the newspaper.

'Could you tell me something of Tom's research? You said there were some issues bothering him.'

'Tom told me the family had fairly good material going back almost three centuries but there were gaps in recent years. It seems it has always fallen on the serving baronet to add the information on his current generation to the records. Unfortunately, Tom's grandfather had let it slip a little and Sir Arthur apparently showed little interest so the young man took it on instead. Tom used to joke he'd not much else to do with his time. But he did wish his father was a bit more forthcoming with information.' At this recollection of happier times, the teacher frowned. 'He was always joking, you know, despite his terrible disability, or perhaps because of it. He once said he always viewed his accident as a tremendous piece of luck.'

'Luck? How could that be?'

'I think he meant he could easily have been killed that day, like his friend. He wasn't especially religious, but he did believe in fate, that things, good and bad, happen and you can't control them so you have to accept them. Quite a mature view of the world for such a young person, don't you think, Inspector?'

I asked her when she'd last seen Tom Barleigh and she replied it had been about a week before his death.

'Did he give you any inkling there was a problem at home or that he was distressed about anything?'

'Not really. The last time I saw him he was as cheerful as ever. He did say his mother had been acting strangely and kept trying to put him off the wedding. She'd become even more forceful in recent days and seemed to be trying to talk to him about something but kept pulling back as if she didn't want to upset him. He was also displaying the usual nerves of any young man about to marry — but nothing out of the ordinary.'

'He gave you no indication of what his mother was trying to discuss with him?'

'I don't think he really knew, Inspector. We didn't speak about it for more than a few minutes. We soon moved on to photographs I'd found of his father and several friends taken a few days before they left for the Front. He was most interested in those and he asked me to point out who they were. Two of the other young men in them, Harry Stenson and Graham Cox, were killed at Passchendaele. Graham was my nephew and had been hoping to join his father's solicitor's practice after the War and Harry wanted to continue his passion for archaeology at university. Such bright futures thrown away.'

I'd briefly seen several photographs on Tom's desk and asked if the ones she'd given him might be amongst them. She thought it was a possibility but said she couldn't swear to it. It's interesting how, in the company of a policeman, even quite respectable people become more cautious. I asked her if there was anything else she could add.

'Not really, Inspector. As I've said, Tom was in fairly good spirits the last day I saw him. He was grateful for the photographs and excited that they might help him with one of the items he'd been puzzling over. He was his normal polite self but I could tell once he'd seen them he was itching to get back home. I think if he hadn't been stuck in the wheelchair he'd have dashed out of the cottage as soon as he had the photographs in his hands.'

I was on the point of thanking the teacher when a knock came on the door. It was Cudlip.

'Sorry to disturb you, Inspector, but a message has been sent down from Grovestock House that Sir Arthur is available if you want to see him this morning. Shall I let them know when you'll be there?'

The man who shambled up to shake my hand was even more of a surprise than Miss Leeming had been. Something in my upbringing had led me to picture landed gentry as tall, elegant, patrician and handsome. People literally head and shoulders in every way above the normal run of humanity. But here was a man for whom pity, rather than admiration, was the immediate response.

He looked to be over seventy, though he was, in fact, only in his fifties. His hand, briefly shaking mine, had a cold limpness and he walked as if one leg was slightly shorter than the other. Though he may have been taller he was now afflicted by a severe stoop which made him appear several inches smaller than me. His most striking feature was his face. The whole of his forehead and right cheek shone red and yellow with long-healed burnt skin.

It was clear he had once been a handsome man and despite his terrible injuries there was still a certain attractiveness in his features; a keen observer would see some of his remaining good looks were the result of recent and competent application of makeup. His lashes had been thickened and his hairless brows made to look less alarming. Within all of this, his eyes still blazed fiercely and intelligently.

'Ah, Inspector, I'm not what you thought, it seems. It is clear in your face.'

'I'm sorry, Sir Arthur, I don't mean to be disrespectful, but no, you're not as I expected you to be.'

'Well, no matter. You're not the first, and doubtless you won't be the last, to be a little surprised at my appearance on first meeting. In my youth, you know, I was considered quite a charmer. The real ladies' man. But then, like for so many of my generation, the Great War put paid to that. We seem to be squaring up for another fight with Germany, don't you think? As if we hadn't taken enough punishment last time.'

We chatted for several more minutes about the situation with Germany. Then, as if coming upon some kind of resolve, he paused and drew a deep breath.

'Well, Inspector, you didn't come here to discuss Mr Chamberlain and Herr Hitler, so let's get down to business. But first, may I apologise for not making myself available yesterday? You'll appreciate, I'm sure, that the last couple of weeks have been quite wretched.' He looked away, staring into the distance through his study window.

'Sir Arthur, if I could avoid putting you through this, please believe me I would. However, I'm sure you understand we need to get to the bottom of what happened.'

'But why, Mr Given? Are you saying your constable and the Coroner got it wrong?'

'No, sir, I'm not. We just need to tie up some loose ends and it would be most helpful if we can just go through a few remaining questions I have.'

'Very well, Inspector, please continue.'

'Firstly, can you tell me where you were when your son was shot?'

'I was in my room.'

'But you didn't hear the shot?'

'Of course I heard the shot, but this is a working estate, Inspector, there's always shooting — whether it's a guest out for sport or one of the staff chasing their dinner — it isn't at all unusual.'

'Wasn't this a little close to the house?'

'I presumed it was Perkins or one of the other gardeners dealing with a rat or something.'

'Did you think the same when the second shot was fired?'

'As I already said, Mr Given, gunshots are not uncommon around Grovestock House, even close to.'

'Could I ask you about the day before the shootings, Sir Arthur? I'm told you had an argument with your wife. What was it about?'

'Are you married, Inspector?'

I shook my head.

'No, I thought not. If you were you'd know domestic disagreements happen all the time but really mean nothing. My wife was on edge because of the wedding. She thought Tom was too ill to be married and wanted me to put a stop to the arrangements. She'd been talking about it for weeks so I merely told her she'd have to like it or lump it. Tom had made up his mind and that was that. She stormed off in a huff but we were talking again by lunchtime.'

'I see. Thank you for that, Sir Arthur. Can we now turn to the shotgun itself?'

'The shotgun? I understand it belonged to George Perkins but I know nothing else.'

'But didn't Mr Perkins report to you it had been stolen, sir?'

'Well, the man came in to see me in a bit of a state just after breakfast, saying his gun had been stolen, urging me to call the police. To tell you the truth, Inspector, I'd just had a bit of good news and was in quite high spirits. I told Perkins not to fuss and that there was a good chance it was one of the lads playing a trick on him. Perhaps if I'd taken him seriously none of this would have happened.'

He put his hands up to his face, pressing them against his eyes. I gave him a moment to recover.

His room was beautifully furnished, with bookcases lining two walls containing leather-bound books, probably collected by his family over many years. One, Salmon's *Ancient and*

Modern Rome, lay open on a walnut desk facing an enormous bay window. This window was the outstanding feature of the room, and provided a splendid panorama of the estate and the countryside beyond. Away in the distance I could see the tower of the village church, jutting skywards above a line of trees. The floor was covered with Turkish rugs and, while I'm no expert, they seemed to be of the finest quality. Although I'd been given to believe the baronetcy wasn't real aristocracy, there had been without doubt a substantial income associated with it.

'My apologies, Inspector.'

'Please don't apologise, sir, it's quite understandable. You were saying you'd had some good news. What was it?'

'Well, I suppose there's no harm in me telling you. It was money.'

'Money, sir?' I looked around the room again, slightly incredulous.

'Yes, money. Don't be fooled by the surroundings, Inspector. My income, in the main, is derived from investments the family made long ago and some of them have taken a bit of a battering in recent times. However, all this talk of war has brought quite a revival to Army spending — clothing, vehicles, armaments and so on — and I'd had news that morning of some very substantial orders received by companies in which I have an interest.'

'But you were only talking to me a few minutes ago how you deplored war and hoped another one might be avoided.'

'Oh, I do, Inspector. Believe me, if I thought there was anything I could do to prevent the conflict I'd do it. I have to be practical. It's not as if I'm newly investing in these industries. We've been with them through the bad times as well. Some people are going to make a fortune if fighting breaks out, so why shouldn't I be one of them?'

It was an honest, albeit callous, assessment of the situation. Could he be just as calculating when two or three deaths were closer to home?

'Indeed, sir, why not? I haven't any investments myself but I know times have been difficult over the past year or so. You would have been relieved to hear of this upturn in your affairs.'

'Quite so, Inspector. In fact, I had to go into town on Tuesday right after I'd spoken to Constable Sawyer. I needed to get to the bank to shore up the money for these ventures. If I hadn't done so they'd have fallen through and I might have been ruined.'

'And someone at the bank will corroborate your visit, I presume?'

'I'm sure they will if you ask them, Inspector, though I can't see why you'd want to bother.'

'Let's return for a minute to the time following the first shootings. You said you were in this room and thought nothing of the shots. Is that correct?'

He nodded.

'So what happened next?'

'Jervis came running in. Without a knock or anything. Most unlike him. He blurted out: "Come quickly, Sir Arthur. It's Lady Isabelle and Mr Tom. They've been shot!"'

'Were those his exact words? No mention that her Ladyship had shot your son?'

'No, I don't believe so. I can't swear those were the actual words he used but they're close enough. I think the poor man was so alarmed he'd just run up to inform me without thinking through the sequence of events. I hurried down to the side lawn with him and saw...' He stared out of the window again.

'So what happened next?'

'I told Jervis to go into the house to phone the police. I think I may have also asked Tom's nurse, who had just arrived, to see if anything could be done, but she confirmed they were both dead. I then told everyone they mustn't disturb the ... the bodies any further because the police would need to inspect them.'

'Was that it then, sir?'

'I left a couple of the gardeners to keep watch. Then I urged everyone else back into the house and went inside myself.'

'And did you all stay together until Constable Sawyer arrived?'

'No, I'm afraid not. I asked Jervis to tell the staff what had happened and then send them about their business as normally as possible, or go back to their rooms if they so desired. For my part, I returned here and stayed until Jervis sent Jenny up to see me.'

'What happened when she arrived?'

'She was looking radiant. It was as though the time away from the stresses and strains of the wedding arrangements had done her good. However, I think she sensed something was seriously wrong, even though I'd given strict instructions to Jervis not to say anything.'

'But wouldn't she have seen the bodies when she was arriving at the house?'

'I shouldn't think so, Inspector, because the side lawn is pretty well shielded from the drive. If the men were doing their job as I'd instructed she may have noticed a group of them standing there chatting, but not much else. If she had seen anything she didn't mention it to me.'

'How did she take the news?'

'Absolutely distraught, almost fainted when the realisation hit her. The poor girl began to tremble and kept saying "what will I do", over and over again. Eventually she calmed enough for me to offer to help her to her room but instead she shook herself away from me then ran out of the door.'

'Where did she go?'

'I presumed she'd gone off to her room. It was ... it was the last time I saw her.'

'Was anyone in the study with you, Sir Arthur, either before or after Miss Bamford returned to the house?'

'Are you asking if anyone can substantiate I was where I say I was?'

'If you want to put it that way, then yes, it would be helpful.'

'I'm afraid not, Inspector. Poor Jervis was in such a flap I didn't think it right to be ringing him to bring me tea or anything so I was quite alone. When Jenny ran out I just sat at my desk and stared out of the window.'

'The third shot — what did you do when you heard it?'

'Initially I thought I was just reliving the horror but realised this was, indeed, another shot and closer by. It seemed to have come from along the corridor so I dashed to Jenny's room.'

'Why did you think it might be Miss Bamford?'

'I didn't. It's just that Jenny's was the nearest, apart from Isabelle's. I knocked but received no answer so I went in. Her room was empty. I looked in Isabelle's room and then Alan Haleson's, because his was next to Jenny's, but both were empty. I went to Tom's after those and found Jenny sprawled across his bed.'

'Had anyone else arrived by then?'

'No, it was a few seconds later when Jervis and young Alan arrived. We checked Jenny wasn't breathing then left, locking the door behind us. There was nothing further to be done until the constable arrived.'

He looked a little pale but asked if he could assist me any further.

'The problem is, Sir Arthur, for the life of me I cannot understand why she'd do it.'

'Why?'

'Yes, sir, why would Lady Isabelle go to such lengths? I do understand she'd expressed unhappiness with the marriage — but to kill him? It makes no sense. With a shotgun? It seems too strong to me, Sir Arthur. What do you think?'

'Can any man understand what goes through the mind of a woman, Inspector? All I know is that Isabelle had gone on and on trying to stop the wedding for a month before she took the drastic action she did.' He once more massaged his temples and closed his eyes before speaking slowly, as if to himself. 'Whatever am I going to do?'

Four

When I'd finished with Sir Arthur, Sawyer joined me and I suggested we take a walk down by the lake. The autumn sun still shone but its power was fading as the days grew ever shorter. Golden leaves skittered across the surface of the water in a final regatta before the winter storms arrived.

Sawyer fastened the top button of his overcoat.

'Any particular reason for this, sir?'

'Not really, Cudlip's breakfast is still lying a bit heavy. He certainly knows how to fill a man up. I thought the exercise might help and, besides, that house gives me the creeps.' I glanced back up the hill and shivered. 'I'm never comfortable surrounded by that much money, especially when the family fortune is built on countless deaths. On top of that there's something not right up there, even *if* the Coroner's version is correct. A mother killing her own son because she didn't want him to marry? Hardly bears thinking about.'

'You said "if" the Coroner's version is correct, sir. Do you still think it wasn't?'

'I'm not sure. We've two of the staff still missing and several people whose whereabouts when the shootings happened can't be corroborated so I'm keeping an open mind. Any news on Collinge or the Sharp boy?'

'Nothing on the nurse yet but I've put the word out as you asked. She'll show up somewhere. As for Billy, I had an interesting chat with his mate, Alf Nash, when I called in to see him about another matter.'

Nash had been accused of stealing some bread and riding away on a bike he'd taken from Charlie Himlet's yard. When Sawyer tackled him, the lad denied it.

'He said it was Billy Sharp, sir. Nash bumped into him just after Billy had taken the bike. Told me Billy was shaking and saying he needed to get away. Claimed someone had chased him in the woods. Only other thing Nash could make out was Billy had been caught with a shotgun in the morning by Perkins, then saw someone take it from the shed.'

'And he didn't tell Nash who it was?'

'Apparently not. As I say, Nash could hardly get anything out of Billy, only that he was trying to escape from something awful. If someone was after him then it's not surprising he was scared.'

'Could he just have made it up, do you think? Trying to muddy the trail?'

'It's possible, I suppose. Young Alf Nash is a bit of a blabbermouth, so Billy might have lied to him.'

We'd walked the whole path round the lake when a cloud briefly blotted out the sun and the temperature dropped dramatically. I paused, taking in the beauty of the scene, the house up the hill to our left and the late afternoon light accenting autumn on the hills beyond the water. Several ducks swam towards their shelter, a magnificent confection in the shape of a pagoda, which someone had taken immense trouble to paint in red, green and gold. A short gangplank rose from the water into the entrance, an easy entrance for the ducks but not for any passing fox.

'Could we get back to the house, sir? It's brass monkeys out here!'

I laughed. 'Come on then, but I need to talk to you about Elizabeth Parry. Did you know she and I have known one another before?'

I filled him in as far as he needed, leaving out my marriage offer and the personal carnage which had followed her disappearance. Even so, Sawyer asked the obvious question.

'Do you think you should be ... well... You know, sir. If you don't mind me asking. Couldn't it be a bit difficult, like?'

I told him the truth; I just didn't know. I wasn't even sure a crime other than the murder of Tom Barleigh by his mother had been committed here. If one had, could Elizabeth be a reasonable suspect? Was my earlier relationship likely to blur my judgement? I hoped not, but Sawyer certainly had a point.

'I think I'll need to cross that bridge when I come to it. Let's keep it to ourselves for now and I'll talk to the boss about it when we get to that point.'

Sawyer looked at me sideways but knew enough not to disagree with his senior officer. I, for my part, hadn't a clue how I was going to raise it with Dyer.

George Perkins' potting shed was neat, tidy, and organised. I'd bumped into him on my way up from the lake and asked him to send up the gardeners to the yard. He'd suggested I went in his shed until he found them. The ten minutes I was waiting gave me a chance to look around where the shotgun had been taken from and find the place in the yard where Billy Sharp might have hidden when he reportedly watched someone take it. Needless to say, the shed bore no evidence of a lock and anyone could be in and out in no time.

Plant pots in rows straight as soldiers stood to attention on a third of a bench stretching virtually the whole length of one wall. I'm no gardener but even I could tell that preparations were already underway for the following season. Strawberry plants and rhubarb crowns were the only ones I recognised amongst the couple of dozen varieties of foliage waiting to be moved out to the cold frames and greenhouses. Every one of them looked healthy and it was easy to see why. The almost black compost in a bin at the end of the bench smelled sweet, earthy, and crumbled effortlessly through my fingers.

A further half of the surface carried evidence of this year's harvest; a wicker basket still a quarter full of apples lay beside a stack of trays of the fruit individually wrapped in newspaper. When completed these would doubtless be transported up to the house to keep Mrs Veasey well supplied over the winter.

I sat down in a dilapidated armchair when the two gardeners came in, holding their caps in their hands. One man was tall and the other small and fat like the pot-bellied stove warming my feet. I asked them their names. The smaller one answered.

'I'm Ted Ward and this here's Dickie Beasley. Mr Perkins said you wanted to see us.'

'You were the two on the gate after Constable Sawyer arrived, is that right?'

Ward, who seemed to be the spokesman, confirmed that they were.

'And no-one went out after that?'

'No, sir, no-one went out.'

'You were there the whole time? Didn't slope off for a quick smoke?'

'Well, we did have a smoke, but stayed on duty like we was told.'

Throughout the exchange, Beasley fidgeted and kept nudging his partner until Ward reacted by flicking his cap at him.

'Is there something you want to say, Dickie?'

The tall gardener looked like he wanted the ground to open up beneath him.

'Take no notice, Inspector, he's just being stupid.'

'I think I'll be the judge of that, Ted. Now come on man, spit it out.'

The gardeners looked at each other and Ward nodded.

'Go on then, Dickie, we'd best come clean.'

Beasley now stared at the ground as if his very life depended on it.

'I said to Ted we should tell the truth from the start, sir. After all, we know Miss Parry can't have had anything to do with what happened.'

'Miss Parry? What are you talking about?'

'She went out, Mr Given. Must have been before we got to the gate and after she'd been with the others in the kitchen, but out she was. She came back again about fifteen minutes after the constable sent us up there. Said she'd needed to get out for a walk.'

After the gardeners left, I headed for the warmth of Mrs Veasey's kitchen. She greeted me with a great deal of fuss and despite my protests soon had me well provided with sandwiches, tea and freshly-baked scones. All of the time she was preparing these the cook was throwing enquiries in my direction. Had I settled into my lodgings? Was I from around these parts? Then the one she really wanted to ask from the start: was I making any progress with my investigation?

'Slowly but surely, Mrs Veasey, slowly but surely. These things take time, you know, everything has to be checked and double-checked before we can be sure that we've got the picture straight. Take your own story as an example, Mrs Veasey.'

'My story, Inspector? I'm certain I told Constable Sawyer the truth. I hope you're not suggesting anything different.'

'Not at all. I don't believe you'd lie to the constable but you might not have told him *everything* you knew. It's just that we don't always see what's important when we're telling a story, do we? Little details might be missed out which make all the difference. That's why I'd like you to go through it again with me, if you don't mind.'

'I don't mind in the least, Mr Given, if you think that I can help in any way but, as I told Constable Sawyer, I wasn't even here when those awful things happened. I was down in the village.'

'Would you normally go out at that time of the day?'

'Only occasionally. If I'm short of anything I'd ask Phibbs, the driver, or one of the lads from the garden to collect it for me but we'd all been up to our eyes in the preparations for the wedding so there was nobody available. Sir Arthur had especially asked for some nice haddock for his dinner so I had to go into the village myself. I could have done without it, I can tell you; it was hectic enough in the kitchen as it was, without losing an hour or so on special errands.'

'It would have taken you as long as that?'

'Oh yes, Inspector. I'm not as fit as I once was —' the cook patted her not insubstantial hips by way of explanation — 'and it would take me around half an hour each way and I'd not get around the fishmonger and bakery without a bit of a chin-wag. I'd have gone out shortly before eleven. Sir Arthur asked me for the fish soon after breakfast, so I had to make up sandwiches and cold meats for lunch before I left because I wouldn't be back in time to do it later.' With this she let out a distressed moan. 'If only I'd gone straight away, right after breakfast, none of this would have happened.'

'How would that be, Mrs Veasey?'

'Well, I'd have seen everything from the kitchen window and might have been able to shout a warning. Perhaps Lady Isabelle would have stopped herself if she knew I was there.'

I did my best to comfort the cook, telling her that it was unlikely that she could have prevented what happened but I didn't sound convincing. Unfortunately it was true she might have made all the difference in the world by being in the kitchen that morning and there was no way of changing that. She hadn't done anything wrong by going later, but circumstances had conspired to make her feel guilty nonetheless. She took a good few minutes to settle down before I could continue.

'You told Constable Sawyer that you saw someone in the woods when you were on the road, is that right?'

'Yes, Inspector, I did. I'd turned out of the gate and been walking for about five minutes when I noticed a man, just standing there peering over the wall. We often have walkers in the woods and I suspect one or two must stop there to have a nosey so I didn't think much about it at the time. He didn't seem to be doing any harm and I left him to it. It was only when I was in the village that a couple of people mentioned seeing someone hanging around and asking questions. I thought then I should have shouted across to the stranger and asked him what he was doing there.'

'Did they say what he'd been asking?'

'Mainly about who lived here and what people thought about them. Apparently he showed quite a lot of interest in Miss Parry, how long she'd been there, what she looked like, if she ever came into the village, that kind of thing. You don't think he could have had anything to do with what happened do you, sir?'

'It's still too early to say, Mrs Veasey. Could you describe him, or was anyone in the village able to tell you what he looked like?'

'I'm afraid I didn't really get a proper view of him, Inspector. As I said, I didn't think anything of him at the time, just noticed he was there. I'd say he was a little above your height, but on the skinny side, and possibly had dark hair, although it could just have looked darker in the woods. No-one in the village described him, only saying that he was young and looked a bit suspicious. Someone said he might have been sleeping rough, by the state of his clothes.'

I asked her a few more questions to try to draw out any further detail, but there was none forthcoming so I left her to her work.

I went for a better look around Tom's bedroom. I needed to verify the upstairs maid's account and to see if there was anything to explain the death of his fiancée in this room. The search after Jenny Bamford had been found was, at best, cursory. The assumption was she'd committed suicide. Sawyer had the body and the gun, so there was no need to look further.

Somehow the maid's account didn't ring true. She said she'd seen both Tom and his mother at the same time but how could that be, given the measurements I'd taken on the lawn and my observations from the window on my first day here?

I spent the first few minutes checking the views and confirming my initial assessments. The walls were thick, the windows narrow and the rhododendron bush hid most of the lawn, except for the few feet around Tom Barleigh. I knew then Clark couldn't have seen what she claimed from her position, standing by the desk. Was she mistaken, or lying?

I began to examine the room from the perspective of the third death. Why would Jenny Bamford shoot herself? And why in this room? I'd already learned from Alan Haleson she wasn't entirely in love with Tom Barleigh, so his demise wouldn't be likely to result in broken-hearted grief. Could it be the loss of a fortune? Hardly. From all accounts the Barleigh's were comfortable but not wealthy, at least not rich enough for Jenny to commit suicide because she couldn't share in their affluence. She'd been a good-looking young woman who'd have found another well-heeled suitor with little trouble.

I found the room exactly how I'd expect a young man's to be, with the exception of the medication stacked on the dressing table. The sheer quantity of painkillers, tinctures, liniments and dressings told the tale of how damaged the poor fellow had been. I envied his immaculately tidy shelves and drawers; one of the benefits of having servants.

His desk was less well organised, with random stacks of paper of varying heights and, in several cases, overlapping each other. However, on closer inspection, it became clear that Tom had been reading up on the Great War, as there were several photographs and written accounts of decisive actions. One pile contained diagrams and family trees, as well as old letters, clearly related to the history of the baronetcy. The rest appeared haphazard, with just personal notes and material on anything which had caught his imagination: cars, aeroplanes, fishing, and the like.

It was plain to see why he instructed the staff not to touch his desk. He'd never find anything again if it was moved. Oddly, there was one corner of the desk almost clear, covered by a single photograph. It was of three young men in casual clothes, as if pulled together in the middle of a game of cricket. I turned it over and discovered three names written on the back. This must be the one given to Tom by Miss Leeming. Below the names, written in what appeared to be a different hand, were what looked like three teardrops with the letters 'BE' above. A note scribbled at the bottom asked "Beatrice?"

I spent a few moments trying to make sense of this with no luck, so put it to one side and began to make notes of what else was on the desk. I moved on to the wardrobe, where there appeared to be nothing unusual. The box containing the revolver had been removed to the evidence store along with the gun itself, waiting for fingerprint tests. There were fewer outdoor clothes than normal, and the indoor garments were perhaps a little larger than a fashionable young man might have wanted, had it not been a necessity when someone else was dressing him. I removed the bottom drawer and lifted it to the bed to examine the contents. As I did so I saw a large manila envelope lying on the floor. When I knelt and reached under to pick it up I heard a footstep behind me.

Then the lights went out.

Five

I think I must have been out cold for around fifteen minutes before I was dragged from my stupor by the screaming of the witless Marion Clark. I told her in no uncertain terms to shut up and fetch the butler to give me a hand. He helped me up and then brought me some sweet tea, along with Elizabeth to tend to my wounds.

The coldness Elizabeth had displayed when we'd parted in the garden seemed to have evaporated. At one point she turned to make sure Jervis wasn't watching and squeezed my hand. I shook my head but she continued for as long as she dared in the butler's presence. It seemed to me that she was willing to continue our relationship where it left off. I was torn. My affection for Elizabeth was still strong, perhaps too strong, and I wasn't sure I wanted to be dragged back into it, to be at the mercy of her whim. What's to say she might not disappear again?

Once they had left me to my own devices I looked for the envelope I'd spotted earlier but, with little surprise, found it gone. I was still feeling a bit groggy but I'd completed my search of the room so went back to my lodgings where I tried reading for a while but developed an almighty headache, so took a couple of Aspirin and fell asleep.

The first part of my next morning was spent in my room at the Victory nursing my bruises, drinking tea, reading the newspaper and dozing. Every time I moved my head started throbbing again. I'm not an idle man by nature but the events of the night before had knocked me back a bit. However, by lunchtime I was fed up with lying around so began to organise the case evidence and consider its validity. Small inconsistencies and questions were starting to creep in, and it made sense to double-check it now before going too far down the most obvious paths.

I love sifting the tiny details which come up in a case and spotting the tenuous links between them, trying to see both the wood and the trees at the same time. I'd normally carry out this exercise in my office, with a desk and tables to spread everything around. Here, I had to make do with considerably reduced space. On my bed I laid out several piles, my interview notes in one, Sawyer's in another. A further one held the photographs and plans, and then a list of the documents I'd found on Tom's desk. On the bedside table, I arranged my scribbled thoughts and questions. Two questions were already jotted down: who hit me on the head, and why?

After sifting through what I'd gathered I wasn't sure I'd moved further forward. I'd identified nothing concrete to indicate the deaths weren't just as they'd appeared to Sawyer, Gleeson and the Coroner. We'd found no witnesses to the killings so far. Billy Sharp, Nurse Collinge and Jenny Bamford's father were missing, and both Marion Clark and Elizabeth Parry were not telling me the truth. We'd also a stranger in the woods looking over the wall close to the time of the shootings but, again, it might be a coincidence. The strongest evidence that things were not as they seemed was that I'd been hit over the head and the material I'd discovered in Tom Barleigh's wardrobe had been taken. Who might have done it? Sawyer was checking where everyone was when I was attacked but I suspected he'd come up with nothing.

Cudlip popped his head round the door then stepped inside.

'There's a letter for you, Mr Given. Says "Urgent", so thought I'd best bring it up straight away.'

Cudlip handed me the letter but then stood waiting for me to open it.

'Thank you, Mr Cudlip, I'll call you if I need anything else.'

He nodded and left, clearly disappointed.

The envelope was of good quality, the address written in a fine hand, and there was no stamp or postmark so it must have been personally delivered. It was from Tom Barleigh's friend, Alan Haleson.

5th October 1938
21 Montague Place,
Bloomsbury, London

Dear Mr Given

I hope this letter finds you in good time as I did not have an address for you and had to trust it would be passed on by the landlord of the Victory.

As promised, I have laid out below what I recall of last Tuesday, but, firstly, may I apologise for my abruptness in the bar. I was already feeling under stress because I should have been in Munich with the Viscount Halifax.

I told you that my friend had been in poor humour on the evening before his death and I had been concerned for him. However, when I joined him at breakfast the next morning, his spirits seemed to have lifted somewhat. We soon settled into easy chat regarding the weather, the quality of the kippers and so on. After a few minutes of this I could contain myself no longer and ventured to ask him about the events of the previous night.

'Oh, that,' he replied, 'nothing to worry you. Just the old black dog pulling me down a bit.'

I pressed him and at last he told me the wedding wouldn't be going ahead. 'Certain issues have come to light,' was all he'd say on the matter.

Tom had always been besotted with Jenny, even before she'd agreed to marry him, so this news came as a complete shock to me. If it had been she to call off the wedding I would have been much less surprised; he was confined to the wheelchair for life, she is an outgoing, good-looking young woman.

For my own part, I believe it was the accident itself caused Jenny to consent to be Tom's wife in the first place.

Perhaps I should explain about the accident. Eighteen months ago, Tom, Jenny, Suzanne Hughes and I had driven out for a picnic for the day. Suzanne came along to make up the numbers. Tom drove us out to near Cleve Prior, around twenty miles from Grovestock House, where we found a nice spot by the river. I'm ashamed to say there was a lot more drinking than eating done and we were all a little sozzled at the end of it. When the time came for us to leave for home Jenny insisted on driving. She had driven before, but not after drinking. A mile before Grovestock House, a deer ran out onto the road; Jenny swerved and before I knew what was happening we were turning over in the ditch. Jenny and I must have been thrown clear. We were lucky to escape with a few cuts and bruises. Suzanne was killed outright, and Tom ended up in a coma at the hospital for months. Jenny visited almost every day, sitting by his bedside. Once he returned home, she agreed to marry him.

I would never have said this to Tom, but I think she wasn't able to forgive herself for what happened.

I fear I may have digressed, but I thought the background might help.

After breakfast, Tom called for his nurse to take him out to the garden, leaving me to my coffee and newspaper. A few minutes later I heard the crunch of the wheelchair on the gravel path, followed by Tom telling Nurse Collinge to leave him where he was. I heard her walk away and then I heard a woman's steps coming down the path again. At first I imagined it was the nurse returning but it wasn't.

I heard Tom tell his mother that he was going to call off the wedding; his words, as far as I can recall were: 'Come along, Mother, let's not pretend that you've not been doing everything in your power to dissuade me. And now I know why.'

There was some brief protest from his mother, which he cut short with: 'Get out of my sight and think about what a mess you and he have caused.'

With that, Lady Isabelle seemed to leave. I left the morning room and made my way out to the garden, hoping I could make it look as if I'd stumbled on Tom by chance. When I reached the spot where he must have been sitting, however, he was nowhere to be seen.

I never saw him alive again. I was in the library when I heard the first shot at approximately ten past eleven, and was then rushing down the hall when the second one rang out. When I ran from the front door I could see Jervis and Miss Parry just ahead of me on the drive. I dashed straight out in front and Jervis went towards the other corner until Miss Parry cried out that we were going in the wrong direction. Jervis then overtook her but stopped at the gate. He called us over to him, where we saw Tom and his mother lying on the lawn. At this point we also saw Perkins, the head gardener, running towards us from the vegetable gardens.

When Sir Arthur arrived he took charge and did everything necessary prior to Constable Sawyer arriving.

I went into the kitchen and grabbed a cup of tea to steady my nerves then returned to the library. A short time later the third shot rang out upstairs. I dashed up and joined Sir Arthur in the doorway of Tom's room, where Jenny was lying on the bed. She had killed herself.

I hope the above assists you in your enquiries. I'm in Birmingham soon for a couple of days, so if you think I can help in any way perhaps we could meet there.

Your faithful servant,
Alan Haleson

Six

It had been a damp journey over to Warwick and made much worse by a freezing wind. The weather had turned with a vengeance. Inside police headquarters I'd been happy to spend a few minutes with the desk sergeant, Tommy Burns, toasting my toes by the blazing fire in his office. He filled me in on a few cases that had been underway in my absence, as well as digging for information from me on the Grovestock House shootings. Most of this went in one ear and out the other until he dropped a nugget.

'I hear a friend of his lordship's been on the phone.'

'Which particular "lordship" are you talking about, Tommy?'

'Sir Arthur bloody Barleigh — that's who! His mate Jack Sumner rang up and gave the boss an earful.'

'On the phone? How do you know? And he's not a lord, just a baronet.'

'Well, lord or no lord, one of his pals called up and, according to that pretty young WPC, he's been throwing his weight about with the boss. She reckons she couldn't help listening in for a bit but I think she does it all the time. I'm always a bit careful when I know she's on the switchboard.'

I knocked at Dyer's door, like a naughty schoolboy heading for the headmaster's cane.

'Enter!' the Superintendent's voice boomed out. He certainly likes to make his presence felt. I've never asked him but I've an idea he must have been a Sergeant-Major at some point in his career.

'Thanks for coming in, Given.' He made it sound like I'd had a choice. 'Take a seat.'

I decided not to let on I knew why he wanted to see me.

'Is it an update you want, sir? On the Grovestock House case?'

'Well, it is and it isn't. I've had a telephone call.'

'A telephone call, sir?' I did my best to sound mystified.

'From Jack Sumner, a friend of Sir Arthur Barleigh. He says you're getting in the way.'

'Does he, sir? And how exactly am I getting in the way?'

'Now, wait a minute, Inspector. Before you start getting on your high horse, just remember I'm the one who has to jump when one of these buggers starts pulling in favours up above. Don't think it won't happen, because it will. So before we go any further, you'd best fill me in on why you're hanging around out there and haven't tied this case up already.'

On the way upstairs I'd been expecting to be hauled over the coals and now here was the boss giving me a fighting chance. The problem was I didn't have anything tangible I could use to convince him.

'You know the basic facts of the case, sir?'

'Of course I do, what kind of police officer do you think I am?' He was still on a short fuse so I needed to be quick on my feet.

'Just rhetorical, sir — and I know how busy you are, so not likely to have read every file.'

'Quite so, James, quite so. But I've plenty of pressure on me to get this one sorted out. Let's see what we know.'

The Superintendent rose from his desk and walked over to a blackboard in the corner. Picking up a piece of chalk he drew four columns, then divided these into three rows. In the boxes down the left hand side he wrote the names Tom Barleigh,

Lady Isabelle and Jenny Bamford. At the top of the second column Dyer placed a single word, 'Why?' following this by 'How?' on the third and 'Who?' for the fourth. He was evidently enjoying this.

'These are the questions we need to answer, James, aren't they? So fill me in on what you've got.'

'The problem I'm having, sir, is I can't figure out the "why". Before I do that I can't get anywhere near the "who". As far as we're aware, there were no witnesses to any of the deaths so any number of "how"s would be possible.'

'So why isn't it just as straightforward as it was reported? Seems to me quite logical the old girl didn't want the marriage to go ahead, for whatever reason, so shoots the lad and then herself. Girlfriend so overcome with grief she takes the revolver and puts a bullet between her own eyes. Never read *Romeo and Juliet*, Inspector?'

'It just doesn't feel right, sir. I can buy the first two, though most likely as an accident, just, but not the fiancée. From what I hear she'd have been glad not to have to marry Tom Barleigh so why should she top herself just because he's no longer on the scene? Then, she uses a revolver. Not really the suicide choice for a woman, is it, sir? Now if it had been poison, or a drowning…'

'Wait a minute. The future mother-in-law shot herself and she was a woman — unless I've been seriously misled.'

'But, if she did shoot herself, she did it with the shotgun she'd just used on her son, so that would be less of a surprise. Jenny Bamford had to go to Tom's bedroom and root round to find his revolver. Even if she knew where it was she couldn't have been certain it would be loaded, or have ammunition nearby.'

'Very well, I'm ready to run with that idea. What else have you got?'

'Well, you said yourself Lady Isabelle didn't want the wedding to take place "for whatever reason" but it would have to be a pretty serious reason to push her into killing her son. Who would do such a thing?'

'All of this is true, but stranger things have happened, James. You know, as well as I do, murders are seldom logical. If they were, we'd have fewer problems solving them, don't you think?' At this he laughed gently and I could see he was only playing devil's advocate, helping me think through the case. I pushed on.

'Then there's the attack on me.' I rubbed the back of my head. The bump had gone down but the embarrassment at being caught out still stung. 'I think someone was trying to warn me off — and the envelope I found was taken.'

'Well, it's obvious whoever bashed you didn't know you well. You're the most stubborn officer I've got and the attack would only guarantee you'd keep digging.'

'Stubborn's a bit strong, sir. "Tenacious" is the word my mother would use.'

'Ha! I think I was right the first time. But you do have a point. It's unlikely anyone would have knocked you out unless you were on to something. I'm more inclined to see that as evidence of wrongdoing than most of the other stuff you've come up with.'

Dyer turned and tapped the blackboard.

'You say you're not sure who could have carried out the killings, so let me hear who the front-runners are. Forget for a while you haven't got a motive. Who are the most likely culprits?'

I could see this wasn't quite settled in the Superintendent's mind.

'First off, sir, I believe it's got to be someone in the household. As far as I can see, there were enough people around the place for a stranger to have been spotted. There's a man been hanging around in the village and in the woods outside Grovestock House but he's not been seen anywhere in the grounds. No-one's mentioned any visitors so far, apart from Haleson, the chap who was supposed to be best man, so I'd say it's a strong bet for family or staff to have been involved. I'm not completely sure about Haleson — I did have some sense he was hiding something. Maybe he was sweet on the girl. Unfortunately, only a few of the staff were able to confirm the whereabouts of anyone else at the precise time of the shootings. The head gardener, George Perkins, seems to be in the clear because he was with some of the other gardeners and they heard the first shot together.'

'Come on, James, who *could* have done it? I'm not interested in who didn't do it.'

'The only family member there, well, the only one still alive anyway, was Sir Arthur. I interviewed him and he's explained what happened but he's no witnesses to where he was when his wife, son and future daughter-in-law died, so he has to be considered a possibility.'

The boss looked worried. 'You watch your step there, son. I don't want this whole episode exploding in our faces. Who else?'

'I can't see it being the butler or the cook, but neither of them have cast iron alibis for the first deaths so they'll have to stay on the list. Likewise Trudi Collinge, Tom Barleigh's nurse, there's been no word on her yet.'

I hated to admit it but this process was clarifying my thinking. Dyer must have been a good detective in his day.

'What about the lad? Sharp, isn't it?'

'Yes, sir, Billy Sharp. He's a bit of a strange one. George Perkins tells me he was always getting into scrapes. Nothing serious but enough for me to wonder. And he had been told off for playing with the shotgun in the past, including on the morning of the deaths. And he did a runner; no-one has seen him since shortly after those first shots but that's not to say he wasn't still around at the time of Miss Bamford's death. He did give a story to Alf Nash that he'd seen someone take the shotgun from the shed but he could have been lying. As a result he's also got to be in the frame. I can't see why he'd do it but, for the life of me, I can't see why *anyone* would have done it.'

'Right, I think you've shown me there might be more to this than first appeared.' The relief tumbled through my insides. 'So,' he said, nodding towards the board, 'if you can get anything sensible in those boxes in the next few days, I'm prepared to give you a bit more time to get it sorted out. I can't say fairer than that now, can I?'

'No, sir. But what about Mr Sumner?'

'You leave him to me. I can't stand bullies. Is that all?'

As I left him it occurred to me to add another name to the list, Jack Sumner. Why would he want me out of the picture?

I found I was in a much better mood when I left the boss's office and made my way downstairs. Dyer had made it pretty obvious I wasn't going to get a big team on this one and I'd have to manage as best I could with Sawyer's help but I was happy enough with that for the time being. On the first floor landing I bumped into Terry Gleeson and I knew my good humour wouldn't last for long.

'Morning, James. Any chance we can have a word?'

Gleeson peered at me with his piggy eyes. He was breathing hard through his mouth and his flabby chest was heaving, even though he'd only walked the few yards from his desk. He was overweight, lazy and bent, and Gleeson and I had a history of being on opposite sides of the fence. To me, he always seemed to want to take the easy way out. If he could rough up some villain to make him admit to a crime he hadn't committed, Gleeson didn't mind, as long as he made an arrest. I'd never witnessed him planting evidence but there were rumours around the station and I wouldn't put it past the man to do it. I sometimes wonder why people like him even join the police.

'What can I do for you, Terry? Is there something not clear in the beatings case files?'

'I've not had a chance to look at them yet. I've been busy.'

I snorted. 'Busy? You do appreciate this is important, don't you? We've just hanged two fellers and they were only the heavies. There's someone much smarter behind this and they won't stop until we find them.'

Gleeson leaned back in his chair, his hands behind his head.

'Personally, I can't see why we're bothering, it's just a waste of time all this Jewish stuff. Hitler has it about right if you ask me.'

I wanted to break his neck more at that minute than ever before, and I'd come close a few times. Instead, I drew a deep breath.

'Well, if it's not about the case, what did you want to talk about?'

'It's this Barleigh shooting. I hear you're still digging around.'

'You make it sound like I shouldn't be.'

'Well, you shouldn't. It's giving me a bad name.'

I almost laughed out loud. 'How's that, Terry? Why is it giving you a bad name just because I'm trying to investigate a case properly? Isn't it possible you missed something?'

'I didn't miss a bloody thing. The local man was on the scene quickly enough and provided a bloody good report. He even took photos, for God's sake. There was no need even to go all the way to the house to see what had happened.'

'Heaven forbid you lift your backside out of your chair and do some proper detective work, Gleeson. Anyway, I don't have much option. Dyer's asked me to have a look at it to please the higher-ups. I can already see there's some things don't add up. You should never have signed off on it and allowed the Coroner to close the case.'

He leaned across his desk and pointed a podgy finger in my direction.

'I agreed with Sawyer's conclusion. And he was right! Tom Barleigh was killed by his mother and she and the girlfriend shot themselves. You're just groping around in the dark trying to make a name for yourself.'

'Grow up. We both know you should have looked into the circumstances more than you did, rather than trusting the findings of a raw country copper. That's why the boss asked me to look at it. It's pretty clear he doesn't trust your judgement on anything important.'

Gleeson looked like I'd slapped him but then gathered himself. The piggy eyes narrowed even further.

'We'll soon see about that, Given. You'll be back here in a few days with your tail between your legs and your career in tatters. With Jack Sumner coming after you from one direction and me from the other, you won't stand a chance. You definitely don't want either of us as your enemy. Just you see!'

I turned and walked out of his office. Although he was full of bluster, he did have more time with Dyer than I did and he'd be criticising me at every chance he got. The last thing I needed just now was the boss on my back. Even though I didn't like Gleeson, he did get convictions and the Superintendent and those above appreciated him despite his flaws. I'd have to watch my back.

Seven

Sawyer seemed like a bright copper and being from the area he'd pick up a bit more on the local stories than I would. He seemed to be relishing his involvement in a serious case, perhaps seeing a promotion in it somewhere down the line. He'd gone off with a definite spring in his step when I sent him to ask some questions around the village in the afternoon. We were now in the Victory sharing what we'd found. I eyed his pint with more than a little jealousy but stuck to my Vimto.

'Did you know him — Tom?'

'Not well, he was a couple of years older than me and we'd not exactly be in the same social circles. Why do you ask?'

'Just trying to get a picture of the kind of man he was and why his mother should feel strongly enough to kill him.'

'I've only picked up she was totally against his marriage, several people have mentioned it.'

'Even so, she doesn't seem to be the kind of woman who'd murder anyone, let alone her son. But if she did, why didn't she just shoot Jenny, which would have been more logical? We're told she was totally devoted to Tom, so there'd be no sense at all in her taking a shotgun to him.'

Sawyer and I tossed some more ideas around on Lady Isabelle's possible motivation, none of which came to anything, though he was still sticking with his original leanings. He'd be no use to me if he carried on without considering any other options.

'The more I look at this, the more I'm convinced it can't have been the way it first looked. We can't see any reason for Lady Isabelle to murder Tom and the idea that Jenny Bamford would kill herself seems pretty unlikely in the circumstances. I want you to start treating this case as if we're trying to find a different killer.'

'But, sir —'

'No "buts", I've decided. So let's look at what you've been doing. Did you learn much this afternoon?'

'I dug around the village mostly, trying to find out if any locals could throw any light. Problem is, because I know them, I'm expected to stay and have a cuppa and a slice of cake at every house. It took an age to get through half a dozen interviews.'

He paused and took a sip of his beer and flipped through his notebook.

'And?'

'Sorry, sir, there were a couple of interesting things came up and I was just trying to get them straight in my head. It was mainly just the usual village tittle-tattle but several people said there'd been a young feller hanging around, asking for information on Grovestock House — who worked there, how long the family had been there, that kind of thing.'

'Did they say what he looked like?'

'People are rubbish at descriptions, aren't they, sir? Some said he was tall, some average height and build. Half of them reckoned he was blond, the other half dark-haired. The only thing everyone agreed on was he looked a bit down at heel, as though he'd been sleeping rough.'

'Is he still around?'

'Everyone I spoke to said they'd only seen him in the village in the couple of days before the deaths and he's now disappeared again. I did bump into Mrs Edwards, her husband farms out at Foxes Spinney, and she was complaining of things going missing. Eggs, bread from the kitchen, milk, that kind of thing. Her neighbours have had the same problem. She said one of them had a couple of blankets and her husband's socks taken from the washing line. I suppose it could be this bloke if he's laying low somewhere.'

'Right, I think we need to find this man.'

'Another thing came up, sir. I was approached by Billy Sharp's mother. She had a note from him a couple of days after he disappeared. She wouldn't let me keep it, said it was important to her, but I copied it down. Basically, he'd got into a bit of trouble and had to leave the area for a while. Didn't say what the trouble was, nor where he was going. Come to think of it, I suppose it might even be Billy who's pinching stuff if he's hiding locally.'

'It might. What did his mum want you to do?'

'She kept on and on how her Billy was a gentle lad and wouldn't harm anyone. She was frightened out of her wits and wanted me to look for him. I told her we also wanted to find him in case he could tell us anything in connection to the deaths. This seemed to put her in even more of a flap so I said he wasn't necessarily in trouble, but we needed to speak to him to straighten a few things out. I thought it best to put it like that in case the lad shows up again and then she'd try to get him to come to see us.'

'That's good work. Anything else?'

'Not much. The rest was, as I said, village gossip. Rumours regarding Sir Arthur and Isabelle, secret affairs, Tom's accident and so on. Everyone round here's known the family for years, but there was nothing much out of the ordinary.'

I found myself feeling jealous of this deep-rooted sense of place. Sawyer, like the Barleighs and most of their neighbours, could trace their families back for generations in the same village or hamlet, perhaps even the same house. How different to my own family.

'It's the gossip we want, John, the "tittle-tattle" as you put it, and you're the man to get it. So go through it again in your notebook and in your head and see what little gems you can pull out. If there's anything you think worth following up then do it. Call in favours if you need to, just so we can make some progress.'

Sawyer finished his pint and left for the night, leaving me to a final Vimto and my thoughts. I was pulling my playing cards out of my jacket pocket, where I always carry them, when Cudlip came in.

'Telephone for you, Mr Given. I think it's your boss.'

It was indeed Superintendent Dyer, and he wasn't in the best frame of mind when I told him we still hadn't got very far.

'Listen, James, I've had the Chief Constable on my back again. The press are still giving him a hard time and he wants some answers. He's told me to give you another couple of days to wrap it up. Then we're going with the official line that after additional investigations by one of our top detectives we still conclude our original findings, etc., etc. So you'd best come up with something new shortly or the case is closed.'

I protested for a few minutes but deep down I knew he was right. We had to draw the line under it sometime, so I told him I'd do my best, then returned to my nightcap, my lonely hand of patience and my memories.

The next morning, I decided to take a trip to Birmingham to meet with Alan Haleson and spend some time with my parents. The drive through the beautiful mist-cloaked countryside to the railway station at Wootton Wawen was restful. Almost every tree and copse provided a cornucopia of red, brown and yellow, and it was with a little disappointment when I arrived at the station in something less than fifteen minutes. My train wasn't due for another half an hour so I walked into the village to find a shop, hoping to buy a newspaper for my journey. There was one next door to the post office and I could see the papers had been delivered but still lay tied up with string on the counter. The shop itself was deserted until a woman, in her sixties, came through, huffing and puffing.

'Oh my, sir, I'm so sorry. I'm all behind with myself this morning. I do hope you've not been waiting long.'

'Not at all, I've a little time to spare yet. Could I take a copy of the *Telegraph* and *Post* when you're ready?'

The woman busied herself dragging the package across her counter then fussed for what seemed like minutes trying to locate a pair of scissors to free the contents. I handed her my penknife, for fear she might disappear into her back room to continue her search. The poor woman then had no change to hand and I was beginning to think I'd never catch the train. Throughout the entire performance she chatted away, digging for any vestiges of gossip she'd later be able to share with her customers.

'You're not from round here, are you?'

'No, I'm not. I'm on my way into Birmingham and thought I'd take a stroll whilst I had time on my hands. It's such a lovely morning.'

'Staying nearby then?'

'Priors Allenford.'

'Ah, it's become quite famous with the recent deaths nearby, hasn't it? That poor family, so much tragedy in their lives, one generation after the other. It almost seems like they're cursed.'

'Do you know the Barleighs, then?'

She told me she'd worked at Grovestock House for a year or so towards the end of the Great War.

'I only knew the son, Tom, as a baby, but I knew his grandparents and met Sir Arthur when he came back from the Front. He seemed like a poor shattered thing and locked himself away in his room for weeks at first. By all accounts he'd been a handsome man when he left, but by the time I met him his face was burned something awful. It was Lady Isabelle who pulled him out of it. She must have been in a terrible way, to do what she did.'

By the time she'd finally handed over my newspaper and the few coppers change, I had to run back down the street. I got to the station with seconds to spare before the train arrived, its green engine gleaming and billowing steam round the platform. I claimed the one empty compartment, where I removed my topcoat and settled down to read the paper. It was full of speculation on the diplomatic developments with Germany, though opinion was divided between praising the Prime Minister for pulling the country back from the brink of war and damning him for delaying the inevitable.

The journey took almost an hour and I played patience much of the way, as we went trundling through fields and open country broken only occasionally by leafy villages, until we hit the outer suburbs. These seemed to stretch forever, merging eventually with the bustle and grime of the metropolis. A few minutes before reaching our destination the train was plunged into darkness as it entered the long tunnel taking it under the city centre. This feat of engineering was originally a simple cutting but had been covered over and built upon many years before using typical Victorian ingenuity and lust for land. The effect was now impressive as the streets disappeared, for the last mile, before the train emerged once more into the light and the fabulously grand Snow Hill station. What the Victorians had achieved with the tunnel had been emulated by their Edwardian successors in this grandest of celebrations of the age of railways. One couldn't fail to be impressed by the buzz of activity, the smoke, the steam, the tiled platforms and the ornate booking hall, said to be the finest in Europe.

I left the station and turned into Livery Street, heading up the hill and over the canal before turning into a dingy side street on the left-hand side. The buildings here backed on to waterside wharfs and were of dark red brick with large windows, suitable for the delicate work of stitching for hours on end, from dawn till dusk. Up and down this street young boys carried bolts of cloth across their small shoulders from the dozens of barrows into the depths of the workshops. And every one of them appeared to be Jewish. Small carters' lorries bearing the names of towns across the country were piled high with boxes taking the finished goods to emporiums in high streets from Penzance to Pitlochry. Birmingham's sweatshops supply caps to factory workers in Lancashire and plus-fours to gentleman anglers on the River Tweed, hats to titled ladies and waistcoats to farm labourers. An odd kind of equality in an unequal world.

Halfway down, I stopped outside one small factory and even above the street noise I could hear the incessant rattle of sewing machines. Over the door was a basic sign proclaiming "Dov Geffen, All Manner Of Tailoring, Bespoke Suits Our Speciality". The door opened into a large room where the racket was deafening. Twenty men were lined up in three rows, their machines driven by belts ripping around pulleys close to the ceiling. Each man wore a yarmulke and was enclosed in his work area by piles of cut cloth and baskets containing "all manner of tailoring". On one side of the room, positioned part way up the wall, was an office with windows set so the occupant could oversee this hive of activity.

I climbed the wooden steps leading up to the office and went inside. Huddled over a set of ledgers and fingering a well-worn abacus was an elderly man who turned and glanced up as I entered. I paused briefly and looked him in the eye before I spoke.

'*Shalom Aleichem*, Father. *Gut Shabbos*.'

'So what are you doing here?'

'Do I need a reason to visit my family?'

'No, son, of course you don't. But you have to admit it's become a little unusual.'

I couldn't think of a way to respond to this. My father's question had shaken my equilibrium. Why had I come? On the train journey I'd told myself it was just to see they were safe. There were such awful stories coming out of Germany in the newspapers that I was afraid the trouble might spill over again into English cities. Even three or four years ago, Mosley and his black-shirted thugs had been allowed to parade the streets until the tide was turned by the people of London's East End. This danger hadn't gone away and there was still Fascist violence in working class districts, even here in Birmingham. Like the brutal killing of the shopkeeper carried out by Peter Bishop and his accomplice.

'You know I come over when I can, but I've had a lot on at work lately.'

Like most fathers he had little idea of the detail of my job and I could see he was at a loss to see how the work of a rural police officer could be described as 'busy'. I knew if I was to have his approval to leave next day I'd have to tell him more of the case currently occupying my time. But it would need to wait until later.

'I know you visit when you're able, Jacob, and we're always pleased to see you. Especially your mother.'

A smile cracked his face as he acknowledged the immense understatement.

Father and I closed up the office and machines at around half past two, as is his custom on Sabbath, and climbed the stairs to the family accommodation up above. The rooms were quite substantial, occupying the whole of the first floor. It struck me how lucky they were compared to many who worked in the area and had to make do with a single room in a basement, or were forced, through poverty, to share a house with several other families. From the moment he'd started work Father had saved almost every penny he could until he'd been able to buy the workshop and set up on his own.

Just inside the door he turned to me and put his finger to his lips, urging me to stay still and keep quiet. He then went through to the kitchen and told Mama she had a visitor. Her shrieks when she saw me would have awakened the dead. She hugged me so tight, with cries of 'Jacob, Jacob', I could scarcely catch my breath and I was grateful when Eli and Sarah came through to divert her.

'See children, your brother is home. Go hug him, go on.'

Sarah didn't need Mama's prompting and soon she had her arms around me almost as tightly as her mother had minutes before. She could barely reach round my waist until she pressed her dark curls hard into my stomach.

'Jacob, where have you been? Are you staying for Shabbat? Are you?'

I couldn't help but look across at Mama. Her head was nodding so violently I feared she'd do herself an injury.

'All right, all right, my little *zhaba*, I'll stay if Mama will have me.'

94

At this my sister squealed then quickly tried to put on her sternest face.

'Don't call me that, it makes me sound so ugly.'

I laughed and tickled her.

'*Zhaba*, *zhaba*, *zhaba*, Sarah's a little *zhaba*.'

When she was born and my father and I saw her for the first time, she was flat on her stomach with arms and legs spread on both sides. He turned to me, smiling, and said she looked like a toad, "zhaba" in his native Russian, and the name had stuck with baby Sarah from then onwards.

Eli was more reticent than his younger sister, staying back, framed by the passageway through to the bedrooms. I saw a flash of annoyance in his eyes. Here was I, the prodigal returned, and lavished with every bit of affection Mama and our sister could muster. It was too late in the day for the fatted calf to be slaughtered but Eli must have thought Father would have done it if he'd had the opportunity. I reached out my hand.

'Here Eli — *gut Shabbos* — won't you come closer and let me see how much you've grown since I was last here?'

He maintained his distance, and his frostiness.

'Don't be so foolish Jacob, how could I have grown much in so little a time? It's hardly six months since you came over last.'

I turned to Father.

'Tell him, he has grown, hasn't he? I'm sure when I came for Passover he was only at Mama's shoulder and now he's definitely as high as her ears.'

Father smiled, responding to my wink.

'You know, I think you're right. I wouldn't notice it myself, of course, seeing him every day, but now you've pointed it out I'm sure it's true. What do you say, Mama?'

She turned and made to put her arm around Eli to pull him to her. The boy dodged away with a grimace but then drew himself to his full height and walked awkwardly forward to take my hand. He even laid his forehead briefly on my chest and slapped me on the back with his free hand.

'It's good to see you, Jacob.'

I was glad he had come round and now seemed genuinely pleased to see me. I think it must always be difficult when brothers are so far apart in age, and in our case this was made more so by my living so far away.

The next hour was spent on their weekly ritual. Washing and dressing, assisting Mama with decorating the table, preparing the lamps to illuminate our lives for the next fifteen or sixteen hours, and several dozen other small jobs which are carried out week in and week out in Jewish homes throughout the world. This was a pleasant time in the family, like making ready the house for the arrival of an important visitor, for in many ways that is how Sabbath is viewed. Each person knows their place and the tasks they are to undertake, each moving quietly, trying to finish everything in the allotted time.

Eventually the work was complete and, as darkness descended outside, Mama covered her eyes whilst reciting the *berakhot* and lighting the *menorah*. This blessing and ritual, with the stillness surrounding it, always signals the formal commencement of the weekly event, before the family leaves for the synagogue.

It was almost a half hour's walk through the dark streets of the city, but this was no lonely quest, with the family's friends and neighbours alongside us. There were no children running around, nor pointless banter amongst the adults, for this is a serious undertaking. Not sad, nor solemn, but a communal opportunity to take stock and prepare oneself to be with God. Such conversation as there was took place in quiet tones and on matters of importance: the news from Europe; family illnesses and deaths; the state of business. Several friends of my father talked heatedly about the attacks on Jewish businesses in the city and berated me for the lack of progress by the police in finding out who was behind it. I tried to explain we were doing our best but it wasn't easy. Even though we'd managed to catch Bishop and Stack this still wasn't enough as far as they were concerned. For the first time I was left in no doubt how much anxiety there was in the Jewish community and once again I was wishing Dyer hadn't handed the case over to Terry Gleeson.

Dotted throughout this procession were groups of men, their dark-hatted heads bowed together, discussing the interpretation of one particular religious text or another. Occasionally one would throw his hands in the air and raise his eyes skyward in clear frustration with his fellow devotees but, generally, this kind of animation was left for around and inside the synagogue itself.

The front and steps of the building were packed by groups of men displaying the liveliness of debate that reared its head on the walk down. Scattered amongst them, sharing stories of home and family, were many women who my mother knew and we separated soon after arriving, she and Sarah joining them, whilst Eli, my father and I congregated with the men. I found myself the subject of much back-slapping and hand-shaking, with a little admonition for staying away too long thrown in. After the service and the long walk back home, which if anything was even more sombre than the one down, we enjoyed a delightful, leisurely meal prepared by Mama earlier in the day.

'Are you still here, Jacob?'

We'd left the rest of the family to clear up after dinner and come through to the parlour.

'Wha— Oh, sorry Father, I was miles away, considering your question.'

'Well? Is there a reason you've come to visit?

'No, not really.' I gathered my courage. 'Frankly, I had to come into Birmingham to meet someone but there is something I want to ask while I'm here.'

He leaned back and looked across at me with some apprehension.

'You have a problem, Jacob?'

'No, not so much a problem. It's just I've recently met a woman again who I knew a while ago. We became very close but then something happened and she left. I still like her and I know she still likes me. I'm thinking it might possibly become even more serious this time and wanted to know how you might feel.'

'What I might feel? What is it to do with me? I'm sure at your age this isn't the first time you've taken a girl out, is it, and I don't remember you asking me before?'

I laughed because he was right, of course. I'd run away to sea at sixteen and hadn't spoken to him for years afterwards. I'd written to my mother from time to time, just to let her know I was alive, but the girls I'd met on my travels weren't often the sort you'd tell your parents about. I didn't start visiting again until the day my father's world fell apart.

The call came on a Saturday afternoon in November 1936 and I knew something must be seriously wrong for him to break Shabbat. I'd read in the newspaper that Franco's forces had inflicted heavy casualties in the battle to control Madrid. My father's tears told me the rest. Ariel, his first born, my brother, had been killed by a grenade, fighting for his beliefs. I'd given up on establishing a Socialist Utopia at the first hurdle, perhaps my heart wasn't in it, or perhaps I just didn't have his raw courage but Ariel had been a trade unionist, a Communist and a freedom fighter, and he'd put me to shame. It was inevitable in many ways that he would answer the call from his comrades in Spain. It was also predictable he'd be one of the ones to die there.

So I'd gone home to comfort my parents and we made our peace. I knew I'd never replace my elder brother but at least I could support my father when he needed it. It was the year after Elizabeth left me.

'No, Father, it's not the first time, even with Elizabeth, but there's something you need to know. She's a Gentile.'

I spoke the final words so quietly I wasn't sure he'd heard them. His silence seemed to confirm this, so I repeated myself, this time more loudly.

'I heard you the first time, Jacob, just give me a moment to gather my thoughts.' He lifted his head and spoke. 'This is not so great a surprise, son, you've been growing apart from us again for a while now.'

I leaned over and touched his forearm.

'I'm not growing apart from you, Father. Don't I come over whenever I can? And I think of you all every day.'

'No, not the family. Whatever else I might think, you are a good son. It's what we are that you're losing. The congregation. Your faith. Your heritage. When was the last time you were at the synagogue before today? When did you last celebrate Shabbat — I imagine it was last time you were here?'

'It's difficult.'

'I know it's difficult, Jacob, that's the whole point. If God had wanted our lives to be easy he'd have left us in the Garden of Eden. We're still being punished for Adam's indiscretion and each day we're required to make atonement. We need to show we're grateful for the gifts he's bestowed on us.'

So, we'd come to the rock and the hard place, he with his beliefs and me with mine. I'd half expected him to shout and rage when he heard my news but this was more his style. Reasonable and conciliatory. He continued quietly.

'I think it's easier for me, here. I have the family, our neighbours, our friends. All the people who work with me are Jews, and most of those I trade with are as well. It's our universe. I could no more miss going to the synagogue than miss kissing your sister goodnight or miss opening the workshop in the morning. I'm sure it's much harder out there in the big wide world. One hears such awful stories.'

He didn't know the half of it. Certainly, my father would see the news and his own experiences in Russia would acquaint him with the hatred of Jews but he'd know little of how it reared its head in polite English society. He'd even seemed bewildered earlier in the evening when we'd discussed the beatings, almost as if he'd been blocking them out of his consciousness. I'd never told him how much I felt it necessary to hide my Jewish upbringing from people in my normal life but it was obvious he had an inkling of the truth. It wasn't difficult to see how he'd have known because I'd never made any secret of my changed name, but there were more subtle alterations I'd made. The way I dressed, the way I had my hair cut, the way I'd transformed my accent away from Birmingham boy with Russian parents to something vague, born out of practice and contact with a dozen languages in a hundred different ports. I'd wandered incessantly where the ships and fancy took me, to places like Scandinavia, Germany, the Mediterranean, America, and even to the west coast of Africa. In those days I'd whiled away my long off-watch hours drinking and playing cards, gambling away the wages I was earning and my only prayers were for a better hand.

The sad thing was I hadn't hidden my faith because of some realisation I no longer believed but simply out of fear. I wasn't strong enough to be taken at face value in the real world. It was perhaps the reason I'd pursued Bishop so aggressively, my personal atonement for abandoning my people when they were constantly under threat.

'You're right, Father, it isn't easy outside this place. And I've seen things which would break the faith of any man. But don't think I've forsaken it just yet. I'm a little bewildered, that's all. This is why I'm asking you about Elizabeth now; I need you to say you understand. That you won't cut me off if she and I take this further.'

He smiled and leaned back in his armchair.

'Jacob, you're my son. The eldest, now Ariel has gone from us. Why would I cut you off? I love my God dearly, but I love my family too. There are many worse things you could do in this world than get yourself mixed up with a Gentile. It's not what I'd have wanted but neither is it my destiny to walk the path you've to walk. If you think you and she can be happy then you have my blessing — but let's keep it from Mama for a while, or else she'll have the wedding planned before you know it!'

We chatted about lighter things for a few minutes but I could see he was bothered by something else.

'You seem anxious, Father, what is it? Is mother all right?'

'She's fine, Jacob.'

'Then you, is it you? Sarah? Eli?'

'No, no, we're fine.'

'So what is it, if there's nothing wrong?'

'I didn't say there was nothing wrong, Jacob. I've had a letter from your Uncle Gideon. I'm really worried for him.'

Gideon was my mother's brother and lived in Germany. When my parents came to England from Russia, Gideon and his family decided not to travel quite so far, hoping, I suppose, things would settle down at home and they'd be able to move back.

'Why, what's he said?'

'It seems they've been told to leave.'

'Who? Uncle Gideon and his family?'

'No, not just them. All of the Jews in Germany are being told they have to go back to where they came from. But Gideon's been there in Bremen for over thirty years now, it's his home. How can they be trying to send him back to Russia?'

'From what I hear he might be better off getting out while he can. The newspapers are full of stories of beatings — and worse — of Jews over there.'

I'd visited my uncle and his family once when I was between ships, just before I changed my name. He'd let me stay for a while until I sorted myself out but it wasn't a good place for Jews even back then. Hitler had just been released from prison and was stirring up trouble everywhere he went. There was even a march by his supporters through Bremen itself to celebrate the man's birthday when I was there. I was glad to leave the place.

'Is there anything you can do to help Jacob? Anything at all?'

I could hear the desperation in his voice and knew my mother must have been asking him the same question.

'Like what, Father? I have no influence in Germany, I'm not sure anyone here in England has any at present.'

'Not in Germany, son, but here — here in England. You must know someone who could help Gideon come over to join us. You're a policeman, an Inspector even, surely you have contacts.'

Although it was a serious situation, it somehow pleased me my father thought I was important enough to be able to help, especially after our conversation earlier.

'I don't have those kinds of contacts, Father, but I'll ask around. I met a man recently who works in the Foreign Office. I'm seeing him tomorrow so I can ask if he has any suggestions.'

He seemed satisfied with this but I found myself uneasy. I hadn't a clue how I, or Haleson, might help. I knew Uncle Gideon's must be just one of thousands of Jewish families trying to leave Germany for England or America. Anything to avoid going back east to the places they'd fled from many years before. It wasn't appropriate for me to be attempting to gain influence through someone I'd met in the course of an ongoing investigation. I was sure to get into trouble if anyone found out but I half-convinced myself Alan Haleson seemed a decent enough chap, and probably not a suspect in the case, so decided I'd chance speaking to him about it the next day.

I found myself thinking of a photograph hanging above my desk at home. It shows a row of wooden houses on the side of a muddy dirt road. One of them has a double door opened to reveal a workshop inside. It's my grandfather's house. Outside, posed with fixed expressions stand two men, my grandfather and my father. An elderly woman is seated by their side and, behind her, linking arms with the younger man, stands my mother. I always imagine, rather than see, the slight bulge which is the beginning of Ariel, my elder brother. In the middle of the street is another family group. It is my Uncle

Gideon, his wife and two children, cousins Anna and Lev. Everyone in the photograph has bare feet, the cold mud oozing up through their toes. I know this scene is no longer there, the homes burnt down by Christian neighbours. Is this the Russia my relatives are being forced to return to?

Eight

Alan Haleson sat across the table from me: a handsome young man, his precise age hidden under the guise of the British civil servant. His formal dark suit, complete with gold chain securing the fob watch in his waistcoat pocket, with an equally dark overcoat smothering the back of his chair, provided him with a gravitas that had been absent when we had met in the Victory. The only flash of colour was his tie, a turquoise and yellow affair probably from some minor public school. Haleson's sombre dress was in stark contrast to the magnificently ornate station buffet in which we found ourselves. Its high ceiling was decorated with plaster vines, cherubs and elaborate bosses picked out in gold leaf, green, red and robin's egg blue. Unfortunately, this splendour was clouded by the pall of smoke hanging in the air, which arose from gusts blowing in from the platform whenever a customer opened the door and from the vapours pouring from cigars and cigarettes all around. Even Haleson himself puffed away on a pipe, smoke wreathing his face each time he exhaled.

'Thank you for meeting me here, Inspector, it's good of you and saves me a little time.'

'It's no problem, sir, I was in Birmingham anyway visiting my family and will be taking the train myself back to Kenilworth later.'

'So how can I help you?'

'There are some things I need to check in relation to where you said you were when each of the shootings took place.'

He said he'd be happy to help in any way he could and we quickly went through the main statements he'd made in his letter. We then went into more detail but he had to admit no one could confirm where he was when the killings occurred.

'So, in fact, you could have been anywhere?'

'I could, Inspector, but I wasn't. I was definitely in the library and I'm afraid you'll have to take my word for it.'

I decided not to press the point because I knew I'd have to ask a favour of him later. All the time he was speaking his eyes darted around the buffet. At one point he tensed when a bearded man in a dark suit came through the door, and then he relaxed again when the man turned and left.

'Let's leave that there for now and look at some of the other things you recall. You reported that in your conversation with Tom the night before he died he said "certain issues have come to light". He didn't elaborate on what they were? No inkling at all?'

'I'm sorry, Inspector, I've thought a lot since it happened. It's kept me awake at night, wondering should I have noticed if something even more serious was amiss than him cancelling the wedding. But, try as I might, I can't think of anything else he said and, as I told you, he seemed almost back to normal next morning.'

'But you also overheard him arguing with his mother after breakfast, telling her the wedding was off and that this should make her very happy. Why would he want to taunt Lady Isabelle in such a way?'

'I think she'd been putting Tom under pressure for a long time. It was no secret she'd become dead set against the marriage. Tom was probably just trying to get his own back.'

'Was she always against it then?'

'Well, she was never happy about it, as I said in my letter; she thought Jenny was just after Tom's money. But over the last few weeks her attitude seemed to have become more hardened the closer the actual day came. She seemed to be trying all sorts of illogical arguments to put Tom off his plans.'

'Did you get the impression she was angered by what her son had said to her or just shocked? Angry enough to take his life?'

'I couldn't truthfully say how she felt. I only overheard the conversation and didn't see her face. I know she was almost obsessively fond of Tom but what had gone on in the previous few weeks had plainly put a strain on the two of them. It's hard to see how finally getting what she wanted would have prompted her to shoot the one person in the world she loved above everyone else. Quite the opposite, don't you think, Inspector?'

A look which I couldn't quite fathom flitted across Haleson's face as he said this. I was having difficulty seeing him as being involved but he didn't have anyone to confirm where he was when the shootings took place. It's been said before that innocent men don't need alibis and possibly it's true, but that doesn't mean that having no alibi is a proof of innocence. I'd need to cross-check with the other statements which had been taken. Would it have been possible for him to get between the library and other parts of the building without being seen and in the required time? Even if it looked unlikely, it still wouldn't prove he was in the library when he claimed he was.

'There's something in what you say there, Mr Haleson, and it's why I'm still investigating, but I believe we can leave it there for now. You've been most helpful, though I may have to come back to you later.'

'There is one other thing, Inspector. I can't believe it's relevant but I do think you should know.' He paused. 'Even though Tom was in a wheelchair and devoted to Jenny, he still had a way with the ladies. Women of any age would melt when he spoke to them. Quite the envy of his friends, you know.'

'I can't quite see what that has to do with his death, Mr Haleson.'

'Sorry, Inspector, I'm not making myself clear. The nurse, Trudi Collinge, for example, was one who fell under his spell. I don't think he intended it, but he told me she'd become convinced he was going to throw Jenny over and marry her. We had a good laugh over it until Lady Isabelle found out. She immediately gave Nurse Collinge her notice so she was to leave straight after the wedding. Tom showed me a note the nurse sent to him, full of anger and pain. She'd said something like "you'd best get rid of Jenny now, or I will do it myself."'

On the table next to us, a newly married couple put their arms around each other and smiled at a friend taking a photograph. The flash made the husband and wife giggle, and threw the cherubs on the ceiling into stark relief. Haleson blinked as the camera popped again. I drained my tea and suggested we leave.

On the platform Haleson continued to look around as if he was expecting someone.

'Do you have another meeting here, sir? Am I keeping you?'

'No, no, Inspector, I'm just a little nervous in crowded places. Is there anything else I can do for you before I go?'

'Actually, sir, there might be.'

I filled him in on the situation with my Uncle Gideon and asked if there was anything he might be able to suggest. He grimaced and thought for a moment or two before responding. Throughout our interview Haleson's speech had been measured, as if rehearsed. Something beyond the clipped inflection of the well-educated. Perhaps the diplomacy and inevitable secrecy surrounding the Munich discussions had rubbed off on him and become a habit.

'You seem to be holding something back, Mr Haleson.'

'Not at all, Inspector. At least no more than is prudent. You must appreciate our position with the German leadership is still very difficult. It wouldn't do at all for me to give too much away of what we do and don't know about what's happening. What I can tell you is it's getting terribly bad out there, and I don't think anyone's going to be safe if they're not on the Fuhrer's side. He has very decided views on who to blame for his country's problems. You leave it with me and I'll ask a few questions around my colleagues. See if we can come up with anything.'

I thanked him and passed over a note containing the details of Uncle Gideon and his family. He read the handwritten sheet and clarified the address with me before folding it up and placing it into his jacket pocket. As he headed off for his train he turned and shouted over his shoulder that he'd get back to me in a few days. All I could hope, not for the first time, was that he was a man of his word.

The compartment was busier than when I'd travelled into the city so I was wedged between an elderly couple and two young boys looking out of the window. Their chatter and fascination with all that was going on around them in the station couldn't fail to amuse. The younger of them asked me if I travelled on the train often and he explained they were on their way to their aunt's in Coventry, where they'd be staying 'for a whole week'.

I leaned over to the window to point to an enormous double-header pulling out on the start of its journey to Edinburgh, the smoke and steam enveloping the entire station. As we shunted away from the platform ourselves, a patch cleared momentarily by our carriage and I glimpsed a face I thought I recognised and hadn't seen for many years. To the astonishment of my fellow travellers I flung myself at the window but he'd gone, cloaked in the filth swirling all around.

I let the phone ring three times then hung up. I counted to five then dialled again. This time I let it ring twice before hanging up and redialling.

'Gerry Costello, locksmith and hardware, what can I do for you today?'

'Morning Mr Costello, I'm having trouble with some continental fittings and wondered if you could help?'

The man on the other end chuckled.

'Morning James, I thought it must be you. You do love your cloak and dagger stuff, don't you? I was going to try to call you sometime this week in any case.'

I'd known Gerry for years, more or less since I'd returned to England. He was Irish, from Galway, and had originally been apprenticed as a locksmith. His aptitude for his chosen trade, plus his intimidating physique, soon found him in demand amongst the petty criminal gangs of his home in London's East End. He could unpick any lock in seconds and be away with any vehicle in only a few moments more. As a result of a couple of mistakes he'd spent a year or so in jail and didn't fancy returning. When I met him he was eking out a living more or less honestly during the winter before getting drunk, losing his job, carrying out a profitable burglary or two and then heading for the fruit fields of Kent. He'd work there until the heat, literally and figuratively, died down, then begin the whole cycle again.

It was Gerry who had introduced me to Heather. I don't know if they'd ever gone as far as being lovers but they were definitely close. Gerry's mammoth fists had loosened more than one set of teeth belonging to men who tried taking liberties with her. Despite his physical presence, and his predilection for thievery, Gerry was a hard man not to like. He had a gentle voice, a ribald sense of humour and once he was in your corner he stayed there. Gerry, Heather and I struck up a friendship almost immediately, working together whenever we could, then laughing and drinking long into the night. They were good days. He'd stayed in Kent to be nearer to London when Heather and I followed the harvest northwards to Worcestershire.

I turned to Gerry when Heather was murdered.

I'd asked Gerry to keep his eyes and ears open for any news of the Sicilians I suspected had killed her and for years he'd done so. I was convinced Benito and Pàulu Demma would gravitate towards the big cities, where they wouldn't stand out in the mix of nationalities and where their particular brand of thuggery would find a steady market. Every few months he'd ring to say one of his contacts had told him foreigners had surfaced in this gang or that but by the time I'd followed it up they'd always disappeared again, fading into the shadows of the criminal underworld.

'Gerry, how are you doing?'

'Mustn't grumble, mustn't grumble — no one listens anyway, even if you do. My old back's playing up again, but, you know, I can't expect anything else at my age.'

I reminded him he'd been about to call me.

'So I was, James. I was out drinking with Dec Spode at the weekend, let's call him a colleague of mine so to speak, said he wanted me to meet an Italian friend of his. Big brute of a man. Dec introduced him jokingly as Il Duce, but I'd be fairly sure it's Benito Demma.'

I could feel my throat tightening at the mention of his name.

'Good God, Gerry, why didn't you contact me earlier? Did you find out where he was staying? Who he's with and what he's up to?'

I knew he was about to confirm what I'd seen from the train.

'He was very cagey, James, I couldn't get much out of him but one thing Dec told me was his mate was shortly heading up to your neck of the woods. To Birmingham.'

My next call was to Terry Gleeson. Needless to say, he thought I was interfering again.

'What can I do for you, Given? Checking up on me?'

'Now, now, Terry, don't be like that, I just have some news I thought you might find useful.'

'Go on then, spit it out.'

I told him about Gerry in London and how he passed information to me from time to time.

'So what's this Demma bloke got to do with me?'

'He's a known hard man and I've been keeping tabs on him for ages. My contact tells me he's been mixed up with Fascist gangs down there over the last year and now he's up in Birmingham. I just thought you'd like to know, in case he surfaces in relation to the beatings you're supposed to be investigating.'

'Don't you think I've enough on my plate without following up every Tom, Dick and Guido you come up with, Given?'

'Only trying to help, Terry. If you do happen to come across him, perhaps you'll let me know. Unless it's too much trouble, that is.'

I put down the receiver before he could reply.

Nine

'How was your weekend, sir?'

I told Sawyer it had been a pleasant enough break and that I'd managed to fit in a further interview with Alan Haleson. 'What about yourself?'

Sawyer grinned like a fool.

'Aha? An encounter with a young lady, I assume?'

'Just someone I met on my way home from the pub. She's called Jane. We had a drink or two in her gran's house. Nothing serious.'

'Don't be apologising; enjoy your time off while you can. Anyway, I presume nothing serious, as you put it, could have happened with her grannie on the scene.'

'Actually, her gran wasn't there, she died a while back and Jane is clearing out the house. In fact, we were talking about how her gran knew the Barleigh family. It might be worth you having her in for a chat.'

'Not so Plain Jane', as the lads at the pub called her, lived in Birmingham and had recently been left the house by her grandmother. Sawyer had been walking home when he'd seen a strange car outside and had taken a closer look. Jane had invited him in, and, several drinks and reminiscences later, she'd provided information which might be useful. I told him to invite her into the station; if nothing else it would give him a chance to show off his uniform.

'Would you ever move to the city, Sawyer? There can't be much chance of promotion out in the sticks.'

'I don't think so, sir, I'm a country boy and, besides, I've my mum and dad to consider. Neither of them is getting any younger and, though he doesn't say much, I know Dad's grateful for the help I give him around the farm at the weekends. When I get the odd weekend off, that is.'

'Well, you had this weekend off, and seem to have made good use of it if this Jane is anything to go by.'

'I wasn't complaining. I like it here and I love my job but the only disadvantage in a small place is you're never really off duty. Like with Jane. I knew the house was empty so I had to investigate when I saw the car. Even our chat has led to me bringing stuff back to you. And there's another thing I heard in the pub before meeting Jane.'

'Something else about the Barleighs?'

'Everyone's still talking about the tragedy, all with their own theories, you know how it is in the countryside. Most of them are completely cock-eyed, though one I heard might be worth following up. Reggie Taylor works for Mr Sumner occasionally, gardening jobs and the like, and was saying he'd heard Mr Sumner and Tom Barleigh arguing one day when he was up near the house. Reggie said it got quite heated. Seems like Tom left with Sumner shouting "you'll be sorry for this" after him.'

Jane Newman was a good-looking young woman. She had a city girl's pale complexion, sharply set off by her smear of crimson lipstick. She was wearing a well-tailored skirt and jacket, beige blouse and shoes more suited for urban streets than country lanes, looking every inch the personal secretary of a successful businessman. I'd have placed her at about twenty-two years of age and her smile lit up the room when Sawyer brought her in.

'Sawyer, here, tells me you're staying in your grandmother's old house.'

'That's right, Inspector, it's where John and I met.' She glanced up at him and I could see she was perhaps closer than he'd suggested. 'He thought I might be a burglar. Came to check me out, he did.'

This time it was Sawyer's cheeks that lit up the room.

'So tell me about your grandmother — she'd lived in the village a while, I understand.'

'Virtually all her adult life. She came to Priors Allenford soon after she married Granddad. He took over the post office, she found a nursing job and they lived above the shop until he died, then she moved in here. According to Mum, they were a totally devoted couple and she was devastated when he passed away at such an early age. It was only her friends and the village gossip got her through it. The time she'd spent behind the post office counter occasionally helping out Granddad meant she knew everyone and everything about them.'

'And she knew a bit about Sir Arthur and Isabelle Barleigh?'

'Well, yes. Gran always said Arthur and Isabelle had a fling long before they were married. She maintained Isabelle was a bit of a naughty girl and extremely fond of the boys in her younger days. She was, apparently, even seeing one of Arthur's friends at the same time she was courting him.'

I scanned through my notebook.

'Would that be Harry Stenson or Graham Cox? Would you know?'

'I'm afraid Gran never said, or if she did I've forgotten. I'm sorry.'

'Not to worry, I'm sure we can check it out.'

'Gran did say that Isabelle shouldn't have been going out with Arthur anyway but she'd never say why. It always seemed there were plenty of skeletons in the cupboard, but perhaps Gran was just spicing up the stories a bit.'

115

'Perhaps. Is there anything else, Miss Newman?'

She looked up at Sawyer again, this time with a little more concern. He nodded to her.

'Well, not to do with my gran, Inspector, but John told me you were looking for someone who'd been seen up near Grovestock House, a man who looked like he might have been sleeping rough. I saw someone like that in the village on the day Tom Barleigh was shot. He was talking to a woman and they seemed very close; at least, she kissed him when they parted.'

'Can you describe her?'

'Pretty, I'd say, possibly late twenties. Tall with auburn hair, that's about all I noticed.'

There was little doubt in my mind. It was Elizabeth Parry.

Ten

I'd never had a clue how Elizabeth felt about me, though we'd got on well enough in the early days with tea, conversation and her all too rare smile. I'd been fairly well smitten from our first meeting but she just seemed to be lonely and filling a gap in her life. Looking after the needs of a country vicar didn't provide much in the way of stimulating social contact for a young woman, so perhaps she'd only seen me as steady, safe.

Even when we'd graduated to a kiss she seemed to be offering it as a reward for some imagined kindness in taking care of her. I should have known then that there was never likely to be any real passion in our relationship. She cared for me but probably didn't love me.

The night before I'd asked her to marry me we'd slept together for the first time. She cried softly into my shoulder afterwards and I knew she was the woman I wanted to spend the rest of my life with. Her actions in the following days showed she didn't feel the same way about me.

After we'd met again at Grovestock House we'd seen one another around the place. Even when I knew her earlier, Elizabeth had always seemed to have a knack of putting me off balance, and this hadn't changed. A few days previously, I was taking an early walk round the village before starting work when I came across her, seemingly doing the same thing, although for a brief moment I thought she was looking for me.

'Morning Elizabeth. I'm glad I bumped into you, do you have a minute?'

'What is it, James? Do you have more questions for me? I'm sure I've told you all I know.'

She'd bowed her head and her long, auburn hair had covered much of her face, though I could still see the sadness behind her eyes.

'No. No more questions. At least not for now. I just wondered … well, I thought…' My brain had screamed at me not to say the words.

She lifted her head again and a smile was playing on her lips. I was prepared for a rebuff but I ploughed on.

'There's a new play on next week. The Kenilworth Players — I've heard they're quite good. It's at the Abbey Hotel and I've been given a couple of tickets for a matinée. Could you … would you come with me?'

She had agreed, and now I was on my way to the hotel to meet her. It had been a fine, crisp afternoon when I'd walked up into the town and the sun was low, throwing the nooks and crannies in the red sandstone of the castle into sharp relief. As I sauntered up the hill I tried to figure out why Elizabeth Parry might have lied to me. Her reticence in our initial interview had certainly raised some questions, and now it appeared it might be because she'd met with a man who we were looking for. This still hadn't given me grounds to suspect her of committing a crime but I held on to a nagging doubt. Had I been smitten, even blinded, or was she just as she seemed — an attractive young woman with a secret she didn't want to share with a policeman? She had a solid alibi for when the deaths took place, so what *was* she hiding? If Dyer found out I was going out with someone associated with a case he'd have my guts for garters.

After I had been waiting around at the Abbey Hotel for some time, Sir Arthur's driver pulled up and Elizabeth climbed out of the car.

'Sorry, James, I'm really, really sorry we're so late. There was a minor emergency at Grovestock House so I was delayed.' She turned back into the car, speaking to the driver. 'Thank you, Peter. Could you pick me up again at about 9.30? Outside here will do. Bye for now.' With this she stepped back to me and smiled. 'Right then, let's see what this play has to offer.'

The Middle Watch was a fairly amusing affair, though a little hammy at times. The small portable stage in the hotel ballroom didn't do much to convey the impression of the vast warship which was supposed to be the setting for the story. But the antics of the captain, the crew and the two errant, pretty young women at the heart of the action did raise a laugh, even though everyone knew warships might not be such funny places in the near future.

I'd booked us a table in the hotel tea-room where we sat after the show discussing the weather and other trivialities.

'You said there'd been an emergency at the house?'

'Oh, it was nothing really, James. Only Sir Arthur throwing one of his little tantrums. Crockery ending up smashed on the floor and staff having to clean up before lunch could carry on. You know the kind of thing. It meant I couldn't leave when I'd intended.'

'Does he often throw tantrums and crockery then?'

'Only occasionally. He can be charming and kind, but I suppose things get on top of him now and again, especially after all that's happened recently. Anyway, it's the kind of thing you have to get used to if you're a housekeeper.'

Domestic servants, of whatever rank, are strange creatures. Amongst themselves they might complain bitterly about their employer but outside they keep their lips well sealed. I knew Elizabeth wasn't going to say any more on the matter when she smiled and changed the subject.

'I often wondered, James, did you always want to be a policeman?'

Her question made me think for a moment before I replied.

'A policeman? No, I didn't. As a child I'd think what fun it would be sneaking around and digging in other people's business, but never thought of it as a career. Always wandering round with a magnifying glass and a notebook, I was. Heavens knows what my mother used to think. I had a friend, Mordi, and we'd play detective games together but he always wanted to be Holmes on account of him playing the violin. I was never cut out for the role of Watson so I'd just play on my own mostly.'

'So how *did* you become a policeman?'

I didn't want to tell her the real reason because I'm not sure she'd have understood about Heather. I didn't lie, I just didn't tell her the whole story.

'I sort of drifted into it. I did a few things when I was younger — travelled around, a series of dead-end jobs, then I decided I needed to settle down and the police seemed like a good option.' I laughed. 'Perhaps I was remembering all the good fun I'd had with my magnifying glass.'

Elizabeth's face clouded and I wondered if I had said something inappropriate.

'James, can I tell you a couple of things? One of them has been bothering me since that first interview, and I don't want it to come between us.'

I wiped a few stray cake crumbs from my chin and stared down at my cup, stirring the tea this way and that.

By her sudden change of mood I suspected she wanted to talk about issues concerning the case. Perhaps she was going to tell me the truth about her trip into Priors Allenford on the day of the deaths, something I was hoping she'd do before I needed to challenge her about it. But now wasn't the time or place.

'Listen, Elizabeth, if this is relevant to the case can we leave it until tomorrow?' I leaned across the table and took her hand. 'It has to be done properly and we can't be seen to be mixing business and pleasure now, can we? It's not fair on either of us. Let's just enjoy ourselves tonight and I'll come and find you in the morning.'

Later that evening, on my walk home, I turned to glance over my shoulder, not for the first time, and saw no-one behind me. The street was dark but the shop doorways were darker. It would have taken no real effort for someone to step into one and immediately disappear from view.

I'm not normally prone to bouts of paranoia but I'd had the feeling of being followed for the last few days. Nothing I could put my finger on, but enough to unnerve me. It might be the case weighing down on me, with no idea of the identity of the murderer, nor even how many murders had been committed, and enough suspects to fill two Agatha Christie books. Perhaps always being on my guard up at Grovestock House had affected me, making me sensitive on the shadowy Kenilworth streets, suspicious of everyone and everything around me.

I scurried down past the park and the silhouetted castle to my front door. My hand was shaking when I turned my key and stepped into the hall, feeling relieved when the bolt clicked across on the inside.

I went straight upstairs to my little office. Without putting a match to the gas lamp I drew the curtains and looked down into the street. Directly opposite, a man was now leaning against a pillar box, staring straight up at me. Bold as brass, he tipped the brim of his trilby and started to make his way towards my front door.

At least this was a real person, not some figment of my imagination. I felt much more able to deal with him than with the terrors I'd had spinning around in my head.

'Who is it?' I shouted through the door.

'Come along, Inspector Given, open up. We need to have a word with you.'

We? Anyone using the plural must either be royalty, have reinforcements hidden from view, or be a policeman. I was fairly sure I could discount the first of these and hoped it was the last one. I took a chance and unlocked the door.

'My name's Spencer —' he flashed me a warrant card — 'Special Branch. Could you get your coat and come along with me.'

There was no question mark at the end of the sentence. It was a command, delivered by someone who was used to being obeyed.

'Can I ask what this is about?'

'I'm afraid you can't, Inspector, not at present. We don't want a fuss out here on the doorstep, do we, so get your coat. You're coming anyway, so you might as well be warm.'

It seemed I had no alternative. A large black car had drawn up at the kerb and I could see the driver and another man next to him on the front seat. Spencer took me lightly by the elbow.

'Get in, Inspector, and we'll be off.'

At the start I badgered Spencer with questions but after an initial "all in good time" he fell silent and stared stonily at the darkness floating past the window. Even though I knew this to be a standard technique to put suspects under pressure it still unnerved me. We travelled like this for nearly half an hour and I was almost grateful when the car slowed down at a sentry post. Spencer rolled down the window and spoke a few words to the young soldier on guard, who raised the barrier to allow us to drive in.

The army camp was well lit and row upon row of barrack huts stood out from the surrounding night. We drove past the parade ground where men were being drilled by a sergeant barking at them, even at this late hour. We stopped outside one of the huts and as Spencer stepped out I discovered my door wouldn't open from the inside. It was only when the others had also left the car and entered the building that Spencer let me out and guided me into the hut.

To my surprise it wasn't the dimly lit concrete clad bunker I was expecting from the latest batch of spy films, with a single electric bulb swinging above a table in the middle of the room. Instead, it was a canteen with rows of wooden trestles and bench seats, probably sufficient seating for sixty hungry soldiers. At the far end an enormous tea urn and the crockery to go with it sat on a long table. My only concern was raised by the windows, which were covered with shutters on the inside to protect the occupants from prying eyes.

The man who'd been the other passenger in the car now sat at one of the tables and indicated I should take a place beside him. Spencer placed himself on the other bench and the driver took up a spot on a single chair by the door we'd entered. Spencer introduced his companion.

'This is Mr Mitchell of MI5, he'll be asking you a few questions this evening.'

The man named Mitchell leaned over and offered his hand. I shook it and noticed how cold it was, even though he was dressed in a good quality overcoat.

'Perhaps it's me should be seeking some answers before this goes any further,' I snapped. 'Why have you got me here and on whose authority?'

Mitchell cut me off before I could protest any further.

'We'll cover that shortly, Inspector. You know the drill. For the time being let's say you're helping us with our enquiries. You don't mind doing that, now, do you?'

'In fact I do mind, but I assume I've no option, so let's get on with it.'

'Thank you so much.' The man offered a cool smile which barely covered a hint of menace. 'You are Inspector James Given of Warwickshire Police?'

'You already know who I am.'

'Just confirm it for the record, Given, and we'll all be out of here a lot quicker.'

I shrugged. 'All right, have it your way. Yes, I am Detective Inspector James Given.'

'And you live at 15 Burton Lane, Kenilworth?'

'Yes.'

Mitchell reached down below the table and pulled some documents from a briefcase. He leafed through them, laid a photograph on the table and pushed it towards me.

'This is you and Mr Alan Haleson?'

The photo showed Haleson and me sitting in the Victory, with Cudlip standing behind the bar. It seemed to have been taken from the direction of the dartboard. I tried to hide my shock, with little success.

'It is, but what's going on? How did you get this?'

'Never mind that for now, Inspector, let's get on, shall we?'

He placed a second photograph alongside the other. It was Haleson and me again, but a different location. This one was in the station buffet, with the two of us deep in conversation whilst a wedding party celebrated in the foreground. I confirmed the obvious.

'So you're not denying you met with the civil servant Alan Haleson on at least two occasions, once in a public house in Priors Allenford and a little over a week later in Birmingham New Street railway station?'

'No, I'm not denying it, why should I?'

'We also understand you've had correspondence with him.'

'Hardly correspondence. I had a letter from him and then I dropped him a brief note asking for the second meeting.'

'Can I ask you what the nature of your relationship is with Haleson, Inspector?'

'You tell me, Mr Mitchell. You seem to have all of the information on me you need.'

'Just humour me, if you would. Remind me why you've been meeting with him.'

'I'm a bloody police inspector! I'm investigating three suspicious deaths and Alan Haleson was present when they happened. Why the hell do you think I've been meeting him?'

Mitchell didn't seem disconcerted by my outburst. He simply nodded and looked briefly across the table at Spencer. He placed two more photographs down, this time outside the Birmingham station buffet. In one I was handing a sheet of paper to Haleson, in the other he was placing the folded document in his jacket pocket.

'Ever been to Germany, Inspector?'

'Germany? Hold on a minute. I'm not saying another word until you tell me what this is all about!'

Spencer stood up abruptly and walked behind me, placing his hands on my shoulders. When he spoke it was with firm, controlled anger.

'Now you listen here, Given, we're going to get through this and you'll answer Mr Mitchell's questions by hook or by crook. You keep blustering and we'll be here for days. If it takes too long and we need to leave then you'll go in a cell until we get back again, and so it will go on until he's happy. Alternatively, you be nice and co-operative and there's no reason we shouldn't have you back home in bed in no time. All you need to understand is I'm a police officer, senior to you, also investigating criminal activity, and we have reason to believe you may be connected in some way. So tell Mr Mitchell about your time in Germany.'

There was no point in arguing. I'd used the same methods myself plenty of times. Unnerve the suspect by how much you know and hope they slip up in the details. I shrugged my shoulders.

'Very well, have it your way. I was in Germany for a few months in early 1925, Bremerhaven mostly. I'd left one boat and was looking to find a berth on another. I was a merchant seaman. If you've really done your homework you'll know I wasn't only there. I went all over — Africa, the Mediterranean, even America — before I finally came home.'

'By "home" I take it you mean England?'

'Of course I do, I'm English.'

'But this isn't really your home, is it, Inspector? You're Russian, at least your dad is. And your mother. Russian parents and a Jew-boy to boot. Hardly English, is it?'

If he'd slapped me it couldn't have stung more. He tapped the two latest photographs.

'Tell me about these, Inspector. We've blown them up as much as we could but the only word we could pick out was "Bremen". That's in Germany, isn't it? Friends with the Nazis, are we?'

'Now listen, I don't know what you're insinuating but I was giving Alan Haleson the address of my uncle who lives in Bremen. You'd know as well as anyone what's happening over there to Jewish people. Haleson's in the Foreign Office and I just thought he might have contacts who could help to get my Uncle Gideon and his family out.'

'So you're interviewing Haleson as a suspect but you'd trust him enough to do you a massive favour? And you expect us to believe that?'

'Frankly, Mr Mitchell, I don't care what you believe. As far as I could see he appeared a decent enough chap and happened to be in the house when the deaths occurred. I was only interviewing him to check out some of the things he'd written to me about. There's a couple of points in his story that don't quite add up, that's all.'

Mitchell and Spencer looked at each other again, but this time a question flashed between them, whether to trust me or not. Mitchell seemed to arrive at a conclusion.

'You'll have to give us a few minutes to reflect on this, Inspector. Mr Spencer here is going to make some phone calls, then we'll finally decide what we're to do with you.'

Spencer stood up and walked over to a door at the back of the room, stepping through to an office. For five minutes or more I could hear his muffled voice before he eventually came back. He gestured for Mitchell to join him and they whispered in the corner until they apparently reached agreement. The two resumed their places at the table and Mitchell indicated to Spencer he should take over.

'It looks as if your story checks out, Inspector. Your Superintendent Dyer speaks very highly of you and our sources confirm your father does have a brother in Germany. As for Alan Haleson being a "decent enough chap" as you put it, you're way off the mark there. We've arrested him this morning for spying for Russia.'

Haleson sat huddled in the corner of an airless cell; the dapper and sophisticated young man I'd met with in Birmingham had all but disappeared. His tie and jacket had been removed and he was handcuffed to his chair. A red welt across his cheek suggested his interrogators hadn't exactly been gentle and I couldn't help feeling sorry for him, regardless of what he might have done. I could be tough enough in interviews myself, quite prepared to raise my voice and act the bully, but I'd never resorted to beating a suspect into submission.

Spencer had brought me here after our little chat. He possibly still didn't trust me but it seemed he was the junior man and it was Mitchell's decision which mattered. As we'd walked from the canteen past several rows of huts, Spencer explained that Haleson had been pulled in that morning following several weeks' observation. He had to stop his story numerous times when groups of soldiers walked past. He displayed a fascinating knack of being able to switch almost imperceptibly from disclosing state secrets to discussing the latest radio shows, and back again, when the men had passed out of hearing.

MI5 had been alerted by the Foreign Secretary's office when it appeared as if the German team had prior knowledge of what was being brought to the negotiating table. Several civil servants had been investigated and Haleson emerged as the most likely suspect when he was seen with a known Russian go-between. What Haleson didn't know was that his contact dutifully passed material down the line but somewhere in that line it was being diverted to the Abwehr, the German intelligence service. It took a little more listening in to

Haleson's telephone conversations and interception of his mail before they could tighten the noose. They were tailing Haleson throughout this time and recorded my meetings with him. It was pretty obvious why they concluded I could be implicated.

Haleson had apparently confessed everything, though Spencer didn't say if it was before or after the young man had been beaten. He was misguided enough to believe the Soviets could prevent the outbreak of war and this had taken him down the path of betraying his country. He had the best of intentions but made the worst of decisions.

I pulled a chair close in to Haleson and asked if he wanted a glass of water, which he refused. For a minute or two he didn't seem to know who I was. Whether they'd also drugged him to get at the truth I couldn't tell but he was evidently not fully in possession of his faculties. I had to speak to him several times before my voice sank in.

'Inspector Given, what are you doing here? Can you get me out of this? Please.'

He sounded pitiful and I decided to play on his need for an ally.

'I'm sorry, Mr Haleson, but there's nothing I can do. In fact, because of my association with you I was arrested myself. They only released me when it was confirmed I'd only been with you because of Tom Barleigh's murder. That's why I'm here. Is there any more you want to tell me now you're in this mess? Get it off your chest?'

This seemed to shock him out of his disorientation. He sat bolt upright in his chair and, for the first time, looked me straight in the eye.

'What are you saying, Inspector? That you suspect me of killing Tom, his mother and Jenny? How could you think I'd do such a thing? Haven't I been open with you in our discussions?'

'I have to admit that I did think you had been truthful, Alan, but now I'm faced with new information. I wouldn't for a moment have suspected you of being a traitor either, though now it seems you are. If you look at it from my point of view you must know I have little choice but to put you in the frame again, don't I?'

'What possible reason could I have for taking Tom's life? He was my best friend!'

'You know, Alan, I've been asking myself the same question — what would be your motive? And it's why you were discounted at the beginning. But now? Well, you're proven to be a liar, with no scruples about providing classified information to another country. I have to conclude that you could murder several people and tell me with a straight face that you're innocent.'

'But you have no evidence! I am innocent — I am!'

My disgust got the better of me.

'Maybe you didn't kill the Barleighs and Jenny Bamford but you're far from innocent. Your actions have put thousands, if not millions, of lives at risk and you know it. What difference would three more deaths make to you? You're right. I have no evidence but I do have a theory and the evidence will emerge if it's an accurate one. You've already said you and Tom were close and I believe you confided your treachery to him. You wouldn't have called it that, of course. You'd have told him you were acting in the best interests of England, that those around you were fools and couldn't see Communism was the best way forward. Even though you were Tom's oldest friend you'd never have guessed how horrified he'd have been at what you were admitting. Seeing his reaction, you'd have to silence him so you waited for your moment, stole the shotgun from the gardener's shed and shot him. Lady Isabelle came on the scene and you had to kill her as well. As for Jenny, you suspected Tom might have told her your secret and you needed to silence her as well, an easy decision once you'd killed twice.'

Haleson continued to whimper and shake his head.

'None of this is true, none of it. I didn't kill Tom, you have to believe me.'

'I don't have to believe you, Haleson, and I will get to the bottom of this. For the time being I'm going to leave you to our mutual friends and see what they can get out of you.'

Eleven

Despite being half dead from my previous night's activity I had Spencer drop me off at Grovestock House when we'd done. Mrs Veasey was surprised to see me at her kitchen door so early but soon had a decent breakfast on the table, which revived me no end. I asked Jervis to find Elizabeth for me and send her to the morning room when I'd finished. She seemed as unsure about how to approach the interview as I was myself when I invited her to sit opposite me in the window seats.

'You were going to tell me something last night, Elizabeth?'

'There were actually two things, James. One is relevant to your investigations and I hope you'll believe me when I say the second one isn't, at least, not directly.'

'I suspect you'd best tell them in that order then.'

'The first is about Marion Clark. She came to see me yesterday because she was worried about something. I can't tell you what it was because she asked me not to, but in all conscience I can't really keep it a secret. I told her she should come and see you, but I think you should have another word with her anyway, if she doesn't. I feel terrible at letting her down.'

'Don't worry, Elizabeth. I already had an inkling she was hiding something from me, she's been jumpy as a kitten every time I've bumped into her over the last few days. I'd planned to speak to her next week anyway.'

I asked what the second thing was she wanted to talk to me about and suddenly the view out across the park seemed of great interest to her. I imagine she'd been rehearsing her words all night but they still gushed like a plug had been pulled.

'On that first day in the garden I told you I'd spent the time after the shootings in my room but it wasn't true. I'd gone up at first then went into the village.'

'Why?'

'To warn my brother.'

'Your brother?' Even though she was admitting she'd lied to the police in a murder investigation, one part of me felt nothing but relief that the man she'd been seen with hadn't been some kind of romantic liaison. 'Three people dead in the house and you leave to spend time with your brother?'

'It wasn't like that. It was serious.'

'How serious could it have been in those circumstances?'

She closed her eyes briefly and took a deep breath. 'Michael has recently been released from prison. He'd fallen into debt and stolen some money to pay his bills. He'd been stupid enough to leave a clue to his identity so his victim found him. Michael's not a violent man but a fight broke out when he was confronted and the other man ended up in hospital.' She paused. 'I was frightened he might be dragged into what had just happened at the house.'

'So you already thought something was suspicious about the deaths?'

'No, not at all, but, you know … people put two and two together and make five. I couldn't afford any kind of scandal. If Michael had been questioned as a suspect and it had come out he was related to me I'm sure I'd have been asked to leave. Like last time.'

'Last time?'

She laughed a brittle little laugh.

'You don't understand, do you, James? When Michael was arrested before, I spoke to Reverend Gardner, hoping he'd sympathize and give me some time off to help Michael.

Instead, he just gave me my marching orders, said I couldn't be bringing any shame onto his position in the parish. That's why I left so quickly. Why I wasn't there when you came looking for me.'

I slumped back in my chair. Deep down I'd always known it would come to this, the professional versus the personal. Now I knew why she'd left me and I was half-ready to forgive her. In the circumstances who wouldn't have acted the way she had? But I couldn't allow that to interfere with my case.

'And you thought it better to hide this, in order to protect your brother and your job, rather than throw some light on three suspicious deaths? How did you know you weren't aiding a murderer to escape?'

'Michael, a murderer? How could you think such a thing?'

'Quite easily. I know you lied to me about meeting him. I've known for a couple of days. But I don't know anything about *him* except what you've told me. That he's violent and been in prison.'

'But he wouldn't kill anyone!'

'How do you know, Elizabeth, how do you know? All you have to go on is your faith in him as your brother. You should have told me about him straight away.'

She glared at me with anger and frustration.

'What? And risk you doing what you've done? Assuming he's guilty because of mistakes he made in the past.'

'I'm not assuming he's guilty! But I do need to speak to him to make sure he's not. You know I have to, don't you?'

Elizabeth stared out of the window again and I sensed a battle going on inside her head about whether to come clean. She remained silent for what seemed like an age until I felt the need to prompt her as gently as I could.

'Now come on, Elizabeth, where can I find him? I assume you know?'

In that moment I could see, as her eyes flashed, she'd come to a decision.

'I'm not going to tell you that, James, and you'll never find him.' She stood up, straightening her skirt as she did so. 'Now, I have work to do, at least while I still have a job, so I think we're through, don't you? And, by the way, I'd appreciate it if you'd keep your distance from now on.'

Sir Arthur had been limping past the door when Elizabeth flung it open to make her exit, with me trailing in her wake, still trying to work out how to retrieve the situation. I let her go on and asked him if he could spare me a few minutes.

'How can I help, Inspector?'

I told him I needed to ask him some questions about his friend, Jack Sumner.

'Sumner? What on earth do you want to know about him?'

'There's a couple of issues that have come up, sir, and I just hoped you might be able to throw some light on them. It seems he telephoned my Superintendent trying to get him to pull me out of the case. Have you any idea why he might want to do that?'

He thought for a moment, pursing his lips.

'I haven't a clue. He's a very good friend so perhaps he thought he was doing me a favour. He never said anything to me about it.'

'The other thing I wanted to talk to you about was an argument Mr Sumner apparently had with Tom shortly before he was killed. Any idea why they'd have been arguing?'

'Tom and Jack? I can't see any reason why they'd have a row, but I can't see why they wouldn't have one either. Jack is my friend but Tom knew him well enough and was getting help from him on the wedding arrangements. One strand of Jack's little empire is a food and drink wholesaler's so he was looking to save us a few pounds.' Sir Arthur chuckled. 'Perhaps they'd disagreed about the wine list.'

Marion was shaking when I beckoned her into the morning room and I could see she'd been crying. Thankfully, she'd given this up before she came through.

'Come in, Marion. Sit down over there.' I pointed to the seat in the bay window where the light was sure to emphasise anything in her face which would indicate she might be lying. 'You're not going to start crying again, are you?'

'No, sir; at least, I'll try.'

She immediately looked like she was going to go back on this promise.

'I think we need a little chat then, don't you?' I fixed her with my sternest look, at least the sternest I could muster for a pretty young woman who was falling apart in front of me.

'I do, sir. I've hardly slept a wink since you were hurt. I didn't know what I should do. I had a word with Miss Parry — she's very nice, you know — and she said I should tell you the truth. I was going to come and see you when you were next in the house.'

'That was very wise of you, Marion, and Miss Parry gave you good advice. Did you know she and I have spoken about you?'

At this the maid clasped her hands over her mouth and shook her head violently.

'But she promised she'd not tell on me! Why should she do that?'

'Calm yourself, girl. She didn't tell tales, she just confirmed what I already knew — and she did it without saying very much at all. Indeed, if you hadn't asked to see me I'd have sent for you myself before the day was out.'

This seemed to satisfy Clark and she regained her composure.

'So come along then, Marion, what have you to give to me?'

'It's this, sir.' From her apron pocket she pulled a large, manila envelope. 'But how did you know I had it?'

Indeed, it hadn't been too difficult to guess something was wrong with the girl. She'd been pleasant and chatty before the episode in Tom's bedroom but soon afterwards seemed scared out of her wits every time she bumped into me. Whenever I tried to engage her in conversation she'd make some excuse about needing to get on with her work and scurry out of the room.

'I guessed it might have been something to do with the envelope I'd found then lost. You, like all the staff, knew I was looking for it — but before we get into that, I want you to clear something else up for me.'

I pulled out my notebook and flipped through to find my record of her earlier statement to me. I didn't hurry and was happy to allow the silence to keep the pressure on the maid. I made great play of carefully reading, and re-reading, my notes before eventually closing the book again and looking up at her.

'When I interviewed you on the day I arrived here, do you remember what you said, Marion?'

'I think so, sir.'

'You told me you'd looked out of the window and saw Mr Barleigh in his wheelchair and Lady Isabelle coming towards him from the front of the house. Is that how it was?'

Marion thought for a moment or two, her face set firm in concentration.

'It can't have been quite like that, Mr Given. Now you come to mention it, there's a big bush hides part of the view. I've always thought it a shame it was there but you don't seem to notice it if you look out of the window every day like I do.'

'So you must have looked one way to see Mr Barleigh, then looked the other way to see his mother approaching, mustn't you?'

She nodded and bit her bottom lip.

'Don't worry about it, Marion; it's only a small detail but one which might be important.'

The young woman cast her eyes to the ground and I felt sorry for her, though we hadn't yet got to the hard part of her revelations. I lifted the envelope from the desk and gave a quick look inside. I'd avoided giving it too much attention when she first handed it over as I wanted her to believe my powers of deduction were greater than they are. All the time we'd been talking I was itching to get at the contents, to tip them out on the table and to examine their secrets. I laid it down again.

'Thank you, Marion. Now let's get back to the reason you've come to see me. This envelope, where did you get it from?'

'A couple of hours after your accident, sir —'

'Accident? You and I both know it was no accident. You mean just after someone bashed me on the head.'

'If you say so, sir. Well, it was then. I was cleaning out the room Mr Haleson had been staying in and I'd knocked over a flower vase. Thankfully it hadn't broken but the water had gone everywhere so I went out to get a cloth from the kitchen. As I was passing Mr Jervis's upstairs cupboard I remembered he kept cloths in there and, though I'm not supposed to go in, it seemed easier than going all the way downstairs.'

I interrupted and asked her where the butler's cupboard was located.

'It's by the top of the stairs that lead down to the kitchen. He keeps all sorts of things in there. His main pantry is downstairs, off the kitchen, but it's full of the stuff he'd use for working in the dining room or in here. He finds it easier to have some items up there to save traipsing up and down stairs all the while.'

'And the envelope was just inside the cupboard?'

'Oh no, Inspector. The cloths are in a box at the back of the middle shelf. I had to lift it out to find one and the envelope was underneath it. It seemed very strange and, because I remembered you were looking for one like it, I had a quick peek inside. I could see straight away it was like the stuff Mr Barleigh had all over his desk, so I thought it must have been the one from his room.'

'So why didn't you bring it to me immediately? Were you protecting someone?'

With this, the floods finally came. Great, gulping sobs, following a pitiful wail.

'I shouldn't have kept it. I knew Mr Jervis couldn't have had anything to do with what happened but ... oh heavens, I didn't know what to think. There was you having been knocked out and three people dead in the house, and this hidden away amongst Mr Jervis' things. I panicked and put it under my bed until I worked out what to do.'

'And Miss Parry helped you "work it out", as you put it?'

'I went to see her and asked what she thought of Mr Jervis, if he'd ever be a violent sort of person or anything like that. Miss Parry told me off for thinking so badly of such a nice man and how kind he'd been to Mrs Veasey who was still really upset, and she said to tell you everything and...' She gulped. 'I thought and thought about this and still couldn't decide what to do. In the end it felt right I should tell you and I came to as soon as I could, sir. I'm really sorry I didn't come sooner. What does it mean, Mr Given, the envelope and the attack on you?'

'I don't know yet, young lady, but I'm hoping what's in here will make it all a bit clearer in the near future. Now, back to your work and don't be keeping any more secrets.'

Jervis and I were sitting in the morning room. He looked perfectly relaxed, his hands resting on the table in front of him, fingers entwined, in the toadying way servants have when addressed by their masters. It made my skin crawl.

'I have some more questions for you, Mr Jervis, do you mind?'

'Of course not, Inspector, how can I help?'

'How long have you been at Grovestock House?'

'For about twenty years, I came here soon after Sir Arthur took over.'

'So you didn't work for his father, then?'

Jervis shook his head. 'No, sir, I didn't.'

'Tell me something. I've often wondered how a man gets into being a butler, always imagined it's handed down father to son. Is that how you came into it?'

'It wasn't quite like that, sir. My father was a farmer but I was the fourth eldest and was put into service. I've three older brothers so there was never any chance of me taking over Dad's land. I worked as footman for Lord Gresham over near Snitterfield but when the war started I joined up, like his Lordship and many on his estate. Sadly he lost his life on the battlefield, as did lots of my friends. I served all the way through, mainly in France, but when I came back the Gresham estate had been closed up, the family having moved to their other home on the south coast. I asked around and heard that Sir Arthur was in need of a butler. When I approached him, and he heard of my army service, he offered me the position.'

'Did you already know him, then?'

'Not really, sir. He'd visited his Lordship on a couple of occasions and I'd served them at dinner but he wasn't a regular visitor. I believe they may have had business connections.'

'Can I take you back to the day of the shootings? You told me you were in the lift at the time when Mr Barleigh and Lady Isabelle died. Can anyone verify that?'

'I don't think so, sir. I'd carried the linen through from the store cupboard on the landing and into the lift. I heard Miss Parry speaking to one of the maids in Mr Barleigh's room but I don't think she saw me.'

'And later, you weren't with the others in the kitchen. You said you were waiting for Miss Bamford to return. Is that correct?'

'Yes, it is.'

'You spoke to no-one other than Miss Bamford herself?'

'No, sir, not after Sir Arthur asked me to wait for her.'

'Now, I want to ask you about an envelope. One that's been found.'

'An envelope? What envelope? And found where?'

'Well, that's the point, isn't it, Mr Jervis? Found where? Found in your cupboard upstairs.'

I watched his face for any signs of recognition but saw none.

'I don't know of any envelope which could have been in there. Really, Mr Given, I don't.'

'Come on, man, it was a large, brown envelope, hidden beneath a box of rags at the back of your cupboard. How could it have got there if you didn't put it there?'

Jervis didn't respond immediately. When he did he was calm and measured.

'It could have been anyone, Inspector. All the staff know I keep lots of things in there. The family would probably know as well. But all I can tell you is, it wasn't me.'

The butler had shown on more than one occasion that he could be a cool customer but what motive would he have to kill? He had no alibis, but there was no firm evidence to connect him with any of the deaths and even the link with the assault on me was tenuous. Anyone could have put the envelope in his cupboard, as he'd said.

'I don't know if I believe you, Mr Jervis. Three people dead and possible evidence stuffed away in your cupboard. Evidence which was so important, you could have felt the need to take the risk of hitting me on the head to stop me from finding it. Well, the envelope will be dusted for fingerprints, and if they find yours, I'll be back to speak to you again. And next time I won't be going so gently.'

Twelve

I'd been delayed by my questioning of Jervis but now I pulled out the wad of documents with all the ferocity of a tramp coming upon an unexpected meal. The pile lying on the table in the morning room appeared to consist mainly of stuff relating to Tom Barleigh's interest in his family's history. Much the same as the items on his desk. But why was this particular material important enough to be separated and hidden at the bottom of his wardrobe?

I gave the envelope one last shake to be sure I'd removed everything. A small package, wrapped in tissue paper, dropped on to the mound of documents. Inside were two small hexagonal discs of what appeared to be coloured leather, held together by a thin strip, also apparently of leather. There was a name and initial stamped on to each disc and I knew one of the names very well. I carefully laid these to one side to return to them later.

I picked up each item in turn, noted what it was and placed it face down on a second pile. At the top were three certificates, two for marriages and one for Tom's birth. A quick glance told me something no-one had revealed so far. Tom Barleigh wasn't Isabelle's son.

Below these certificates was another, smaller envelope, addressed to Tom Barleigh. The letter inside, which comprised a number of pages, was folded several times and the ink had soaked through the cheap paper, leaving dark blotches all over the back. It was signed in different, shakier, handwriting by Fred Turner, who, the opening paragraphs revealed, had been

George Perkins' predecessor as head gardener at Grovestock House. It was dated a month before Tom was shot.

It opened with an apology and an explanation that Turner had not replied earlier to Tom's enquiry because he'd needed to wait for his daughter, who was a secretary, to visit and read it, and then write down his reply. It appeared Tom had contacted Turner during the summer with a number of questions relating to his research into the family history. The former gardener explained he knew little but did offer a few bits and pieces about Tom's grandfather. A gentleman, always polite, a credit to his title, and so on. I began to think the letter was going to be of little use until I scanned the last couple of pages, where I finally spotted something. I paused briefly to double-check the names on the tags I'd put to one side before returning to the letter.

I well remember your father as a child. He, like his father before him, was gentle and softly spoken, with no airs and graces, unlike his friend Harry Stenson. Arthur and Harry were like brothers, together all the time they were growing up and so similar in many ways. The big difference was their attitudes. Harry was often bad-tempered and rude to the servants, even though he himself was of no great station in life. I couldn't really understand why Arthur stayed friends with him, but he did. Right the way through school and even joining the army at the same time. Even the same company and the same battles, Arthur as captain and Harry one of his lieutenants. It was a real shock to Arthur when Harry was killed in action, coming so soon after his father's death. I think it changed him, that and the horrors he'd seen on the front line.

There's not much I can tell you about the family after the War because I wasn't there for long afterwards. While your father was recovering from his wounds I carried on trying to keep up the gardens, which had fallen into a terrible mess. We'd had to make do with myself, one other gardener who since died a year or two back, and boys from the village. At this time, Sir Arthur, as he now was, always seemed uncomfortable with me around. Perhaps I reminded him of happier times before the War or perhaps he was unhappy with my work. He was especially cross with me if I mentioned Harry Stenson for any reason and even cursed me once, shouting that I shouldn't ever speak his name again. He let me go soon after that, saying he had plans for the gardens and would want a new, modern man. He said he felt I'd be too old to manage such a project.

The letter closed with the usual good wishes and the offer to answer any more specific questions Tom might want to put to him. Beneath the letter were news-cuttings. Several from local papers covering Sir Arthur's injuries, his bravery under fire and his return home. There were also a few cuttings relating to the friends of Sir Arthur mentioned by Miss Leeming and by Fred Turner. Two were the brief announcements in the *London Gazette* of their deaths in action. The others were their obituaries, again in a local newspaper. The remaining items were photographs, mainly of someone I assumed to be Sir Arthur in his younger days. A couple showed him in uniform and the others were with friends, playing tennis, rowing or relaxing in the sunshine. One other item of interest was an unsigned brief message in what appeared to be a woman's hand.

My dearest T.
You know you have to get rid of her soon. If you don't, I'll have to do it for you.

I was almost certain the 'T' in question was Tom Barleigh. Was this the message from Trudi Collinge which Alan Haleson had referred to?

Before I could consider this much further Jervis came in to tell me Sawyer had telephoned to say he'd found Elizabeth's brother hiding out in the village and was bringing him down to see me.

Michael Parry had his sister's good looks, though his time in prison had added a few lines and a wary, sullen expression. I judged him to be about seven or eight years older than Elizabeth. This surprised me because she had spoken about him as though she was looking out for a younger brother. The hair at his temples and in his moustache was tinged with grey and his skin carried the paleness caused by a shortage of sunlight. His clothes were creased and he hadn't shaved for several days.

'Been living rough, have we, Mr Parry?'

He shrugged. 'Why would I hide? I've done nothing.'

'I didn't say you were hiding. Were you?'

Another shrug.

'Listen, we know you've been in prison. Bit of a bad temper, we hear. We also know you met your sister in the village shortly after three people died. So why did you meet Elizabeth, and why run away?'

At the mention of his sister's name Parry flinched.

'This is nothing to do with her. All she's done is try to help me.'

'And how exactly was she helping you?'

'She knew you fellers would come after me if you knew I was in the area. Try to pin something on me just because I've been inside. Lizzy only came to warn me to lie low until it had all blown over.'

The fact that he hadn't run far, he'd been picked up in the village, suggested he was telling the truth. At the time they'd met, Elizabeth wouldn't have known all the circumstances surrounding the deaths so could easily assume we'd be looking for a possible murderer.

'Could you tell me where you were before you met your sister?'

'You know where I was, I'd just come out of Shrewsbury prison. She'd written to me every week I was inside so I made my way over here to see her. It took me about a week.'

'What about the day she came to meet you?'

'I was hanging around in the village for a couple of hours waiting for Lizzy to arrive.'

'Anyone see you there? Did you talk to anybody?'

'I don't know. There were one or two about. Someone might remember me but I can't see why they would. Do I need an alibi, then?'

I told him he didn't. I decided I'd let Parry go and just have him checked out along with everyone else.

'But you stay nearby, you hear me? I may want to talk to you some more. Stay in contact with your sister every day and make sure she knows where you are at all times. Clear?'

Parry nodded. As I was seeing him out of the door I glimpsed a frown on Sawyer's face. He wasn't happy about something.

'And these were in with the papers?' Sawyer held the leather straps by the end so the two discs dangled in the light of the window. 'They're not leather, you know, sir.'

'Sorry?'

'Leather, you said they were leather discs. In fact they're some kind of cloth with asbestos, so they don't burn. My dad has one like them, except his has a serial number on it, so I think these must have belonged to officers. Really proud of it, he is. Always says it was a comfort that he'd got through the

War unscathed. Whenever he's going on any journey he'll take it out of the drawer and wear it like a St Christopher. Hopes it'll keep him safe after all they've been through together.'

I took them back and turned them over in my hand.

'There's a story here, Sawyer. I can see why Tom might keep his own father's army identification tags but why those of his father's friend, Harry Stenson? A man he'd never met in his life.'

'Perhaps Sir Arthur just had them as a token to remember his dead friend, then passed the whole package over to Tom at some point.'

'That's a possibility. I'll ask the good baronet next time I see him.'

'Do you remember it, sir? The War? My only memory is of Mum crying a lot while Dad was away. When I was older, Dad told me the conditions were awful. Right chaotic, as though no one understood what was going on or how to handle it all.'

'I was old enough to understand that if I went out there my chances of survival would be slim. Frighteningly it looks like we might be heading that way again before too long.'

'My dad was in the same regiment as Sir Arthur, you know. It might be worth you having a chat with him, see if there's anything from that time would lead to what's happened.'

I asked him to arrange it and was once more envious of his links though the generations. I could understand why he'd be reluctant to give all that up and replace it with the anonymity of urban life.

I told him I'd discovered from the birth certificate that Tom Barleigh wasn't Isabelle's son.

'So Lady Isabelle was Sir Arthur's second wife? What happened to the first — divorce?'

'No, she died when Tom was born. According to the certificates in the envelope from Tom's room, Sir Arthur married Beatrice, his first wife, in early 1914, then Isabelle when he came back wounded from the Front. It seems the boy was brought up by his grandfather, or more likely the servants, whilst his father was away. Doubtless he was packed off to boarding school after that.'

This seemed like a good point to tell Sawyer about my little episode with Mitchell and Spencer. He was as shocked as I'd been about Haleson's treachery.

'So this puts Haleson high up on the list of suspects, does it, sir?'

'I'm not sure. He strenuously denied any involvement in murder, even though he'd admitted passing secrets to the Russians. I have to say he seemed pretty broken by the time I saw him, so I think he'd have come clean if he'd had anything to do with the killings. He can only be executed once. We'll leave him on the list for now, but perhaps not near the top.'

'And you're in the clear — sorry, sir, I mean you're no longer under suspicion?'

'As far as I can tell. Mitchell let me go after they'd had words with Dyer and made a couple of phone calls, though you never know with those boys. Anyway, let's get back to this stuff in the envelope.'

'Did you find anything else interesting, sir?'

'I went through these papers from top to bottom and I couldn't get much else from them. I'd say they were to do with Tom's genealogy research but I still can't work out why they'd be kept apart from the rest of the things on his desk? What is it about them that's so special? There seemed to be quite a few items about his father's dead comrades. Photographs and news cuttings about their deaths, that kind of thing, but I can't see any connections.'

I knew we might be chasing a red herring with the envelope, although if someone tried to keep the information from us by bashing me over the head it must be worth something.

'Speaking of photos, do you have any more you took in the garden or Tom's room?'

There'd been something niggling me in the ones of Lady Isabelle. I'd looked at them over and over and knew I was missing something. Like a bird flashing past the corner of my eye, it was there, yet I couldn't describe it.

'I do have some more, sir, but they're a bit grainy so I didn't put them in with my report. I thought they might not be good enough.'

It was nice to think he was proud of his work.

'Well, you'd best let me have what you've got and I'll go through them with the others. You never know, there might be something there. Drop them down to me as soon as you can.'

Sawyer sent the extra photographs over to me, using some village lad as messenger, and I put them on the table with the others. Each row focussed on a different victim, starting with Tom at the top, Jenny at the bottom and Isabelle in between.

There seemed to be nothing new in those of the murdered young man. The angles were slightly different in the ones Sawyer had hung on to but that was all. The flash had worked its magic on the indoor pictures, so there were only two new ones of Jenny and both were virtual copies of some I already had.

In those of the mother he'd included a close-up snapshot of her face, her expression captured at the precise moment of her demise. Her eyes wide and lips held in a perfect circle, almost as if she was surprised. Even though she was in her late forties I could see she would have been a beauty in her youth. Certainly quite a catch for Sir Arthur, whose good looks had been burnt away by the time they married.

Suddenly it struck me. I could see Lady Isabelle's face in the photograph. I was sure she *had* been murdered.

Thirteen

I'd rung Dyer's office as soon as I'd come to the conclusion about Isabelle Barleigh's murder. I wanted to see him urgently but was told he was out in Stratford-on-Avon at a Superintendents' meeting for two days. I was thinking of attempting to go over to Stratford to find him when I received a call back from WPC Fallon. She told me she'd managed to contact Dyer and he'd see me on Wednesday afternoon at his office in Warwick when his meetings were finished. She said I wouldn't be able to speak to him before he returned so it made sense to get on with other things and I'd arranged with Sawyer to see his father.

If I'd seen Sawyer and his father standing side by side anywhere outside their home I'd never have guessed they were related. Dave Sawyer was dark haired and thick set, the complete opposite of his son, with a farmer's complexion, leathery from long days spent outside in all weathers. His grip, when he shook my hand, was strong and calloused.

'Good to finally meet you, Inspector. John talks about you all the time.'

Sawyer Junior let out an exasperated, 'Dad!'

'It's a pleasure to meet you too, Mr Sawyer, John's a fine officer.'

My colleague blushed even more and it would have been fun to carry on embarrassing him. However, I needed to interview his father alone, so I sent him out for a while.

'John tells me you were in the same regiment as Sir Arthur Barleigh, is that right?'

'It is. Lots of us around here joined up together, all in the same mob, "pals" battalions they called 'em. I can think of at least twenty men who came with us, including Sir Arthur and his mates, Graham Cox and Harry Stenson. Those two, and another eight or ten, never came back. They stopped that happening later in the War, too many men from the same area being slaughtered. What a waste. Why do you ask?'

'I was wondering if you might know of anything in Sir Arthur's past which might explain why someone would kill his wife and son. Anyone with a grudge, that kind of thing?'

Dave Sawyer sat back in his chair and thought for a minute.

'No-one comes to mind, Inspector. No-one who'd murder someone, anyway.'

'It's often hard to tell who'd commit such a crime, Mr Sawyer. If you can think of anyone at all who'd dislike Sir Arthur, or Lady Isabelle for that matter, just tell me and we'll check them out.'

'As I said, many of the men from that time never came home. Of those that did, I only ever heard one say a bad word about Sir Arthur. Wally Bailey.'

I wrote down his name.

'Is he still local?'

Dave laughed. 'You could say he's local and always *in* the local.' He continued chuckling at his own joke.

'This Mr Bailey likes a drink then, does he?'

'Aye, he does that. Nicest man you'd ever want to meet when he's sober, though that's rare enough these days. When he's had a few he's loud and rambles like my old donkey. Now and again he'll go on about how Sir Arthur's a fraud and how he hates the man.'

'A fraud?'

153

'Hard to be sure what Wally's going on about because he rambles, as I say. But as far as I can make out he reckons Sir Arthur got all the credit as a war hero when he came back, just because he'd been injured. Wally himself was decorated, saved some blokes out of no-man's land, and resents the fact he never got the recognition he deserved. As far as I'm concerned, they're both heroes. From what I know, Sir Arthur paid a high price for his time at the Front.'

He wouldn't go so far as to say he thought Bailey meant Sir Arthur any harm so I just got from him where the man did his drinking, and asked if he could think of anyone else.

'Only other person I can think of, and it might be something and nothing, was a woman who came round about eighteen months ago, just after young Tom's accident. There was quite a bit in the papers about it at the time and all sorts of people came hanging around. Our John had to chase a few of them off, they were such a nuisance.'

'So who was this woman? Why did she stand out from the others?'

'She latched on to me one day when I was in the post office. Fine looking woman, though she'd have been in her fifties. Must have been a stunner when she was young. Well dressed. Looked like a city type, not from round here. Started asking me questions about the Barleighs. I thought she was just another sad woman getting her thrills from someone else's misfortune so I told her to sling her hook. Then she apologised and said it wasn't Tom Barleigh she was interested in, but his father. After a couple of minutes she started going on about how he owed her something, how they'd been very close in the past but he'd left her. She said she needed to see him to pay him back. The poor lass seemed to be in quite a state about it.'

'So what did you do?'

'I felt sorry for her and decided it was up to him to sort out his own affairs, so just gave her directions up to Grovestock House. She went off and I didn't see her again.'

Sawyer and I left his father's house and ensconced ourselves in a back room of the Victory which Mr Cudlip continued to allow us to use as an office. He kept us well supplied with cups of strong tea, biscuits and occasional sandwiches. I suspected he'd gossip with his regulars about any little scrap he might get from us. As a result I made sure everything was taken away each day. If I needed a rumour to be spread I could, in a moment of rare forgetfulness, leave something in the room for him to pick up on.

I liked Cudlip. He appeared to be a good honest man trying to eke out a living as best he could. He was over six feet tall, a veritable giant amongst the local farmers and workmen who mainly frequented the pub, and cut a comical figure as he ducked and bowed under the low beams and doorways, going about his business. He was a mine of information and always ready with a funny story he'd picked up from a customer or someone he'd met in the town. Cudlip was a useful, if unknowing, assistant to have as he fed me all the bits of tittle-tattle he'd heard. None of them had proved important in the case so far but they helped to paint a fuller picture of the village and its residents.

I filled Sawyer in on how I knew Isabelle had been murdered.

'So you're saying, sir, that if she'd held the shotgun under her own chin she'd have had the barrel against her body and would have blown off her face when she pulled the trigger? Couldn't she do it any other way?'

'Well, possibly, but this is the most likely — the most comfortable way of holding the weapon. She'd have had to hold the weapon at arm's-length at an angle to just destroy the back of her head, and that would be far from easy. One thing I'm having trouble working out is, if Isabelle didn't kill Tom but was shot after him, why she couldn't run off to raise the alarm when Tom was murdered? If she had, then the killer would have shot her in the back from a distance and not been able to stage a suicide.'

'Perhaps the murderer was holding her hostage with the gun under her chin.'

'But surely she'd have struggled and escaped. Unlikely he, or she, would be able to hold on to Isabelle effectively, shoot Tom with any degree of accuracy, and then get the weapon back under her chin.'

'You're now assuming, then, that Lady Isabelle was shot first?'

'I'm coming to that conclusion, John, I can't seem to make sense of it any other way. The problem then thrown up is whether her ladyship was really the main target, rather than Tom.'

At this point the landlord came in with our lunch. After some pleasantries he confided he'd heard a rumour regarding Tom Barleigh and his nurse. Cudlip's informant had assured him it was "the gospel truth" that Miss Collinge had a deep and consuming crush on Tom. She'd apparently convinced herself he'd soon throw over Jenny Bamford in favour of her.

Cudlip left wearing a satisfied smile. Sawyer added to the list in front of him.

'He's a useful source of information, don't you think? Nothing stays secret in a village pub and he's just confirmed what Alan Haleson said. It also almost guarantees the threat I found in Tom Barleigh's envelope came from Collinge.'

'So she could have done it? Hell hath no fury, etc?'

'I suppose if Tom eventually made it clear he was only interested in Jenny Bamford, the nurse might have decided to wreak revenge on the two of them. But why would she go for Lady Isabelle as well? And why would she shoot two people with the shotgun and then go to the trouble of finding another gun to kill the fiancée?'

'Perhaps she didn't know how to reload the shotgun? She could have pinched it from the gardener's shed already loaded, then not known what to do, or had no more cartridges when she'd emptied the two barrels.'

'That's a possibility, John, a little unlikely, but we'll keep it in mind. In any case, we'll have to leave Nurse Collinge on the list until either we can find her or discount her properly. We were just going to go through the others when Mr Cudlip came in, so who are they?' I noticed him smile briefly as I called him by his first name.

'It's becoming quite a long list now, sir. The ones I have are Billy Sharp, Michael Parry, the mysterious man in the woods and, now, Trudy Collinge and Alan Haleson, plus the ones Dad mentioned, Wally and this woman who came looking for Sir Arthur. I suppose we always have Mr Jervis as well. After all, the envelope was found in his cupboard and he has no satisfactory explanation about how it got there. I know those Victorian melodramas always have the butler doing the dirty deed, but it would be nice and tidy if this time he actually had!'

I laughed. If only life was as simple as that. We went on to consider Haleson as a suspect. He, at least, had a possible motive for getting Tom Barleigh out of the picture, if he had indeed told his friend of his treason.

157

'But isn't that at odds with your idea of Lady Isabelle being the first one killed, sir? And anyway, even if Tom was the target and Lady Isabelle came upon the scene by accident, why should Haleson go on to murder Jenny Bamford? It's the same reasoning as for Trudi Collinge.'

'I know, I know, John. Of course you're right but we'll need to leave him somewhere near the top of your list for the time being. Doubtless our friends at Special Branch and MI5 will get it out of him if he was in any way involved. I notice you don't have Sir Arthur on your list?'

'Sir Arthur? Why would you think it could be him, sir? What possible motive would he have?'

'I don't know, John, but somebody did it and he'd as much opportunity as anyone else, though I agree, I can't see why he would. It might just be my natural mistrust of the landed gentry but let's also add him to your list till we can take him off for certain. What about Billy Sharp?'

'On the face of it Billy's the most likely for using the shotgun, either as an accident or in a fit of anger for being told off. It was fairly well known the lad liked to play around with the gun, and he has taken off and gone to ground. But there's still the problem of the third shooting, the same as with the nurse and Sir Arthur. Why would Billy, having killed Tom and Lady Isabelle, find another gun, then chase after Jenny Bamford and pop her off as well?'

It occurred to me that Jenny's death might be a bit of a distraction. Did she commit suicide after all? Or could she have been murdered by someone other than the person who killed the others? Two murderers? Highly unlikely but still a possibility to be considered. I shared this with Sawyer.

'Good God, sir, do you really think that's possible?'

Until recently all the young fellow had needed to deal with were petty crimes and the occasional drunk and disorderly. Now he was faced with the picture of two killers walking the streets of his sleepy parish.

'Relax, John. The chances of Grovestock House harbouring two homicidal maniacs is a bit remote, I'll admit, but we don't want to have to backtrack later to make all the pieces fit together.'

With this reassurance Sawyer seemed to calm down slightly and we moved on to Michael Parry.

'I don't know about this one, John. There's no doubt he's a bad egg but it's only been minor stuff in the past, usually just getting into trouble after drinking or losing his temper, until the latest incident with the theft. He has no alibi but I'm still inclined to believe he had nothing to do with it.'

Sawyer started to reply but changed his mind.

'Go on, John, what is it?'

He was still hesitant and I had to urge him again to speak.

'Do you think you might be being a bit light on him because he's Miss Parry's brother, sir? I ... I mean, with you and her going out, so to speak.'

I held my temper, though I was seething at his suggestion. I'd asked him to speak his mind, so now he had there was no point in bawling him out for it. At least it was better out in the open than festering throughout the investigation.

'We've not known each other long, have we?'

Sawyer hung his head. 'No, sir, we haven't.'

'So you'd not know whether what you just said was reasonable or not?'

'Sorry, sir, I only meant —'

I cut him off. 'When you know me a little better you'll see me for what I am — a bastard when it comes to catching criminals. I've even considered if Elizabeth Parry herself might have been involved in the murders in some way but she has cast iron alibis. I would exclude no one, not even her, let alone her brother, if I had the slightest inkling they were implicated. If you can show me any firm evidence linking Michael Parry, I promise I'll show no mercy. Do you have anything, Constable?'

'No, sir, I don't. All we have is he was in the area at the time, he, like Sharp and Collinge, has disappeared, and he has a record, a prison record, sir, for violent crime.'

'Good points, John, and well made. Never assume that older, more experienced officers have all the answers. Being a good detective is being able to see the things others can't see. Tell you what, when we're finished here you can pull him in again and we'll have a second go.'

Sawyer brightened at this, though I could see he was still a bit annoyed at the dressing down. Still, he'd get over it. We agreed I'd also follow up on Wally Bailey and ask Sir Arthur about his lady friend when I got a chance.

'There's also Jack Sumner, you know. I've had no proper explanation about why he wants me off the case or why he was arguing with Tom Barleigh. He's another long shot so I'd best interview him at some point.'

This was becoming silly. A list of suspects as long as my arm and none I'd be confident to put in court. And the roll call was getting longer by the minute.

'Finally, we have the man in the woods. What have you got on him?'

'He's a right mystery, sir. All we know for sure from the cook is someone, she thinks it was a man, was standing at the far edge of the woods looking over the wall of Grovestock House when she went out to the village. The person was too far away for her to see anything distinctly, and she didn't give it too much thought as there are often walkers passing through there.' He hesitated. 'Do you think it might have been Michael Parry?'

'If it was he could have been there for any number of reasons. Perhaps he was trying to make contact with his sister. Have you been over to see what the man was looking at?'

'I took the cook out with me to find the spot where she'd been, and once she'd pointed out the general direction I went over to the wall myself. There was a patch a couple of yards wide where the grass was heavily trampled as though someone had been there a while and had walked up and down, perhaps trying to get a better view. There are several paths through the woods, one just a couple of yards from where our man had been so it wasn't possible to tell which way he'd entered and left.'

'Did you look over the wall?'

Sawyer gave me a look suggesting he wasn't impressed with my question. He referred to his notebook.

'A few stones are missing from the top so the wall is fairly low there, only about five feet high. It would be easy for a man of average height to get a decent view but it's only really possible to see the hedge around the side lawn and the front door of the house. No one would have seen what took place behind the hedge. I had a good search on the ground and along the path but there didn't appear to be anything of interest. A few odd cigarette butts, all different types, had been flicked into the grass but they could have belonged to anyone.'

'I'm taking a walk back to the House that way later so I'll do a bit of looking around myself, see if I can spot anything missing.'

I was pleased with the progress we'd made on reviewing the suspects, despite our little spat. Even though we hadn't got very far in thinning out the pack, at least we'd clarified who needed following up. And we'd cleared the air a bit in terms of my relationship with Elizabeth. Sawyer was a bright copper and it was right of him to question me, even if it did get me riled.

The lunch provided by Cudlip had been as expansive as always. Platefuls of sandwiches with pie on the side and, as if we needed more, a dish of apple tart. We could hardly keep our eyes open after all this, though we did manage to struggle through the last few points before giving up for the afternoon. The day was sunny, with a light breeze rustling the branches, occasionally dislodging one of the few remaining leaves to float down.

I was glad I'd decided to walk back to Grovestock House; the exercise wouldn't do me any harm and I'd take the opportunity to have a look in the woods as I'd promised. Sawyer told me how to find the place from the House but because I was walking from the opposite direction I had to look for an alternative route in. With the trees and bushes now mainly devoid of foliage it was relatively easy to see the start of the wall through the woods as I approached the estate. I'd already passed several footpaths where they joined the lane and I could see Sawyer was right in his assessment. Any of them could have been used for access or escape.

About a hundred yards ahead of me was the fallen pine tree Sawyer said marked the spot opposite where our mystery man had been seen. I stopped for a moment to trace the line from the road, squinting down my left arm and index finger, to locate the point on the wall where the stones were missing. When I reached the end of my imaginary line, there was someone by the wall again. I stood stock still. He paced up and down, then placed his hands on top of the wall to scrabble up to get a better view.

I pushed through undergrowth at the edge of the wood, catching the back of my hand on a thorn. A stream of bright red trickled down to my fingertips, summoning a picture from an earlier time and a different woodland. A girl, Heather, spread-eagled on the ground, blood oozing from the stab wound in her breast. I shook away the memory, edged in behind a tree to conceal my presence and crept forward, foot by painstakingly slow foot, in the hope I might get close enough to catch him. I reached within ten yards when the inevitable happened. A branch, long fallen from the canopy, cracked beneath my size nines. The man turned around, saw me and, in an instant, was crashing away through the undergrowth. I was caught off guard by how quickly he fled, which meant he'd gained vital yards before I set off after him. He had the added advantage of seeming to know where he was going and all I could do was try to keep him in sight as he weaved through the many paths.

After a hundred yards it was obvious I wasn't going to catch him and so I had to stop and listen to him making his way off into the distance. I lay my back against a tree, gasping for breath, and resolved that when this case was over I'd commit some time to getting back into shape. More exercise and fewer of the Cudlip-style lunches would be the order of the day.

By the time I finally walked back to Grovestock House I was beginning to wish I'd telephoned for the car. The chase as well as the walk was much more than I'd bargained for. I contemplated sitting down, in the hope that someone would offer me a lift, but there was little traffic and this would only delay me.

As was my habit now I went into the House through the kitchen door and wasn't surprised when the cook asked me to join her in a cup of tea.

'Don't mind if I do, Mrs Veasey, I'm fairly beat.'

I told her what had happened on my walk back and it wasn't long before she laid the cakes out as well as the tea. So much for my earlier resolve to cut down.

'Could I check something with you, Mrs Veasey?'

'Anything at all, Inspector, what can I help you with?'

'It's something you mentioned in your statement. You said the man you spotted in the woods was standing looking over the wall. Do you remember? Saying he was standing, as if he was quite tall?'

'Oh yes. He stood very still, as if watching but not wanting to be seen. As I said to Constable Sawyer, there are often people in the woods and I expect you can get a good view of the house from by the wall, so I never really thought anything about it, just that he was so still.'

At this point the door opened and the butler joined us. Mrs Veasey immediately clucked around him like an old mother hen, spilling out everything I'd told her. I couldn't tell if she was scared, excited, or in love with the man but I'd have preferred it if she hadn't been so free with my information. Especially to a man who was possibly still under suspicion. I should have stopped her, but she was halfway through before I could open my mouth. When she paused for breath he pulled a note from his pocket.

'I'm pleased I found you, Inspector, the constable rang and left a message. Asked if you could call him back when you've chance. He said it was concerning the young man you sent him to look for.'

I cursed under my breath, though was grateful for Sawyer's discretion with Parry's name.

'Thanks for that, Mr Jervis, I'm most grateful and I'm glad you've joined us. Could you please ask Sir Arthur to make himself available in about fifteen minutes and tell him I won't keep him more than is necessary?'

'What is it now, Inspector? I thought we'd dealt with everything last time we met.'

Once again the arrogance of the man got under my skin. We were in his library and he'd remained seated when Jervis brought me in. I was left standing, like one of his servants, but I took a seat anyway.

'Sorry, Sir Arthur — you don't mind if I sit down, do you? — but I'm afraid we might need to have these little inconveniences from time to time until these three murders are sorted out.'

'But you're not even sure there were three murders, are you? The only one you're actually certain about is Tom's. Don't you think you're trying to bend and shape the bare facts a little too far to fit your theory?'

'Unfortunately, Sir Arthur, we now know you're wrong in one very important respect.'

'And in what respect would that be, man?'

'I can show that Lady Isabelle was murdered.'

He slumped back in his chair. 'Murdered? How? I mean … what makes you think that?'

'I'm afraid I can't tell you, Sir Arthur, but let's just say evidence has come to light which makes it fairly certain. So everyone is now a murder suspect unless they can prove otherwise.'

He seemed to regain his composure. 'All right, Inspector, let's get this over with. What is it you want to know?'

'Thank you, Sir Arthur, there are a couple of points I need to clear up. Firstly, I'd like to ask about some identity tags we've found amongst Tom's things. Do you know the ones I'm talking about?'

'You're talking about my army identity tags?'

'Yours and those of a Mr Harry Stenson.'

'Lieutenant Stenson, Inspector, not simply "mister". He was my lifelong friend and served with me in France. I saw him blown to pieces in front of me at Passchendaele.' He touched his face. 'That was where I picked this up. Burned so badly even my own mother wouldn't recognise me. Lost two toes as well, and a piece of shrapnel the size of a golf ball lodged in my back. Did you know that, Inspector?'

'They were terrible times, sir.'

I had to pity the man for what he'd been through. He turned away and looked beyond the window into the far distance, as if trying to capture something lost.

'As you say, Inspector, terrible times. For months I was in hospital with men dying all around me. I was supposedly one of the lucky ones. I was in France until I was well enough to be moved back over to England. When I started to get back on my feet I came home to Grovestock House to recuperate. But then the old man died and I was expected to take over running the place. I didn't think I'd have the nerve to go to the Front again but I needn't have worried. By the time I was anywhere near fit enough to consider getting around on my own the whole show was over.'

Sir Arthur shook his head and turned back to face me.

'I picked up Harry's identification tag on the battlefield, even though I shouldn't have. Just something to remember him by.

I've kept mine and his together all of those years, here, in a drawer in my library. When Tom started his research into the family, my wife told him he could look around to see if there was anything relevant. He must have picked up the tags then. I didn't know he'd got them.'

'Could I also ask you about Billy Sharp, Sir Arthur?'

'Billy Sharp? Oh, the lad who helps out in the garden? Can't say I really know anything about him. Perkins handles all of that side of things.'

'You didn't see him on the morning the murders happened?' I emphasised the word 'murders'.

'I hardly saw anyone, Inspector; I've told you, I was up in my room before it all happened and went back up again afterwards before I went out. Is it important? Do you think this Billy Sharp had something to do with it?'

'Not really, sir, although it is a possibility. I just think he might have seen something and run off because he was frightened. I hoped someone might have seen him so we can discount him as a suspect. It would also be useful for us to find him as a witness if he did see the murderer.'

'Well, I'm sorry, Mr Given, but I didn't. Perhaps one of the staff might have. Now, is there anything else I can help you with?'

'Actually, sir, there is one other thing.'

I asked him about the woman who'd been looking for him and who'd been directed to the house by Dave Sawyer.

'That would be Agnes Black. She was a nurse in the hospital where I was convalescing. Very attractive young woman at the time and we became friendly. More than friendly actually. But it meant nothing, at least not to me. For some reason she started writing to me a couple of years ago saying all sorts of crazy things.'

'Such as?'

'That she was in love with me, always had been. Said she'd had a child but he'd died. Then she started making demands, saying I owed her something. Next thing I knew she had turned up on my doorstep. Fortunately I'd already told Isabelle about the letters so the two of us confronted Agnes and sent her packing.'

He looked upset when he mentioned his wife's name.

'And did she stop?'

'No. The letters kept coming so about nine months ago I'd had enough and had my solicitor write to her threatening legal action if she didn't desist.' Sir Arthur stopped short as a thought seemed to have come to him. 'You don't think she could have had anything to do with this, do you? My God, I know she was a little irrational, but murder?'

I said I didn't know, but she might be worth following up. He gave me the last address he had for her and asked if I needed anything else. I told him there wasn't and thanked him again for his time. I couldn't decide if I believed what he'd told me but had no real reason not to accept it as the truth. At least for the time being.

I'd wanted so much to believe Elizabeth that her brother had nothing to do with the murders. Regardless of Sawyer's misgivings I'd released Michael Parry and now he'd gone. I rang Sawyer and I could hear the exasperation in his voice.

'He's in the wind, sir. Seems he was seen with Miss Parry shortly after we released him, then jumped on the bus to town. What do you want me to do?'

I told him to put a call out to the police stations around the county to keep an eye out for Parry, then to get on with other stuff until I called him.

I was fuming. When I found Elizabeth in Tom Barleigh's room she was clearing the dead man's clothes from his wardrobe onto the bed before packing them in tea-chests. She looked up and half-smiled when I walked in; but when she saw my mood, her expression tightened.

'Where is he?'

'Who?'

'Don't play games with me, Elizabeth. Where's Michael?'

'He's gone and you'll not find him again.'

'Gone? Gone where?'

'America. I gave him some money I'd saved up and told him to get away.'

I lashed out at the pile of clothes on the bed, scattering them onto the floor.

'How could you be so stupid, Elizabeth! Do you know what you've done? He must have told you I'd interviewed him and was satisfied enough to let him go. Things have changed so I needed to talk to him again. Now I'll have to issue an arrest warrant and have him brought back. Then it will look much worse for him for running away.'

She bit her bottom lip and stared me coldly in the eye.

'You do what you have to do, *Inspector*. I've told you Michael is innocent.'

Elizabeth picked up the debris from the floor, threw it back on the bed and pushed past me onto the landing. She spat her final words over her shoulder, shaking her head in desperation.

'I think it's better if we keep our relationship as it is. You just come looking for me when you have police business to discuss.'

Wally Bailey was exactly where Sawyer's father had said he would be: propping up the bar of the Rose and Crown, surrounded by like-minded philanthropists supporting the brewery. It was only half an hour after opening time so I was hoping he'd still be coherent when I introduced myself and asked if we could have a word. His drinking companions exchanged knowing looks and Wally was trembling so much he spilled half his pint as we made our way to a table in the corner. Sawyer had told me he'd been pulled in a few times for being drunk and disorderly but had been sent home without charges once a few hours in a cell had quietened him down.

'So, Wally, a little birdie tells me you don't like Sir Arthur Barleigh, you shout your mouth off about him all the time.'

He cast his eyes around the bar at his mates, who now all seemed to have something more interesting to look at on the other side of the counter. Despite his shaking he tried to tough it out. 'Who told you that?'

'It's true then?'

'What if it is? What's this all about?'

'Answer the question, Wally. Do you have a grudge against Sir Arthur Barleigh?'

'I wouldn't call it a grudge. I don't like him much, never have, not after what he did.'

'And what was that?'

'He came back here, loads of local lads shot to pieces, and takes all the glory just because he's badly injured and still alive. Even his two best mates killed and he gets himself in the papers like a big brave man. Then he comes into money and marries a beauty while some of us have to scratch a living like always. Mentioned in despatches out there, I was, and you know what, Inspector, I didn't sleep a full night through for two years after I got back, shells exploding in my head all the time.' He held out his shaking hand at full stretch. 'What do you think caused this?'

He wasn't the first man I'd seen with shell shock but I couldn't help thinking back to what Dave Sawyer had said. They were all heroes. Men like Wally Bailey had come home expecting their lives to be different and they were, though not necessarily better in the way they'd hoped. Who knows, he might have drunk himself senseless and railed at the world even if he hadn't had his experiences in the trenches but, then again, he might not. Either way, all I could see in front of me now, with drink-flushed cheeks and a half empty glass quivering in his hands, was a sad, middle-aged man carrying a chip on his shoulder. Not a murderer.

We carried on with routine questions for another few minutes, though my heart wasn't in it. When I asked him where he'd been on the day of the murders he called the landlord over.

'Here, Geoff, tell the Inspector where I was when Tom Barleigh and his mum were bumped off.'

The landlord shrugged. 'I expect you was in here as always. What day was it?'

I gave him the date and time.

'Oh, definitely, he was in. He'd had a bit of luck on the races the day before and spent his way through it. Passed out by lunchtime he was.'

I didn't bother to point out the pub shouldn't have been open long enough for him to be drunk by that time. Villages have always been a law unto themselves as far as that's concerned. Consequently I gave Bailey the usual "don't go anywhere because we might want to talk to you again" speech then left him to his beer and friends, wishing I could have stayed and joined them at the bar.

Fourteen

The next morning, I made my way to Jack Sumner's office on the first floor of a rather dingy warehouse on the edge of Warwick. A secretary, who I'd been told was his wife, Marjorie, showed me into his office. She called him "Mr Sumner" and he dismissed her like some Eastern potentate dismissing a servant. I took an instant dislike to the man.

His room belied the building which housed it and reminded me of the only slightly grander room of Sir Arthur Barleigh. Sumner was seated in a plush leather chair behind a desk he could hardly reach across when he stood to shake my hand. I was intrigued by the oil painting of Jerusalem on the wall behind him.

'Good morning, Inspector Given. Marjorie tells me you wanted a word.'

I explained that the case had now turned into a murder investigation so I'd been wondering why he'd felt the need to contact my Superintendent to have the investigation stopped. I could see him bristling at the impertinence of my question.

'Apologies if this upset you, Inspector.' He didn't look remotely contrite. 'It seemed to me you were sniffing around at Sir Arthur Barleigh's place all the time, making yourself a nuisance. I understand you demanded Sir Arthur stay in the house until you'd interviewed him, telling the butler it was routine — but it was obvious you were digging around for dirt. I thought there must be a promotion in it somewhere for you.'

'Well, at the time it *was* just routine, Mr Sumner. But now it's different and I can't help thinking perhaps you knew that already.'

He laughed. 'What? You think I had something to do with this whole affair? As far as I was concerned it just wasn't good enough. Sir Arthur wanted to be left alone to put his life back together. It appeared obvious they were acts of madness by two hysterical women. One murder and two suicides. Everyone but you agreed with that and I wanted you out of there.'

'I was proved right though, wasn't I? Lady Isabelle, Tom Barleigh and Jenny Bamford were shot for reasons unknown by persons unknown. *Was* it you?'

'Why? Because I tried to protect the feelings of a good friend? Don't be ridiculous, man.'

'But you also had a row with young Tom, didn't you, shortly before the day he was murdered? I hear it was quite serious and when you left you were telling him he'd regret it. What was that about? Did you make him regret it?'

Sumner looked like he'd been slapped and some of his earlier arrogance left him. He leaned forward with his elbow on the desk and rubbed his forehead.

'Inspector, Tom Barleigh was his father's son and we were very close. Sometimes it felt to me as if I was back in my early twenties and it was Arthur and me talking. I was devastated when he died, still am. But you can be close to someone and have major disagreements. I have to say I'd agreed with Isabelle that he shouldn't be marrying Jenny, I didn't like her at all. Thought her most unsuitable. So when Isabelle asked me to try one last time to dissuade him about the marriage, I agreed. And that was it. He called me a few names I'd rather forget and it all ended acrimoniously.'

'So you parted on bad terms and soon afterwards he was dead. How do you think that looks, Mr Sumner?'

'I have to admit it doesn't look good. I had been poking my nose in where it wasn't wanted and we both said things we shouldn't, but Tom rang me later to apologise. I did the same and we made up.'

He confirmed no one could verify the reason for the argument, the telephone call or its outcome, because both Tom and Lady Isabelle were dead. I didn't like Sumner but his explanations sounded plausible. He then told me that he'd been in the office all day when the murders took place, although the only person who'd be able to corroborate it was his wife. I knew she would if I asked her so it would mean very little.

When I stood up to leave I asked him about the picture of Jerusalem.

'Have you been there, Inspector?'

'No, I haven't, but it looks beautiful — at least in the painting. Have you been yourself?'

'It is, and I've been many times. I try to make pilgrimage and pray at the Western Wall every two or three years.'

I should have known better but I was surprised that he was Jewish. I mentioned the beatings case I'd been working on and asked if he'd had any problems.

'Not so far. I think perhaps my business is a bit too big for them to get to me. Too many of my men about the place most of the time. It's a bad affair, though; your colleague, Terry Gleeson, mentioned it to me.'

'You know Inspector Gleeson?'

'Oh yes, I know him very well.' He jerked his thumb at the painting. 'But don't mention what I said about this to him, if you don't mind.'

I arrived at Warwick headquarters after lunch and asked the front desk to let me know when Dyer was back. After they rang me I gave him five minutes before dashing up to his office, before he could get embroiled in anything else.

He looked as smart as ever I'd seen him, in his best dress uniform, patently only wheeled out when he was trying to impress. He was also not in the best of moods.

'Bloody silly games these people play, James. It's not about good policing these days, only about office politics, who can get one over on who. We're here on the edge of a war, with the whole country on alert, and this damn meeting spends most of its time bickering and in-fighting. I felt like getting up and walking out.'

I wasn't sure if what I was about to tell him would put him in a better frame of mind or a worse one but I had no alternative now he'd arrived. However, he was already one jump ahead of me.

'What's this MI5 nonsense you've got yourself mixed up in? I'd just gone to bed when I get a call from some man — Spencer, I think he called himself — claiming to be from Special Branch and saying he's thinking of arresting one of my officers.'

I gave Dyer the whole story and said I was sorry he'd been put out.

'What the hell do you think you were playing at? Even if the chap hadn't been a spy you shouldn't have been talking to a witness in a potential murder case and being pally for your own personal reasons. I should have you put on disciplinary charges, and might even do so when the case is finished.'

I drew a deep breath. 'It's no longer just a *potential* murder...' I went through my reasoning and thankfully he seemed to consider it accurate, even if he wasn't entirely happy with the result.

'I have to say I'm having difficulty getting this straight in my head, James. I send you down there to check a young copper's conclusions about a particularly nasty double suicide and you've brought me back a triple murder — with no certainty about who the primary victim was or why they were killed. God knows what the Chief Constable will say when I pass the news on to him. He's a friend of the family, for heaven's sake.'

'Speaking of friends of the family, sir, I interviewed Jack Sumner earlier. He'd had a fierce row with Tom Barleigh the day before he was shot so I thought I should see him. Didn't like him one bit and I'm not sure I trust his alibi.'

'Sure you're not suspicious just because he's Jewish, James? I wouldn't have had you down as an anti-Semite.'

'I'm definitely not, sir, and I resent the suggestion that I would be. I didn't like him before I even knew he was a Jew. He's arrogant and bad mannered to his staff. And the only one who can substantiate where he was on the morning of the murders is his wife.'

'Well, he'd not be alone in that now, would he? If that was the only thing we had to rely on then half the male population would be on the list of suspects. I don't like Sumner myself very much but I can't see him being a murderer.'

I decided to chance my arm about the next steps and asked Dyer for more time to follow up my suspicions. He considered for a second or two then shrugged his shoulders.

'What else can I do, James? I'll give you a few more days but no more manpower. You can hang on to Sawyer, but that's it until you find something more conclusive.'

Dyer began to leaf through the letters waiting for him on his desk. This meeting was over. As I stood up and headed for the door, he gave me his ultimatum.

'Wrap this up quickly, Inspector. I'll cut you as much slack as I can but this can't go on much longer. And if upstairs says it has to stop, then it has to stop. Understand? Besides, I want you back on the beatings. Gleeson's getting nowhere and his latest cock-up is beginning to make *me* look incompetent.'

'What's happened, sir? I haven't heard anything.'

Dyer told me there'd been a raid on a club the night before. A tip-off had been received that several of the key suspects would be on the premises and they'd have evidence with them on their next plans.

'Gleeson charged in with all guns blazing, so to speak. You could hear the police car bells from miles away. Needless to say, the club was deserted when they arrived. I need him off the case and you back in charge.'

I nodded my agreement and told him I'd passed some information from my London contact on to Gleeson then I left. There was no point in being annoyed at Dyer about the time limit. He'd already explained the office politics he had to play and I was sure he'd do everything he could to support me. My difficulty now was to pull all the pieces together as quickly as possible, with only Sawyer to help with the legwork.

I decided there would be no point going back to Grovestock House that afternoon and I could work as easily at a spare desk in the canteen as at the station in Kenilworth. I wrote up a few notes, rang Sawyer with Agnes Black's address and spent another two or three hours scribbling various ideas and possibilities in my notebook until my pen ran out of ink. I checked the drawers of the desk but could only find a couple of empty bottles so nipped to Gleeson's office to see if he had any. He, showing his usual dedication to duty, had left the station dead on five o'clock but his door wasn't locked so I went in anyway. His desk top was completely clear. In fact, the entire office was spotless with not a paper out of place.

I opened his top drawer and laughed to see it as neat as the room. Someone had once said to me that a tidy desk is the sign of a sick mind and it now became clear what he was talking about. I couldn't help thinking how much fun it would be to rearrange the drawer and watch Gleeson's reaction next morning. I even took a first step towards this prank by picking up his notebook with view to leaving it open so it would be the first change he'd see. As I leafed through it I noticed my name in the pages towards the back. Alongside each entry was a date and a brief note. At the head of the section were a name and a telephone number. Several were those of suspects I'd have known in the beatings case, others I didn't recognise. One was dated the morning after my trip to Birmingham.

I returned home and walked over to draw the curtain across the window. The sun was setting over the fields beyond the castle, highlighting the sandstone ruins with a red blaze. How magnificent the scene must have looked on an evening like this, when Robert Dudley wooed Elizabeth I, lavishing entertainments worth a King's ransom on her during her visit in 1575.

I was glad I'd found my way here after I returned to England, and even happier I'd found this cottage where I could set up an office in an upstairs room that captured the evening sun. It isn't a large room and the ceiling is low. Still, I've managed to fit in a table to serve as a desk, a couple of bookcases and a small wooden filing cabinet I rescued from my father's workshop when he was going to throw it out. I usually prefer to work at my desk — I find it keeps my mind focused — but occasionally I'll take to the armchair in the corner if I need to read or ruminate over information I've gathered.

This armchair is a great luxury and helps me avoid working in the rest of my home. It's the curse of the detective, especially when working on complex cases, as I do. I have no control over my thoughts. They turn round and round in my head day and night, slotting this piece here and that piece there until the picture emerges. Or at least until it's clear there are no pieces missing. So it's not really possible to limit my thinking to one room, but I try. I'd go quite mad if I didn't.

My reverie over the sunlit scene was soon broken when the telephone rang on my desk. It was the Special Branch officer, Spencer.

'How did you get this number?'

'Come, come, Inspector, don't be so naïve. You know the times we're in — all I have to do is utter the word "spy" and I can get almost anything I want. Besides, your Superintendent Dyer still isn't happy about you chatting to a possible suspect, supposedly for personal reasons. He's not at all convinced you're not a threat to the realm. Are you sure he doesn't know your background?'

I almost slammed the phone down on him, but thought better of it. If he, and Dyer, still had suspicions it was better to try to clear them up without antagonising him too much. It wouldn't take a great deal for him to implicate me in Haleson's little game if he decided I wasn't being sufficiently co-operative.

'Understood, Mr Spencer, it's been a long day and I'm a little sensitive about who has my home number. What can I do for you?'

'It's rather the other way round, old man. Haleson is here and he wants a word. Already spilled the beans to us, and verse. Names, dates, the lot. Seems like you're in the clear so there's no harm in him talking to you and I've said he can.'

Before he put Haleson on I asked Spencer if they'd made any more arrests.

'Only small fry really, just the messengers, he's the really important one. Frightening how much access he had to top level information. Anyway, I'll hand you over. As I said, you appear to be blameless in all of this but I'll be listening in on the line, just in case.'

Alan Haleson sounded like a broken man. His breathing was laboured and his voice trembled as he spoke. He told me he'd been able to make some enquiries on my behalf between our meeting in Birmingham and being picked up by Spencer's crowd.

'But why are you trying to get this for me now?'

'I just want to try to make things right, Mr Given. Tom was my best friend and I'd never have done anything to hurt him, Jenny or his mother. They were like my own family.'

I could have told him it wouldn't be the first time families had fallen out with it ending in bloodshed, but I'd had doubts about his involvement right from the start. He was under enough pressure without me adding to it. Instead, I told him his denials meant very little to me and it was the evidence which would count in the end. I also said I had no influence whatsoever on Spencer or Mitchell, so not to think I'd be able to do any pleading for leniency on his behalf. I sensed Spencer himself chuckling on the other extension at my admission of his power.

'Of course, I understand all that, Mr Given, but I feel a need to make amends where I can. I'm afraid I didn't turn up anything specific on your Uncle Gideon or his whereabouts before they pulled me in but I'd urge you to contact him in any way you can. All of our intelligence in the Foreign Office leads us to believe Hitler is about to orchestrate a big show against the Jews. We don't know what it is yet but it's going to be widespread — national — and aimed at all of the Jewish shops and small businesses. I'm assuming your uncle is Jewish, isn't he?'

This was one more person who knew something of my past I'd rather wasn't too public, though I had little choice but to confirm what he'd said.

'Hitler will want this to look like a popular demonstration against the Jews, rather than coming from his direction, so he's had his henchmen meeting for weeks in secret up and down the country. We think something's likely to happen in the next fortnight so anyone who can get out, should get out.'

At this point the phone was taken away from Haleson and Spencer broke in.

'I'm afraid that's bordering on the hush-hush, Inspector, so I'm going to need to stop it there. I'll say goodnight now.'

The line went dead and my mind began to race. How could I get word to my uncle that he and his family are in even more danger than they suspected? I hadn't a clue where they were, and even if I had, I'd no way of getting a message to them.

I glanced at the clock to check if it was too late to telephone my father. As I reached out to pick up the receiver the telephone rang again.

'Hello again, Inspector.' It was Spencer. It was barely five minutes since our previous conversation had ended.

'Good evening, Mr Spencer. To what do I owe the pleasure of another call so soon? Actually, before you answer, thanks for letting Haleson speak to me. He didn't have much information but at least it was something. And forewarned is forearmed, so I'm grateful to you.'

'Good of you to say so, Inspector, especially taking into account our earlier meeting.'

I told him I knew he had a job to do. What I didn't say was I wished he hadn't pursued it with such relish. There's a very fine line between putting on an aggressive act to browbeat a suspect and in letting your feelings of disgust get the better of you. I still wasn't sure if Spencer was a consummate actor or simply a bully boy.

'Contrary to what passed between you, me and Mr Mitchell, Inspector, I'm not an anti-Semite, my wife is Jewish and her family are in the same boat as yours. I just have to put on this little show sometimes when interrogating people. Adolph Hitler needs to be stopped. He has it in for the Jews and there are thousands, if not tens of thousands, going to be hurt. If I can help just one of them in some way I hope I'll have done my bit.' He paused, and I could imagine him looking around before he continued. 'Mitchell has chaps all over Germany working underground. I dare say if *they* can't find your uncle no-one can. If it's all right with you I'll ask him if he'd mind putting the word out to see what they can come up with. I can't promise anything, old man, but at least we can have a go.'

I thanked him profusely, almost embarrassingly so, before he agreed to get back to me as soon as he could and we finally said our goodbyes.

It was now almost dark. I looked up at the photograph above my desk and lifted the receiver again to telephone my father.

Fifteen

Blue gingham tablecloths, each topped with a neatly typed menu card, glass and chromium cruet set, willow pattern jam pot, complete with spoon, and neat place settings, made Martha's Tearoom look like every other one I'd been in. Martha's name was picked out in bold maroon letters on the front window, the bottom half covered by a net curtain, affording customers privacy from prying eyes in the street. I smiled as it occurred to me this flimsy screen would provide no protection whatsoever from the gossip machine which chugs and churns in every small town and village. My life would be so much more difficult without it.

A young waitress with shockingly red hair tumbling from a starched white cap wandered over to take my order.

'Tea for one, is it, sir?'

'Please.'

I returned to reading my papers but the girl stood there until I looked up.

'Anything else, sir? We've some lovely scones, freshly baked. Or perhaps an iced bun? They're my favourite.'

Her smile was so engaging as she pointed over to the rack of cakes in the counter-top glass display I was almost tempted to order something.

'No thanks, just the tea. Trying to lose some weight, you know, and I don't think they'd help much, would they?'

Her smile turned into a good-natured laugh as she placed her pad and pencil back into her apron pocket.

'I expect not, sir. Tea it is, then. I'll be back in a jiffy.'

In the few minutes I was waiting for her to come back, my mind wandered. Thoughts of Elizabeth, and what I was going to do about her, crept in. Should I say I was sorry for suspecting her brother and hope we could get back on good terms? Did I want this? Truth was, I didn't know what I wanted. Elizabeth had hurt me a lot when she'd left the first time but I'd now realised I still had strong feelings for her.

True to her word the waitress emerged from the kitchen with a steaming teapot in the same blue and white as the crockery already adorning the table top. I scrambled to move my documents to make space but, without waiting, she leaned past me to place the pot down and several drops of hot brown liquid splashed from the spout on to my open notebook. The girl's eyes widened and she gasped as the ink blotched and ran. Before I could say or do anything she'd whipped her tea-towel from her waistband and was flapping at my pile of papers. Inevitably this made things worse and was only brought to an abrupt halt when this over-vigorous flailing resulted in half of them falling to the floor. The waitress, now a half-mad thing, fell to her knees and attempted to scoop everything up. I had to stop her, to save my own sanity as much as hers.

'Please leave them,' I said, 'just leave them alone. They'll be fine. I'll pick them up myself.'

With this, she stopped and looked up at me, her eyes brimming.

'I'm so sorry, sir.'

A woman shouted from the counter. 'Bridget! What are you doing? Stand up at once and into the kitchen with you, girl!'

The older woman, who I had to assume was Martha herself, walked over, knelt, shuffled my papers into a single stack, and put them in my hand. She was attractive in a way which seemed to come from an innate confidence rather than anything recognisable as traditional beauty. She was, like me, a little overweight, though she carried it well.

'There you are, Inspector. I hope the silly girl didn't do too much damage.'

'I'm sure they'll be fine, Mrs...?'

'Kendall, Martha Kendall.'

'Well, as I was saying Mrs Kendall, I'm certain the papers will be fine, it was only a few drops of tea. Don't be too hard on the girl, she was trying to do her best — just panicked a bit that's all.'

'It's very kind of you to be so understanding, Inspector.'

'That's the second time you've used my title, Mrs Kendall. We've not met before, have we?'

'No, we haven't, but everyone knows who you are. No secrets in a place like this. I wasn't a hundred per cent certain it was you when you first came in, but then the headings on some of those papers confirmed it.'

'I could use someone as observant as you in the force — have you ever considered joining?'

'Get away with you, Inspector! I'm happy enough in this place and get all the excitement I need trying to help my customers choose between ham and cheese in their sandwiches!'

'Well, if you ever change your mind, you come and see me.'

'That I will, sir, though I don't think it's going to happen.'

Even though this was a natural break in the conversation the woman appeared reluctant to leave.

'Would you like to join me in a cup of tea, Mrs Kendall? I'm sure there's plenty here for two, even after what the waitress spilled.'

She pulled a chair away from the table and sat down. I made ready to pour her a drink.

'No tea for me, thanks, but we're not very busy so I'll sit down with you for a minute or two. You're investigating the deaths up at Grovestock House, aren't you?'

'Yes, that's right.'

She shook her head. 'Terrible, terrible.'

'It is a sad state of affairs indeed, Mrs Kendall.'

'And people are saying it wasn't Lady Isabelle who shot poor Tom Barleigh. That it was someone else who murdered the three of them. Are they right?'

So, the word was out. I might have known it wouldn't remain secret for long.

'Well, we have to explore all the possibilities, don't we, and we're not ruling anything out.'

She leaned further over the table towards me and dropped her voice to a whisper.

'Do you have any idea to who it might be?'

'I'm sure you'll understand I can't discuss it with you, Mrs Kendall. Do you know something about what happened?'

'Oh no, not me, sir. It's just that my daughter, Alice, used to work up there before she married, that's why I'm interested, and the things she heard might make your hair stand on end.'

'What sort of things?'

'I don't think I should be saying, Inspector. It would be second-hand, wouldn't it? But I've been nagging Alice to have a word with you, and I think she'd be happy to come in and tell you herself.'

'You're Alice?'

The young woman arrived about half an hour after Martha Kendall had sent a note to ask her to meet me. She had her mother's good looks and confidence.

'Alice Brown, now, was Alice Kendall. Mum said you wanted to have a word.'

Martha had allowed us the use of her rooms above the café so her daughter and I could talk without being overheard. The living area echoed the orderliness she displayed downstairs, with very little clutter beyond family photographs and a few knick-knacks. We had settled ourselves into armchairs either side of a large bay window.

'Your mother told me you used to work at Grovestock House. What did you do there?'

'I was the upstairs maid. Well, that's what they called it, even though there was no downstairs maid at the time, just me. Most of the work was making the beds, setting fires in the rooms and so on. Mrs Veasey would keep the kitchen tidy and the butler would look after the dining room and morning room, apart from lighting the fire and sweeping.'

'And this was before Marion Clark took over as maid? Before Tom Barleigh became confined to his wheelchair?'

'That's right, Inspector.'

'Why did you leave, Alice?'

Her cheeks reddened, and she turned to look out of the window.

'Why do you need to know? You don't suspect I had anything to do with this horrible affair, do you?'

'No, not at all, Alice, put that out of your mind right away. I'm simply trying to build up a picture of the house and the family. Your mother seemed to think you might be able to help me do so. You don't have to say why you left if you don't want to.'

'Well, I suppose it can't do any harm. Not now. I left because her Ladyship found out her son had been making advances.'

'Tom Barleigh? But wasn't he engaged?'

'Not at the time, Inspector, but he had been seeing Miss Bamford for quite a while. It wouldn't have stopped him anyway, he was well known for it before his accident.'

I sat back in my chair and chose my words with as much care as I could.

'So you're saying you had an affair with Tom Barleigh and Lady Isabelle found out then gave you the sack?'

'No, no, no, Inspector! Not an affair. I never said that! And she didn't give me the sack, I left of my own accord. I was courting, so I wouldn't have had anything to do with Mr Barleigh. But he was always making excuses to be in the same room and putting his hand on mine, that sort of thing.'

'Tom Barleigh was a bit of a lady's man, then?'

'I don't like to speak ill of the dead, Inspector Given, but he most definitely was.'

This put a different complexion on the man, one I hadn't seen before. Could this provide some motive for his death? It was bothering me that, while I was now certain the three deaths had been murders, I couldn't fathom a reason for them. Even if someone had killed Tom Barleigh as result of his philandering, why would they go on and kill his stepmother and fiancée? At least, for the time being, it might offer another line of enquiry. I underlined Alice's comment in my notes.

'If, as you suggest, you were able to resist Tom's advances, why did you leave?'

'It's as I said, Mr Given — Mr Barleigh was always trying to get me alone in the room with him. One day I was dusting in the morning room and he came in, followed by Mrs Veasey with a pot of tea. After she left I was foolish enough to agree to sit down with him and take a cup. Next thing, he grabs my hand, pulls me over to him and plants a kiss on my cheek. It all happened so fast I couldn't stop him. I pulled myself away as quickly as I could and saw his eyes widen as he looked over my shoulder. When I twisted round I saw, staring straight through the window at us, his mother. I could tell she'd seen the kiss.'

'What did she do?'

'She just gave me such a look, scared the life out of me. It makes me shake to think it might have been me she'd taken the shotgun to if I'd stayed around!'

It surprised me Alice hadn't heard the latest rumours from her mother, or perhaps she had and her earlier experience with Lady Isabelle had made her discount them as meaningless.

'So you left?'

'I did, quick as I could. Frank and I were talking of tying the knot and I wouldn't have been allowed to stay when we did in any case. Against the rules you know. So I gave in my notice through Mr Jervis and stayed out of the way of Mr Barleigh and his mother afterwards. There was no way I wanted to meet her, not with her temper.'

'She could be bad tempered then, even before this happened?'

'Oh yes, Mr Given, she was always flying off the handle, even over small things. Mr Jervis came through to the kitchen one evening most distressed because she'd found a speck of dirt on her fork and thrown it across the room at him. Swore and told him he was a useless fool, she did. She often shouted at the staff if everything wasn't quite right and one time I even heard her screeching at Sir Arthur behind closed doors. Personally, I think she was a little, well, you know ... unhinged. But she'd never have shot Mr Barleigh. He was the only one she didn't rage at. Even with the little incident in the morning room I'm sure she blamed me and not him.'

'Did you hear what she and her husband were arguing about?'

'You'd hardly not be able to hear it when it was going on. He was always a calm and well-mannered man but this time he let fly back at her. I heard him shout at her he was fed up with the charade and was sorry she'd managed to force him into it.'

'Charade? Is that the word he used?'

'Well, I believe it was. I remember thinking at the time it was a strange word to use. It's a party game, isn't it?'

'And what do you think he might have meant by it?'

'I'm sure I don't really know. I thought he meant their marriage. Like he was sorry he'd married her but they were still pretending to the outside world. Everyone in the house knew he couldn't be happy with a witch like her as his wife. I thought he was a saint myself.'

Alice became silent, as if she'd realised she had, contrary to her earlier intentions, spoken ill of the dead. She looked around as if expecting someone to have overheard her indiscretion even though we were alone in her mother's flat.

'I'm sorry, Mr Given, I shouldn't be saying such awful things about Lady Isabelle. Nor about Tom Barleigh. I don't think there's much more I can tell you and I must be getting back to get Frank's dinner ready; he'll be home from work before long.'

I thanked her for her time and said she'd been very helpful. As I followed her down the stairs and out of Martha's Tearoom, a doubt began pecking away in my head. Could Isabelle have shot Tom and Jenny after all — was she mad enough?

Later, when I met with Sawyer to exchange information, he came off the telephone, shaking his head.

'Another blind alley, sir; that woman, Agnes Black, is dead. Committed suicide nine months ago. Must have been soon after she received the letter from Sir Arthur's solicitor, I imagine.'

Before he could give me more detail the phone rang again. Gerald Bamford had presented himself at the front desk asking to speak to me. I told Sawyer to go down, take Bamford through to the interview room and stay with him until I arrived.

Bamford sat bolt upright on the hard wooden chair when I entered, his hands clasped on the table in front of him. He was a small man, shorter than me by a few inches, and carrying more pounds than was healthy. His clothes were poor quality, though his shirt collar was clean and well pressed. The single exception to this was his shoes. My mother once told me to always buy good shoes and a good bed, because if you're not in one you're in the other. Here was a man who appeared to adhere to this adage and to spend a lot of time on his feet, if his footwear was anything to go by. They also carried a dazzling shine.

I asked Sawyer to leave us.

'Take yourself back upstairs, constable, and carry on with that filing. I'll call you down when I need you.'

Sawyer clearly wanted to stay but did as he was told. It would be easier to draw information from Bamford if I was on my own.

I quizzed him first about where he'd been and why he hadn't been in earlier. He gave me a story about working away a lot and only thought about contacting me after being chased through the woods.

'So that was you I was chasing? Why the hell didn't you stop?'

'I didn't know you were the police. Anybody could have been charging at me through the undergrowth. It was only later I realised who you might be, but I did know it might look suspicious if I was discovered hanging about Grovestock House.'

'Well, you got that right, it looks extremely suspicious. What were you doing there, exactly?'

He told me he'd simply wanted to spend time looking at where Jenny had died. He'd had a run-in with Sir Arthur years earlier so wasn't welcome at the house, even though they'd almost been in-laws. Trudging through the woods and clambering up the wall was the only way he'd get a decent view. Apparently he'd been there about half an hour, watching quietly, when I spotted him. He was adamant this was the only time he'd been there.

Bamford said that, to his eternal regret, he'd not seen his daughter for about two months, though he'd seen Lady Isabelle more recently.

'I met with her about three weeks before Jenny committed ... before Jenny died.'

Unsurprisingly, he could barely speak.

'Go on, Mr Bamford, where was this?'

'In a café in Stratford.'

'Had you arranged it, or had she?'

'Oh, it was me, definitely. I'd needed to speak to her face to face. Couldn't risk her being overheard on the telephone. She was late. She'd always be late when we first met but now one half of me was hoping she wouldn't come, the other half hoping she'd arrive soon so it would all be over.'

'But she did turn up eventually?'

'Yes. Oh, yes. She apologised for being late, said she just couldn't get away without him becoming suspicious.'

'By "him" you mean Sir Arthur Barleigh?'

'Yes, of course. Who else would it be?'

'Now, now, Mr Bamford, don't get shirty, I was only checking. Carry on.'

'Well, we ordered fresh tea and got down to business. She said she knew I hadn't arranged to meet just to tell her about my "rather dull life", as she put it. You know, she smiled sweetly when she said it. She was right though. That's why I didn't get annoyed, I suppose. My life *is* boring. I travel up and down the country, knocking on people's doors, trying to sell them shoe brushes and the like from an old suitcase. Different town every week, different rooms every night. Fifty different lodgings every year and only home at weekends. Don't get me wrong, I've always enjoyed my work and made a decent living but it's hardly like being a fighter pilot, is it? Jenny's mother, Barbara, stuck it as long as she could but it was inevitable she'd get fed up and find someone else. At least she waited until Jenny left school and was old enough to understand what was happening. Living in Australia now, she is. Very happy by all accounts.'

I listened to his assessment of himself and couldn't help feeling sorry for the chap. An ordinary working man, trying to earn a few shillings to keep his family together but despised by his wife. And now he'd lost his daughter as well. However, I shook away these feelings of pity as quickly as they'd come. This was an interview about three murders and no place for sentiment.

'Let's get back to your conversation, Mr Bamford.'

'Yes, of course. I told her the wedding would have to be cancelled. I was quite calm and ... assertive about it too — not like me. I wish I'd been as assertive years before, when we met more often and when she'd made unreasonable demands.'

'Demands?'

'Oh yes, Inspector. Isabelle was a very spoilt young lady; she could twist men round her little finger. She'd say "Take me here, take me there, buy me this, buy me that", constantly, and we'd all jump to be first in line to give her what she wanted.'

This was a side of her Ladyship I hadn't picked up before.

'Why would they call the wedding off?'

'Ah, Inspector, that's the big question, isn't it? First I'll need to give you a bit more of the background so you can make sense of it.'

Bamford had quickly turned into a man in control. He sat back in his chair with his features relaxed and now I saw the hint of a smile, something of the salesman in him. I was intrigued to witness the two sides of his character in so short a space of time and made a mental note to be careful of which face to believe.

'No rush, Gerald. You don't mind if I call you Gerald, do you?' I didn't wait for his reply. 'Good. We've got all day if you need it. Neither of us is going anywhere until this is all explained. So, go on. What was her reaction to what you'd said?'

'Well, first off, she laughed and asked the same question as you, saying: "They're so happy, at least he is, and that's all that matters to me." I told her she was being selfish and Jenny didn't want to be tied to a cripple in a wheelchair. Isabelle hit back by saying Jenny was a stupid girl and should have moved on ages ago but now she'd made her bed and would have to lie on it. I knew then I'd have no alternative but to tell her the truth and be damned with the consequences.'

'So it was you who persuaded Isabelle the wedding should be called off?'

'I did, more or less, and I did it for both of them. The stuff about Jenny not wanting to be tied to Tom was nonsense, really. Certainly she wasn't happy but she had a real sense of duty and felt she owed it to Tom for putting him in the wheelchair in the first place. I just said it, hoping Isabelle would see sense and take Jenny's side.'

'You'd better fill me in with more of the background, Gerald, I'm getting lost here. Why would splitting up the marriage be of benefit to both Tom and Jenny? Jenny, I can understand, but Tom?'

'I'll do my best, Inspector, but we'll have to go back a good few years so bear with me.'

'As I said, we've got all day.'

'Fine. Tom isn't Isabelle's son.'

'I know that. I understand she always treated him as if he was.'

'From what I know she loved him better than if he'd been her own. She idolised him and never had a cross word.'

Here, again, Bamford was confirming what others had indicated. Nothing would have induced Lady Isabelle Barleigh to kill her son.

'You have to understand something about Isabelle. If you think she was attractive, Inspector, you should have seen her in her younger days. She was like a film star. Isabelle could have had any man in the county she wanted and did have a good few of them before she married. Including me.'

I was slightly surprised, mainly by the thought he must have been a very different man in his youth. It was hard to conceive of any great beauty being remotely interested in him now.

'Isabelle was a fortune seeker. She'd come from a nice middle class background but she wanted more. She'd had flings with a few eligible bachelors with prospects, but their parents all knew her reputation and soon steered their sons away. It was only someone like Arthur, who would certainly have trouble attracting a new wife and could see Isabelle would look after his baby son, who would settle down with her. I know they'd also had a bit of a thing going when his first wife was ill, before he'd lost his good looks.'

'If she was so focused on winning a rich husband, why would she be interested in a salesman like yourself, Gerald? Or are you just trying to look better than you are?'

My words stung him, exactly as I intended.

'I didn't say she wanted to marry me. She didn't want to marry most of the men she dated as long as they'd a few bob to spend on her and weren't too hideous. I wasn't half bad looking twenty years ago and I had a good few pounds in the bank — until she relieved me of them!' Bamford spat out the words.

'So you'd have a motive to do her some harm.'

Bamford roared with laughter at this suggestion.

'You're saying I'm so mad with Isabelle for giving me a good time, helping me spend my money and throwing me over for another fool, that I wait a generation before killing her. Then for good measure I murder her stepson? Do me a favour.'

'Believe me, Bamford, I've seen lots of murders and I've learned this: sometimes fury erupts at once, but often it smokes and smoulders on a slow fuse, waiting and waiting until the inevitable explosion. The question is, could Gerald

Bamford, either in a fit of rage or in a cold, calculated, fashion, commit murder? That's what I need to find out.'

Something of his original meekness returned as he realised he was being considered as a serious suspect.

'Do I need to call a solicitor?'

'That's your privilege, Gerald, but perhaps there's no need yet. We've not arrested you and you're only helping us with our investigations into three suspicious deaths.'

'Three? You can't mean you think Jenny was murdered as well? And you imagine I'd do it? I adored the girl. I never told her when she was alive, you know, but I did. I'd never do anything to hurt her.'

Sawyer placed three mugs on the table, one in front of Gerald Bamford, the others on our side. I'd asked him to join us so he'd be able to see any discrepancies in Bamford's story, particularly in relation to local events. I was hoping he'd be smart enough to decide what he should challenge and what should be saved for use later.

Bamford had calmed down by the time the tea arrived but I let him drink in peace, so he could mull over where my next line of questioning might take us. Part of the craft of interviewing is to understand when to bombard a suspect and when to stay quiet, gradually letting the pressure mount until the truth bursts out. I decided to change tack.

'Remind us where you were on the day of the deaths, Gerald.'

'I was away working, in Leeds.'

'Is that where you went on the day of the funeral, as well? Strange you didn't stay around.'

Bamford took another body blow.

'No one told me about Jenny until I got back the night before the funeral. I'd been on the road ever since she died. I told you I don't get on with Arthur so I didn't feel like hanging around and, anyway, I can't afford not to be working.'

'Why don't you get on with Sir Arthur, Gerald?'

'Just a business deal, that's all.'

'Go on.'

'It's years ago. I had the opportunity to make an investment and I approached Arthur to lend me the cash. He refused, saying he didn't think it was sound enough. Later, I found out he'd gone behind my back and invested himself. Made a real killing. I went round to see him and we argued. He threw me out, laughing, and told me never to go to his house again.'

'You must have been pretty angry.'

'I was.'

'Mad enough to take it out on his family?'

Bamford didn't respond.

'So you're saying you were in Leeds on the day of the murders. Can anyone vouch for you?'

'I expect I knocked on nearly two hundred doors, like I do every day, so someone would remember me. Problem is, I couldn't tell you exactly which streets I'd been in, except it was probably in the Burley area.'

'A little convenient, isn't it?'

'Have you ever been to Leeds, Inspector? Street after street of terraced houses, all of them looking exactly the same. I've even found myself going back to the houses I'd done the previous day if I haven't made a note of where I finished off.'

Sawyer interjected. 'So you do keep a record of where you've been, Mr Bamford?'

'Not really. When I remember I scribble the name of the street I've covered last on a scrap of paper. I leave it in my case but throw the old ones away each night when I tidy up and restock. I'd keep a note of anyone who particularly asked me to call back but they're few and far between. Not much money in that part of Leeds you know, and blokes like me calling door to door are ten a penny.'

I picked up the questioning again. 'If, as you say, so many doorstep salesmen are around, no one's going to be able to pick you out in particular, are they? Where were you staying in Leeds?'

'Same place I always stay, a cheap commercial digs near the station. Mrs Bradley's the landlady. Does a nice breakfast and minds her own business. Lots of these women are really nosy cows, always prying. I suppose they only take in lodgers so they can pick up on bits of gossip to share with their friends.'

'You'll give Constable Sawyer here details of how we can contact this Mrs Bradley. We'll check your story, but let's get back to what you were saying about Lady Isabelle and your meeting with her. You said you'd have to "tell her the truth and damn the consequences". What was that truth?'

Bamford seemed to have recovered his composure and leaned back in his chair again, his brow furrowed and his hands pressed prayer-like under his chin. He waited several seconds before he spoke.

'I can only make this clear one step at a time, Inspector.' He was now plainly relishing the drama once more. 'The next thing you need to understand is that Jenny wasn't actually my daughter. My wife and I had been trying for a child of our own for a while without any success so our doctor suggested we try to adopt. He put us in touch with an orphanage run by nuns in Warwick and they had a pretty little toddler who had been with them since she was born. I fell in love with her the minute we met and persuaded Barbara we'd be as happy with her as we would be with a baby. The nuns told us nothing of the child's background, except that she'd been left when she was a few days old because her mother hadn't been able to keep her. We took her gladly and raised her as our own.'

'And did Jenny know she was adopted?'

Bamford hung his head.

'No. We never got round to telling her. We always thought we'd need to break the news one day but the time never seemed right. When we first had her I was soon away in the War and she was a child so Barbara thought she'd be too young to understand. Later, when I got back, Barbara and I had so many troubles of our own — we were breaking up and it didn't seem right to explain to Jenny she wasn't our child after all. I fully intended to tell her the truth before she got married but then the letter arrived.'

'Letter?'

'I'd been working in Wolverhampton for a couple of weeks and when I got back home there was a letter waiting for me from the orphanage. It explained they'd received a note from one of the nuns who used to work there and she'd asked them to forward it to me. It seems that Jenny was Isabelle's daughter.'

Now it was my turn to sit back in my chair to take in this latest bombshell. Sawyer and I looked at each other and I nodded for him to take over the interview.

'You may think I'm being a bit dense, Gerald, but I still can't see how it might have been an impediment to Jenny and Tom getting married. It's not like they were related, is it? We already know Tom wasn't Isabelle's son.'

Bamford leaned forward and stared Sawyer straight in the face. His eyes had a slightly demented look and he choked with emotion as his next words spewed out.

'That's it entirely, Constable. They *were* half-brother and half-sister! The dates tie up. Jenny was the child of Isabelle and Arthur.'

Sixteen

Cudlip was pouring my nightly Vimto when the telephone rang behind him. We'd been discussing the prospects for a war and his concerns for his sons, both of whom were old enough to be called up. The landlord himself had been in the last one so had experienced at first hand the dangers they'd face. He put the half-full glass down on the bar.

'I'll just get this if you don't mind, sir.'

I nodded as he turned away and picked up the telephone.

'Evening — yes, he's here, I'll get him. It's for you, Inspector. Constable Sawyer, says he needs to speak to you urgently.'

Cudlip, exuding curiosity, got on with cleaning some glasses.

'Sawyer? What is it? Are you coming up to join me for one?'

'No, sir — you need to get here, a boy's body has been found.'

The night was terrible and Jack Cudlip, the eldest of the landlord's sons, wrestled his father's car down the country lanes in the driving rain and wind. From time to time he'd have to swerve to avoid branches which had fallen into the road. Whenever we passed a clearing in the trees the vehicle would rock violently as the gale slammed into its side.

The car finally swung into a farmyard and I wished I'd had the foresight to bring boots. There was a sea of mud all around and the stench from the barns was almost unbearable, even through the closed windows. I stepped out and was soon up to my ankles in the mire. Freezing water filled my shoes and the cloying sludge prevented me from running for shelter into the cowshed. By the time we were all inside I was soaked to the skin.

Sawyer quickly filled me in on events. Earlier in the evening he'd been chatting to a friend in the village who told him he'd heard Billy Sharp was hiding in a barn owned by Alf Nash's uncle. Nash had been drunk and shooting his mouth off a couple of nights earlier about knowing where Billy was hiding. So Sawyer headed over to try to find the young gardener. When he arrived he bumped into a farmer, who turned out to be Nash's uncle, coming out of his yard in a very disturbed state.

'He said he'd gone out to put his cows away for the night and found the boy's body in his barn, his skull caved in. He had no telephone himself so was going to run up to the parish church to ask the vicar to make a call to the local police station. That's when he met me and I came in here to find this. I told him to go back over to his house and I cycled up to the vicarage to call you.'

The farmer hadn't had to look hard to find the body. It was sprawled in the centre of the shed at the bottom of a ladder; on its back, face caked in blood. It was a young man in his late teens with a large gash above his left ear. Going by the clothes and the boots, he'd been a labourer of some sort. Closer inspection showed he was also missing two fingers from his right hand, recently severed. Jack Cudlip had followed us inside but soon he was outside again, retching in the pouring rain.

'Nasty. How do you think he died, John?'

'I couldn't say, sir, I might have thought he'd fallen from the ladder if it wasn't for the missing fingers, but with those it doesn't look much like an accident, does it?'

'Certainly doesn't. We'll need to get an opinion from the police doctor when he arrives. Nip up and ask the farmer to come back over, if you would. And tell him to bring some more lamps with him.'

Albert Pardow certainly looked the part, with his face furrowed and tanned, wearing Wellington boots and a tattered tweed jacket which had seen better days. He carried with him two storm lanterns, immediately throwing long shadows into all corners of the barn. I asked him to hang one of the lamps on a beam and to hold the second one over the boy's body. I carried on with my examination whilst we spoke.

'Thanks for coming over, Mr Pardow. This must have been quite a shock for you.'

'Aye, it was. A rare shock. Poor lad. Only glad it was me found him and not the wife. She'd often bring the cows up for milking in the evening but she's away at her sister's, helping with the kids till the new one's born.'

'So there's only you here at present? No-one else on the farm today?'

'Farm's not big enough to support more than the two of us, even though when she's away I'd welcome the help. That's why I was a bit later than normal coming up here, I got tied up fixing a fence over in the bottom field.'

'So what time did you find him?'

'Round about half six. It was after dark, although it was murky enough an hour or so before with all this rain, so a bit hard to tell for certain. I then had to chase up to the vicarage for the telephone, 'cos we don't have one here yet. That's when I bumped into the constable.'

'And when would you have been in the barn before that?'

'Just after it got light, as usual. This morning it was about seven o'clock. Tell you the truth, it must have been a few minutes after, 'cos I listened to the news on the wireless before heading out. Takes me about an a hour to get the cows milked and sorted before taking them back down to the field, so I'd say I wouldn't have been in here between half past eight this morning and half past six tonight.'

'And where were you the rest of the day?'

'Well, after I'd left off the cows I cleared out the pigs and hens. It was fairly dry in the morning so I started ploughing the ten acre field. That's when I discovered the fence between there and the bottom field was damaged from last week's winds. I came up to the house for a bite in the middle of the day then went into town to buy stuff to mend the fence. I got back about three o'clock and set about fixing it. As I said, with this weather it took me longer than I expected so I was down there until dark, then fetched the cows back up.'

'So you didn't hear or see anything up here earlier? Would you know if anyone came into the yard when you were down in the field?'

'Not likely I would, unless they made a good deal of noise. Even from the house the shed and yard are well hidden so I might not have heard anything from in there either.'

'Thank you for your help, Mr Pardow. I'll need you to go through it in detail again with Constable Sawyer, so we have a proper record, but it shouldn't take too long. Pass me the lamp and I'll let you be on your way out of this awful night. The constable will go up with you, and perhaps you might offer young Mr Cudlip a cup of tea, or something stronger? He looks like he could do with it. We'll want to be around for a while — the doctor, then the ambulance, I'm sure you'll understand — so it might be helpful if you could arrange to keep the yard and shed clear until we're done.'

With Sawyer, Jack Cudlip and the farmer gone I examined the barn in more detail. Above the milking stalls there was a hayloft so I climbed up to it. In the dim glow of the lamp I could make out a makeshift straw bed in one corner, where the lad had been sleeping. Protruding from another pile of straw was a pair of handlebars. I carefully moved the straw aside and, sure enough, a bicycle had been covered over to hide it from view.

Back down the ladder I studied the area around the body. I lowered the lamp and confirmed what I'd suspected almost since we arrived inside. There was a clear track in the mud where the body had been dragged into the cowshed. I followed its line, noting the dark stains where the killer had paused for breath, allowing the boy's blood to seep down onto the earth. As I stood in the doorway and raised my arm to spread the glow as widely as possible, two lighter objects were illuminated in the sea of muck. I bent down and wiped the spattered mud away. I shuddered as I picked them up and placed them in one of the bags I use for preserving evidence.

'So you reckon he was murdered outside, sir?'

Sawyer and I had returned to the Victory after the police doctor had done his work and the murdered boy's body had been removed for a post-mortem.

'I'd say so. We'll have to wait for the doctor's opinion but it looked to me like he'd been struck on the side of the head. He must have lain there with the blood running down his face until the killer dragged him by his feet into the shed where he was left lying on his back.'

'And you found his missing fingers in the yard?'

'Well, they completed the grisly picture.'

'How did he lose them, any idea?'

'I imagine he put his hand up to protect himself and they were chopped off by whatever struck the lad on the head.

From what I can see of the state he's in, it was something heavy, sharp and narrow. Like an axe or the corner of a brick. We'll know better what it was when the doctor's cleaned him up. With a bit of luck we'll also be able to have him identified formally when that's done, but for my money it has to be Billy Sharp.'

'The bike seems to match the one stolen from Charlie Himlet on the day of the shootings, so looks likely. I expect we can now take Sharp off our list of suspects as well. Did you find anything else in the yard?'

I laughed grimly. 'Not a chance. The ground was so chewed up with the rain, the cattle and the car, we'd even have been lucky to find the body if it had been left out there.'

'Do you think this one is connected to the other deaths then, sir?'

'If this *is* Billy Sharp then I'd put my shirt on it, though I'm not as convinced as you he's no longer a suspect. He was there when the shootings happened, he disappeared and he's been hiding, and we also know he'd been caught playing with George Perkins' shotgun earlier in the morning. Perhaps someone suspected Billy had killed Tom, Jenny and Isabelle and decided to be the judge and jury — and executioner. Anyway, you might as well get off home, there's not much more you can do tonight and we'll have a long day tomorrow checking out all those alibis again. I'll need to go round to see Billy's mother as soon as I've finished here.'

It's the hardest thing imaginable to have to tell a mother her son has died. I've done it several times but the person has never been a child, always a grown man or woman who's had an accident or been killed in a pub brawl. Sometimes you can sense it's expected, as if the parent has known the lifestyle of their offspring was going to lead unerringly to an early grave. Usually, though, there's a profound expression of shock. Each time I've had to do it I've been overwhelmed by being unable to reach out to the bereaved to comfort them; to say: 'don't worry, everything will be fine'. Because it won't.

Polly Sharp reacted in a way I least expected. The second the words: 'I'm sorry, Mrs Sharp, but I have some bad news,' had left my lips, she stepped forward and slapped me hard across the face.

'Sorry? I told you something was wrong. This is your fault!' With that she collapsed onto a chair. My surprise at her attack quickly gave way to concern. I took a seat until her grief ebbed. The kitchen displayed all the hallmarks of country poverty. A well-worn wooden table, six chairs of mixed parentage, a home-made dresser displaying a range of pots and pans, and a stew bubbling and steaming on a black stove. The air reeked of long-boiled cabbage and damp washing. In another room lay a baby gently gurgling. Billy's mother eventually spoke, her voice still shaking with emotion.

'I'm sorry, Inspector, I shouldn't have done that.'

'It's all right, Mrs Sharp, you've had a terrible shock. What did you mean when you said you'd told me something was wrong? We've not met before, have we?'

'Not you yourself, Inspector, but your constable, that John Sawyer. I told him. When he came round looking for my Billy. I said to him Billy is a good boy and something must have scared him to make him run away like that. And now you're going to tell me he's dead.'

I could see hope in her eyes for me to tell her she was mistaken, he'd only been hurt in an accident, or we'd arrested him. I could do no more than nod an affirmation and she broke down again.

Seventeen

I was up early, largely because the events of the previous evening had left me troubled and sleepless. Also, taking Polly Sharp to identify her son might prove even more stressful than having to inform her he'd died.

I'd sent a police car to collect her and meet me at the mortuary. She looked like she hadn't slept much, though she was calm and dignified. The only display of emotion was her briefest of gasps when the shroud was drawn back from Billy's young face. She nodded when I asked her to confirm it was her son then went back into the police car without a single word.

'I think we need to pull Bamford in again, sir.'

Sawyer had collared me as soon as I got back from the business with Billy Sharp's mother.

'How so?'

'Leeds rang back while you were out. It seems his story is confirmed by the landlady, except for the night before the murders.'

'If it's the night before, how does that help us?'

Bamford reportedly always left his digs straight after breakfast and returned in the evening around seven o'clock, knocking on doors until the light gave out. His landlady was happy to be flexible with his meal-times because he was a good and regular customer. On the day of the murders he'd left in the morning as normal but said he'd be eating out that night and not to wait up for him. She said she hadn't seen him again until seven the next night. Bamford told her he'd left early in the morning because he had a couple of good prospects lined up a few miles away in Bradford. He apologised for not leaving her a note.

When Sawyer had heard this from the Leeds police he'd made several quick calculations. He figured out Bamford could have driven down from Leeds anytime on the Thursday, slept in his car, carried out the murders and easily been back by early evening. He'd probably even have had time to knock a few doors on both days so he'd have an alibi if he needed one.

It seemed plausible enough. I asked Sawyer to arrange a car for us to go to see Bamford, hoping he hadn't left the area again.

'Before we go, sir, I had another couple of calls this morning. One was from the doctor, confirming Billy's cause of death. He says the young feller died from a blow to the side of the head, probably caused by a kick from a horse as far as he can tell. He thinks that's how the fingers were lost as well. He's suggesting it was a front hoof, rather than a back, because of the shape of the wound.'

'What was the other call?'

'It was from the fingerprint boys. Disappointing, but they said they've got quite a bit on at present and it might be two or three weeks before they can get any tests done on our stuff. I pressed them but they weren't budging.'

Gerald Bamford's small, run-down home couldn't have been more different to Grovestock House. It was easy to see how his daughter would have grabbed Tom Barleigh as a catch. The front garden was overgrown, the gate hanging off its hinges, and the paint was peeling off the front door. A dilapidated Austin Seven sat outside. Sawyer rattled the knocker and we waited. He tried again, this time banging with his fist and shouting Bamford's name through the letterbox.

Gerald Bamford opened the door, looking like a mole burst unexpectedly into the outside world, his eyes screwed up against the light. He was as dishevelled as his house, unshaven, without a jacket or tie, and I caught the distinct smell of alcohol on his breath.

'Hello again, Gerald, mind if we come in?'

I pushed him gently in the chest to move him into the hallway and at once regretted leaving the fresh air. The place stank of unwashed dishes and cigarette smoke.

'Cleaner's day off, is it, Gerald?'

We appeared to have woken Bamford and his embarrassment became obvious as he revived. He buttoned his collar and ran a hand through his hair to tidy it.

'What do you want now, Inspector? I don't have anything else I can tell you.'

'I'm afraid you do, Gerald. You didn't exactly give us the truth last time about where you were, now, did you?'

He looked sheepish but tried to bluff his way out of trouble.

'I told you I was in Leeds and that's where I was. You should ask my landlady.'

'Oh, we have, Gerald, we have. And she tells us you disappeared the night before the murders and didn't arrive back until late the next day. Plenty of time to get to Grovestock House and back.'

'I was in Leeds. I was. I never drove all the way down here then back again.'

Sawyer stepped forward and pushed Bamford so hard against the wall I heard the salesman's teeth rattle.

'If you *were* in Leeds you weren't at your digs. So where were you?'

Bamford considered his options for about fifteen seconds and sensibly decided Sawyer was too big, too young and too fit to have a realistic chance of any resistance. He dropped his shoulders and exhaled long and hard.

'If I tell you, it's to go no further. Understand?'

Sawyer looked round at me and I nodded to let Bamford loose.

'Go on, Gerald, spit it out.'

For the first time since we arrived a brief smile flittered across Bamford's face.

'Actually I was with a lady friend. But she's married and her husband mustn't find out or he'll knock her about and probably come after me as well. We nipped over to Harrogate for the night while he was away.'

He gave us her name, and the address of the bed and breakfast where they'd stayed, repeating his request for us to be discreet when checking his story.

'That's one question out of the way, Gerald — now, what about yesterday? Where were you?'

'Yesterday? I was here at home after you let me go, apart from an hour in the evening.'

'Anyone see you?'

'Not after about eight o'clock. I called round to the Cock and Bear for a few jars then came home and polished off half a bottle of Scotch. Fell asleep in the chair and only woke up when you two started banging on my door.'

From the smell and look of him it was a plausible enough story.

'What about the afternoon?'

'I've told you. I was here. Look, what is this? What am I supposed to have done now?'

I told him about Billy. Bamford kept on denying he had anything to do with it.

'That's all well and good, Gerald, but we have four murders on our hands now and you without an alibi for when any of them happened. I'm afraid I'm going to have to take you in until we get your story cleared up.'

The clothes iron thudded as I dropped it on the table.

'Any reason you had this in your car boot, Gerald?'

Bamford shook his head without speaking.

'Strange place to keep it, don't you think? Sort of thing you might keep handy if you wanted to clout someone round the head. Is that what you did, Gerald, drive up to Pardow's farm, pull Billy Sharp out of the loft then beat his brains in with this?'

Another shake of the head.

'We'll easily find out, you know. It already looks to me like this is the weapon that could have killed him. The pathologist will look in more detail and if the shape fits the wounds that will be it, we'll have you. Now, do you want to tell me the truth? You'll feel better for it.'

He slumped forward in his chair with a look of resignation and I thought I'd got him.

'Believe what you want to believe, Inspector, but I didn't do it. Why would I kill a young lad I'd never met? Ask yourself why I'd kill my lovely Jenny? I can't remember why I had the iron in my car but it wasn't there to murder anyone. If you can't accept that I'm innocent then I suppose there's not much I can do about it.'

A couple of hour's further questioning of Bamford in the cells produced no more results so I left him there to stew and just hoped the experts could match it to how Billy Sharp was killed. Then we'd have to go through his story again and find the links to the other murders.

I went over to Grovestock House to re-interview everyone about their whereabouts the previous day, sending a message to Sawyer to meet me there. He was waiting in the morning room when I arrived.

'Afternoon, John, what have you got for me?'

'I've been busy since I left you, sir, but not great news, I'm afraid. First off, I went into the village and asked a few more questions about Michael Parry. Apparently he was seen in a couple of places at the time Jenny Bamford was shot.'

'So we think he's probably out of it now?'

'Well, sir, only if we're sticking with the theory that all three were killed by the same person. Personally, I think it must have been him in the woods earlier so he might just have had time to kill both the Barleighs but not Jenny. If Jenny Bamford did commit suicide, Parry's still a possibility.' He paused as if concerned about what he was going to say next. 'And we only have his sister's word he's now out of the country.'

I bit my tongue, and asked him to carry on with his report.

'Next, I called round to see young Alf Nash again. I thought he hadn't entirely come clean last time I spoke to him. He'd already been told about Billy and was petrified so it wasn't too difficult to get him to open up. Billy had slipped back home to leave a note for his mother and met Alf when he was coming away. He told Alf he'd seen someone with the shotgun leaving through the kitchen door. Thinking they might have seen him, he legged it over the wall and ran for his life.'

'And he didn't tell Alf who he thought it was?'

'No, only that he thought it was a man. Alf also said he'd told Billy I'd been looking for him and he'd been frightened out of his wits so Alf told him about the uncle's barn, where we found him.'

'So it seems like the lad died for nothing if he couldn't identify who the man with the shotgun was.'

'Sounds like it, sir.'

'Is that it, John? Anything else?'

'Afraid so.' Could it get any worse? 'I called into the station earlier and there was a message from Leeds police. It seems Gerald Bamford was in Harrogate like he says.'

I swore and shook my head. Blind alley after blind alley. I'd felt sure we might be on to something with Bamford. Now I had no alternative but to let him go and to keep digging.

Mrs Veasey almost dropped the teapot as a crack of thunder echoed round the kitchen and hailstones rattled the window.

I'd sent Sawyer off for the day to write up his notes and found my way down to scrounge a cup of tea before I began my interviews. The cook was in a terrible flap about Billy's murder and was convinced everyone in the house would soon be killed off in their beds. It seemed she'd already heard several versions of events as news trickled in from the village, and now she was pumping me for more information but I wasn't prepared to give anything away. It was safer to stick with the weather.

'Fairly pouring down out there, Mrs Veasey. Do you think it's ever going to stop?'

'Terrible, isn't it? Rain, rain, rain for the last three days. Everyone's coming in soaked and dripping all over the place. Miss Parry's at her wits end trying to keep the house clean and they tell me the whole countryside is like a swamp.'

'I can vouch for that, Mrs Veasey, the roads are treacherous.'

'Why, even Sir Arthur came off his horse yesterday and he's a very good rider.'

'Was he hurt?'

'Only his pride, I think, but he'd cut his face and was covered in mud. He took his boots off in the kitchen, naturally, but he dropped dirt all through the house on his way to his room. Staff weren't at all happy but he pays the wages, so he can do as he pleases, I suppose, and he apologised later in any case. Said he was just angry at himself for ruining his good clothes.'

We carried on in this vein until I'd almost finished my tea, with the cook repeatedly returning to Billy and his murder.

'We all knew where Billy was hiding, Mr Given. In Alf Nash's uncle's barn, wasn't it?'

'And how, exactly, did you know this, Mrs Veasey?'

'It was all around the village days ago. Someone said Alf was drunk and sharing secrets in the pub. Doesn't take long for news like that to get round, not here anyways.'

It didn't take much intelligence to guess who had helped spread the story.

'Shame you didn't feel inclined to pass it on to me, then. Perhaps Billy might still have been alive if we'd got to him first.'

I was annoyed at the cook, but not half as annoyed as I was with Sawyer and myself for not having picked it up ourselves. There'd be no point in quizzing the other staff about where they'd been when the young lad was killed. Mrs Veasey knew enough about his hiding place, death and discovery and would certainly have passed these around freely. Everyone, from the under-gardeners to Sir Arthur himself would know it all and would have had enough time and information to concoct a plausible alibi. The stupid reluctance to tell the police had cost a boy his life.

With Gerald Bamford and Michael Parry out of the frame, it had to be someone who was in the house at the time. Unless, heaven forbid, it was somebody we hadn't even looked at yet.

Even Alan Haleson had been in custody for the last week so couldn't have murdered Billy Sharp. Both sets of killings were obviously connected but had the same person carried them out? There was still no guarantee they had, so Haleson was still a remote possibility. Apart from him, we had the missing nurse and not much else.

I left the cook in the kitchen, mulling over what I had said to her and made my way to the morning room to telephone Sawyer about my lack of progress. Elizabeth was coming through the hall from the other direction and turned on her heels as soon as she saw me. I called after her and asked if we could have a word.

'Why would I wish to speak to you, Inspector?'

'Because I want to apologise, Elizabeth. You must know by now we think Michael probably wasn't involved.'

As soon as the words left my lips I knew I could have phrased it better.

'Probably? You only say "probably" and still think your apology is enough? Michael *definitely* wasn't involved and I won't accept any apology from you until you acknowledge that.'

'Elizabeth, you know I can't rule him out altogether. This whole thing is a mess and we're not certain about anything. We have four deaths, that's obvious, but do we have four murders? Three murders and a suicide? One murderer? Two murderers? I wish to God I knew what was going on.'

'That's no reason for you to doubt my word. Now, perhaps I'll just get on with my work, and you can get on with yours. Goodbye, James.'

Eighteen

There'd been no progress on the Grovestock House case for a few days so I was relieved when Sawyer rang to say Trudi Collinge had been found working in a nursing home in Leamington. He'd put the word out that we were looking for her, and an off-duty copper visiting his mother in the home had recognised the description. He discreetly asked the matron a couple of questions before calling us.

I told Sawyer to arrange for Collinge to be picked up and brought over to Kenilworth, where he should join me after arranging to have her room searched. Mountains of paperwork had been building up in my absence, so I dived into these until the front desk rang to tell me Trudi Collinge had been put in an interview room.

The woman sitting before us was completely different to how I'd imagined her. The picture in my mind's eye of the nurse was of a middle-class, dowdy and slightly overweight woman in her early fifties. But here was a striking brunette, at least ten years younger, slim and elegant, dressed in clothes of the latest fashion. I felt a slight tremor in her fingers when she stood and offered her hand and put this down to nervousness. Although she smiled I could see she was putting on a brave face. Whether she'd ever been inside a police station before I didn't know, but even the most hardened criminals can't help being anxious when they're hauled in for interview.

She was perfectly open about her movements after the deaths of the Barleighs and Jenny Bamford. After she'd left Tom on the side lawn she went up to her room and began packing. She was leaving anyway straight after the wedding because Lady Isabelle had fired her a few days earlier. Collinge said she heard the two shots but assumed, like Sir Arthur, that it was nothing out of the ordinary. It was only when she was sent for and went downstairs she realised, as she put it, 'her world had fallen apart'. She had returned to her room and finished packing, leaving the house shortly afterwards. She apologised for not waiting to talk to the police but said she'd been devastated by Tom's death and needed to get away as quickly as possible. I found it odd she used the same excuse as Gerald Bamford but I suppose it's a normal enough reaction in those close to anyone suffering a violent death. Different folks react differently: some need to stay close to their loved ones, others seek the solitude of their own thoughts and grief.

'I went to stay with my sister in Leamington and after a few days I met up with an old friend who told me of the possibility of a position in the place where she worked, a private nursing home close by the Royal Pump Rooms.'

The spa waters were not as popular as they'd been fifty years ago, but enough elderly people will still pay good money to stay where they can regularly 'take the waters'. As a result, several establishments catering for them exist in that part of the town. They vary in quality from decrepit lodging houses to swanky establishments with all the grandeur of the better class of hotel. I asked the nurse about the one where she was now employed.

'It's one of the middling ones, looking after what the matron calls "faded gentlefolk": teachers, accountants, low ranking army officers and the like. Many of them are seriously ill and trying to find any way they can to prolong their lives. Clinging to their belief that the mysteries of the spring waters will succeed where all the doctors have failed.'

'It seems a strange choice of position for you to take up, having fled from three deaths only to now find yourself surrounded by them virtually every day.'

She simply shook her head and said she'd always tended the sick and dying but it was the violence at Grovestock House that had made her run away.

Collinge had been working in the hospital Tom Barleigh was taken to after his car accident. He'd been close to death several times and the medical staff held out little hope for him surviving.

'Some said it would be a blessing if he went as he'd never walk again, but I could never accept that view. He was a fine looking young man, right at the beginning of his life, why should it be snatched away so cruelly? Though he was unconscious or drugged and I'd never spoken to him, even from those early days I knew we'd be friends if he could just make it through.'

There was an intensity in her voice that was somehow disturbing. Both Cudlip and Haleson had commented she'd been besotted with Tom Barleigh and believed he would throw Jenny over for her. Her eyes darted about the room as she spoke and her mood seemed to shift from being calm to being extremely agitated.

'I stayed up with him night after night until he was through the worst. As he recovered we became closer. I was the one he trusted to take him for walks, read to him, and to select his clothes when he had visitors.'

'And you stayed with him when he left the hospital? You gave up your secure employment to follow him to Grovestock House?'

'You make it sound strange, Inspector. What else should I do? Tom trusted me and there was a job to be done. Who better than me to do it?'

'It sounds like more than simple devotion to a sick patient, Miss Collinge. Were you a little bit in love with him? Is that what it was?'

She sat up straight in her chair and fixed me with her deep brown eyes.

'*We* were in love, Mr Given, not only me!'

'Did he tell you that?'

Trudi Collinge laughed sharply. She sounded on the edge of hysteria suddenly, fleetingly.

'Tom didn't have to tell me how he felt. I'd see it in the way he looked at me and spoke to me. He told me I was his one true support and he didn't know what he'd do without me. If that's not a sign of love I don't know what is.'

Sawyer, who was standing behind the woman, caught my eye and made a circular motion with his index finger against the side of his head. He moved to the side wall and picked up on my thread, trying to shake her up even more.

'But surely he simply meant he needed you to look after him. The poor man was useless himself, couldn't even get in and out of bed on his own.'

'No, no, that's not how it was! He was going to finish with his fiancée and marry me.'

'Don't be stupid, Miss Collinge, Tom was never going to marry you.' Sawyer moved in close. 'You're just a sad, lonely woman who's fallen for one of her betters and made a fool of herself.'

Sawyer never knew what hit him. In a flash, Collinge swung her hand up from her knee and slapped him full across the face. Next thing, she was cursing and gouging chunks out of his cheek with her nails. He made to slap her back but I got between them, pushing her back into her seat and him against the wall. Collinge's handbag fell to the floor, its contents spilling everywhere.

'Sawyer! Stop! And you, calm down!'

Fortunately, he quickly regained his composure and I was able to hold Collinge's wrists until she'd done the same. I told Sawyer to clear up the handbag while we all relaxed. Only when I was sure it was safe to do so, I let Collinge free and stepped back.

'Is that why you killed them all?'

'What?'

She made as if to jump from her seat and attack me this time but Sawyer was behind her in a second, pinning her arms to the chair. Although I was loath to do it to a woman, I ordered Sawyer to use the handcuffs. It seemed the only way of keeping her temper in check. The nurse struggled briefly then stopped and looked up.

'Why would I murder Tom? He and I were going away together. I loved him and he loved me. There was no need to hurt anyone.'

'If that were true I wouldn't have pulled you in here, would I, Miss Collinge? But it isn't true, is it? When Lady Isabelle heard of your infatuation with her son she dismissed you. When Tom Barleigh himself tried to put you off, you wrote to him threatening to kill Jenny. That's really the truth of it and it looks a very strong motive to me.'

'No, it's not true. I didn't threaten to harm Jenny Bamford. Who told you I did?'

'You wrote a note to Tom saying he'd have to get rid of his fiancée or you'd do it yourself. Sounds like a threat to me.'

She bowed her head.

'The note was a mistake. It was a threat, Inspector, but not in the way you mean. I just wanted to scare Tom into action. All I meant was I'd tell Jenny about us if he didn't. That's all.'

'Do you think she did it, sir?'

Sawyer had been to get his face cleaned up and joined me in the canteen for a cup of tea. Collinge was down in the cells whilst we considered what to do next; if nothing else, she had assaulted a police officer.

'I'm far from certain, John, I really am. She's the only one we've found so far who had any reason to kill anybody, but it doesn't mean she did. She certainly seemed to fly off the handle quickly enough, so she has a temper on her. How's the war wound, by the way?'

He gingerly stroked his left cheek and flinched.

'Bloody hurts, begging your pardon, sir. Hope her nails were clean.'

'Well, at least she doesn't seem to have done any permanent damage.'

'I was thinking about how she exploded like that, sir. Could I ask you if you thought she had a cold?'

'A cold? Not that I noticed. Why?'

'It's just when I was picking up the stuff from her bag I noticed she had three nasal inhalers.'

'Maybe she had a cold and just forgot to take them out of her bag.'

'But three, sir? Why three?'

'I'm not sure what you're getting at, John, you'll have to enlighten me.'

'I was reading about them recently, sir, and the drug they contain, Benzedrine, is apparently addictive. The article I read said it keeps you awake and one of the other side effects for people badly hooked is they have wild swings of mood. Calm one minute and raging with anger the next. Sounds like Collinge, don't you think?'

'So you think she might have murdered Tom Barleigh and the others in a frenzy brought on by this drug?'

'I doubt it would have been enough on its own but if she was already angry it may have pushed her over the top. But it wouldn't explain why she killed Billy, nor really why she'd kill Jenny. What would be the point? If he's dead there's no need to murder the girlfriend as well. I can see why she'd have gone after Lady Isabelle, just to get even for humiliating her and giving her the sack, but not the others, unless she really was off her head and decided to put an end to Jenny for causing all of this.'

Once again Billy's murder proved a stumbling block. Could it be, after all, that Billy's death wasn't connected to the others? Was it an accident? I asked Sawyer.

'I don't know, sir. Are you suggesting Billy bashed his head in the yard, badly enough to cut off two of his fingers, fell semi-conscious to the ground and then dragged himself into the barn to die? Hardly seems likely, does it?'

'Not when you put it like that, John, I suppose it doesn't.'

Nothing resembling a weapon emerged from the search of Collinge's sister's house, though the nurse could have disposed of it anywhere. Needless to say, she continued to deny any involvement in the killings of the Barleighs and Jenny Bamford. We didn't have any firm evidence against her so had to let her go after letting her sweat for a few hours.

Apparently, Sawyer's hunch about her addiction was correct. She was climbing the walls of her cell when he went down to talk to her, shaking and swearing in equal measure, though her earlier violence didn't return. When she was released and given back her things, she dived into her handbag and pulled out a Benzedrine stick. She took in two long draws before even putting on her coat. As a result of this show, Sawyer wanted me to pull her back in again but I told him we'd leave it a while. He argued with me for some time, saying she was the strongest suspect we'd got. I had to agree with him but we had nothing, other than confirmation of her addiction. He wouldn't let it go so I had to put my foot down and insist we move on to something else.

So we were back to square one, now with up to four murders and no viable suspects. What was I missing? The same questions kept coming back over and over again. Could Billy's death be unconnected to the others? Did Jenny Bamford kill herself in grief as reported, not for the loss of Tom Barleigh but for losing the financial security which went with him? If Billy had been killed by a second person then we were going down the completely wrong path and Gerald Bamford and Trudi Collinge were still in the frame. If Jenny had committed suicide, the picture and the possibilities changed again. It felt like a good time for Sawyer and me to take a fresh look at everything we'd discovered. So I let him go for the night, asking him to prepare for the job next day.

Adkins popped his head out of the public bar.

'There you are, Inspector, I've been keeping my eye out for you for a while. Do you have a minute?'

I followed him into the snug, which was deserted, and sat down with him, declining the pint he offered. What he told me made my skin run cold.

'I thought I should have a word, Mr Given. There's been two men looking for you. Normally I'd have just pointed them in the direction of your cottage but I didn't really like the look of them. Wops, they were. Shiny black hair and dark skin. Spanish or Italian possibly. Asking all sorts of questions about if anyone knew you, where you worked, where you lived, that kind of thing.'

'Did anyone tell them anything?'

'I don't think so. At least, not when I was there. Old Tommy Barber was about to say something but I gave him a filthy look and he buttoned his lip. I expect if they came in here they'll have been in other pubs as well so someone might have told them something.'

I thanked him for letting me know and asked him to contact me straight away if they came back. So, on top of everything else, the Demmas had caught up with me. There were only three people who knew I was looking for them and could have told them where I was. I couldn't believe it would have been Gerry Costello or Dyer, which left only one other person. Terry Gleeson.

A few hours and several pubs later, I was sitting in the smoke room of the Blue Pig on Kenilworth high street. The landlady, Jessie Phipps, confirmed that a couple of 'Italian-looking gentlemen' had been frequenting her establishment for the last two weeks, drinking and playing cards until closing time each night. She'd overheard them asking questions about someone who she thought, from their description, must be me. She wasn't aware of anyone giving them information but was happy enough for me to hang around to see if they came back. I have to say I wasn't too sure what I'd do if they did.

Jessie let me use her telephone to ring Gerry. There was no answer. Over the next half hour I tried him again several times with the same result. Nothing.

At the next table was a group of men playing cards, manual workers by the looks of them. They appeared to have come in straight from work; the faces of two were covered with dirt and their clothes were far from their Sunday best. They also laughed out loud and poured scorn on each other's tactics, driven, I suspect, by the substantial quantities of beer they'd consumed. One, in particular, seemed to be losing heavily but still kept his place at the table and pretended the same high spirits as his companions.

A gambling habit's a strange thing. It's hard to work out whether playing or winning — or losing — is the most important. To a non-gambler it would look like the lure of the big prize drags the gambler in, but his compulsion is more about pitting his wits against the odds. Against an opponent who has drawn a luckier hand or on a horse that has as much chance of winning as every other horse in the race. It's the thrill of possibly losing everything or winning everything. One man I knew once said the best part for him is when he has no money left, so he *has* to stop. Because he can't stop on his own account. A helpless gambler will often give most of his winnings away, only keeping enough for his next stake. So it's not about acquiring wealth either.

I have this addiction. I used to drink all night and play anyone willing to shuffle and deal the cards, anyone who'd put a few shillings on the table and play his hand against mine. Sometimes I'd win and sometimes I'd lose. As I became more experienced I fancied I'd win more often but really, deep down, I knew I always lost in the end. I was a loser because I wasn't in control. I was good at the game. I'd a memory for numbers and sequences and could often read what my opponent might have in his fist and be planning to play next. So this gave me the illusion I was in charge. Then, out of the blue, he'd play something different, or would hold cards I hadn't imagined he had. Then the excitement would really begin. My mind would spin with all of the combinations that might take me to be the victor, rather than the defeated, in this battle of wills. But it was all illusion. Cards come out of a pack entirely by chance, not through any mathematical rules. To be able, in reality, to discern what cards an opponent might hold borders on the magical, rather than the logical. I'm intelligent enough to know this but it still didn't stop me.

Then Heather came along. She believed something was missing inside me which made me continue with this drinking and gambling. She also seemed to know it wasn't about whether I won or lost but about getting back my dignity. So I might see myself without the cards or a rum bottle on the table in front of me.

She didn't quite succeed, but at least now I don't drink and when I pick up a pack I play against the cards themselves. I play patience. I deal the cards. I turn them over. If I'm lucky, the sequencing allows me to complete the game. If I'm not lucky, I can accept I've made a mistake or the cards weren't right in the pack in that game. I've lost no money. More importantly, I've maintained my self-respect and I'll always be in Heather's debt for it. She once told me if I was deluded enough to think I was the best card player around I might as well play against myself. That way I'd always be guaranteed to win.

I don't even play patience often any more, but when I do it can go on well into the night. When I've a particularly difficult case I occasionally feel the cards can provide the distraction I need. I find it helps me focus more effectively when I return to the task in hand.

I watched these men at the next table dealing their hands of cribbage, laughing and joking. They marked their progress with matchsticks in a well-used board, swapping pennies as each round was completed, and mocked the mistakes of their opponents. And I ached to join them. I stood up and walked across. I wanted so much to sit down, roll up my shirt sleeves and feel the thrill again of turning the cards with like-minded companions. Instead, I headed for the door and out into the night to hide and wait for the Sicilians in a nearby doorway. An hour later there was still no sign and the pub was emptying. I tried Gerry one last time from a nearby telephone box but with no luck so I called it a night.

The castle and the streets around it were in total darkness, the lights from the town not extending this far. I reached my front door and immediately tensed. It was open. I went inside and put on a light. My living room was in complete chaos. Papers were strewn around the floor, cushions ripped open and cupboards thrown to the ground.

I ran upstairs and the same scene greeted me in my office, absolute disarray. I went through to my bedroom. At first I thought it had been spared. Then I noticed the file on Heather's murder lay on my pillow, a carving knife stabbed through it.

I almost jumped out of my skin when the phone rang. A police inspector giving his name as Tony Pettifor was at the other end. He asked my name and I told him I was also a copper.

'I'm calling from Spitalfields in London, Inspector. It seems we have a mutual acquaintance, Gerry Costello. Can I ask how you know him?'

His tone told me there was something seriously wrong. I explained my connection with Gerry and how I'd been trying to phone him all night.

'Then I'm afraid I've some bad news for you. A neighbour found him this afternoon. He's been stabbed several times and it looks like he's been lying there for a few days. Poor feller's unconscious and in a pretty bad way. He had your number in his waistcoat pocket.'

Nineteen

I was late into the station next morning. Other than preserving my nocturnal visitors' calling card for fingerprints, I'd decided to leave the mess they'd left until daylight. I may as well have done it the night before for all the sleep I got. My mind had been racing about the stake-out, my wrecked house and the kind message left by the Demmas in my pillow. They'd smashed in my front door, breaking the lock in the process so I'd jammed a kitchen chair up against it which would have proved no resistance to the Sicilians had they come back to finish the job. Not a recipe for a peaceful night and I didn't drop off until around four a.m.

As a result I slept in later than normal, then spent a couple of hours tidying up. By the time I did arrive at the station my mood wasn't enhanced by the jokiness of the desk sergeant. Sid Miller and I had worked together for a time before I was promoted. In fact, he'd been a sergeant long before me, though I'd risen through the ranks to overtake him. Still, he was a solid copper and well suited to his present job.

'Come in sometime, then, Inspector?'

Needless to say, my reply was less than polite, which only served to encourage him.

'It's only that while some are sleeping, others are out arresting wrongdoers, that's all I'm saying.'

'What are you talking about, Sid? Who's arrested who?'

'Your young friend, Constable Sawyer. Been here half the night, he has. Dragged in that pretty nurse again. She's locked up in the cells as we speak.'

I took the stairs to my office three at a time, having shouted back to Miller I'd have his guts for garters if he warned Sawyer I was coming. He obviously didn't because Sawyer almost jumped out of his skin when I burst in.

'What do you think you've been doing, Sawyer? I tell you not to re-arrest Collinge and you go ahead and do it anyway. Just thought you'd take no notice, did you, because you know best?'

Half of me expected Sawyer to shout back at me, the other half thought he might look sheepish and apologise. Instead, he stood up to his full height, fixed me with his eyes, and spoke calmly.

'There was new evidence, sir.'

This took the wind out of my sails but I wasn't going to let him off too easily.

'What new evidence?'

'After I left you, I wasn't happy about Collinge's release and thought she was hiding something, so I went over to keep an eye on her sister's house. As I arrived, Collinge was going inside in a hurry. I hung around to see what she was up to and I didn't have to wait long. A quarter of an hour later she came back out carrying a suitcase, so I pulled her in. I found her passport and a wad of cash in her case when I got her back to the station. I interviewed her briefly, then left her in the cells until you arrived.'

Collinge had admitted she'd been up to Grovestock House to beg for assistance from Sir Arthur. She'd told him Tom had been in love with her and she needed to get the police off her back. Sir Arthur had taken pity and given her some money to get away to the continent. She was heading off when Sawyer stopped her outside her sister's house.

The young copper was openly pleased at his result. I still wasn't happy that he'd gone against my wishes, even though he'd shown initiative, and I told him so.

'But sir, we already had her down as a suspect and her running away seems to confirm it. Would you rather I'd have let her hop on a boat to France? Or did you just want to arrest her yourself?'

Whilst I was waiting for Collinge again to be brought upstairs Tony Pettifor phoned and told me Gerry Costello had died during the night. I rang Terry Gleeson straight away about the call from Pettifor. He said he was sorry to hear about my friend but couldn't see why I was ringing him about it. My blood was boiling.

'Don't give me that shit, Gleeson. I know you're up to your neck in this. I've half a mind to go to Dyer right now and tell him what's happened.'

Gleeson laughed down the line at me.

'Do what you want, Given. If you had a shred of evidence you'd not hesitate. With what you've got, Dyer will see it as what it is, another one of your little theories and nothing to back it up. Let me know when you've found something and we'll go to see him together.'

'You won't have the chance to come with me by that time — I'll have you in the clink with the key in my pocket.'

'I'll look forward to you trying. In the meantime, perhaps you'd best think about what you're going to do when your mate's killers come looking for you.'

Collinge sat glaring across the cell at Sawyer. Despite the way he'd challenged me I was letting him lead on the interview; not strictly procedure considering that he was uniform and pretty junior. So far she'd only reiterated her story from the night before but now Sawyer returned to the day of the Grovestock House killings.

'Tell me again about your movements when Tom and Lady Isabelle were shot.'

'I was in my room. I heard two shots. I thought it must be one of the men killing something close to the house. There's always vermin in the yard. It was only when I was called down to the garden I found something was terribly wrong.'

'And you were able to confirm that neither of them was still breathing?'

Collinge covered her mouth as if to stifle a flood of grief.

'It was one of the hardest things I've ever had to do. Lady Isabelle had no chance of surviving. The back of her head was blown off. But I tried and tried with Tom to find a pulse, anything which would give me the slightest prospect of bringing him back, but there was nothing. Nothing.'

'Then you went back up to your room and calmly began packing again?'

This was when the glare came.

'What do you know? I was anything but calm. The man I loved had just been shot and was lying dead on the ground outside. I wanted to run and never stop running, to get away from that awful scene.'

'So you packed, then what?'

'I told you before.'

'Tell me again.'

'I finished packing, left the house and caught the bus to my sister's in Leamington. I didn't know where else to go but I had to go somewhere.'

'When did you leave?'

'It only took me ten or fifteen minutes to finish clearing my room so I'd have left immediately afterwards.'

I chipped in. 'Did anyone see you leave?'

'Perkins, the gardener, was at the front of the house when I was going out. He said I should stay and wait for the police, but I told him I'd be back later, that I needed to go out for a while. I then hurried up to the village and caught the bus into town.'

'What was the hurry?'

'The buses are only every two hours and I knew there was one due at about half past twelve. I didn't want to miss it.'

I nodded to Sawyer to join me outside the cell and told him to check Collinge's story with George Perkins and to contact the bus conductor. Back inside, Collinge seemed pleased that Sawyer had gone. She obviously didn't like him much. I told her he would be talking to the gardener and if we found she was lying she'd be in serious trouble. In the meantime she'd be staying in the cells.

It took a while for Sawyer to get answers to back up Collinge's story because Perkins had no telephone, so had to be contacted through Jervis at Grovestock House. The gardener corroborated the nurse had left the house before Jenny was shot. Sawyer also confirmed the timetable information given to us by Collinge but had to wait an hour until the conductor was back in the depot before he could contact him.

The conductor verified he'd been working on the lunchtime bus from the village and only two people had boarded there, one of them a good-looking brunette with a suitcase. I told Sawyer to let Collinge go.

'I think you're wrong, sir. Collinge could easily have doubled back after she saw Perkins, killed Jenny Bamford and still made it to the bus stop on time. It would be the perfect alibi.'

'John, "reasonable doubt" is all a jury will need. We have to have it solid before we can charge her with multiple murders. Now, just confiscate the passport from her and let her go. If anything else turns up we can soon drag her back in.'

'If you're going to release her, Inspector, then you should charge Perkins with wasting police time. He should have informed us that Collinge had an alibi and he didn't bother.'

I understood his frustration but nothing was going to be served by taking it out on a gardener.

'Come on, let's put this one down to experience. Perkins wouldn't have believed Collinge had anything to do with the murders. Why would he? Seeing her leave the house and then hearing Jenny was killed after the nurse left would only have confirmed that view. In his mind she wouldn't have needed an alibi.'

I'd never have thought Sawyer one to sulk if he didn't get his own way but for a minute he looked like he was on the verge of it. I needed him back on my side and it wouldn't happen unless I took evasive action.

'You've had a long night, John. Even though we didn't get the right result you did some good detective work, far beyond what might have been expected. Now head off home and get your head down for a few hours, there's a little job I'd like help with later. And you can have a couple of pints while you're at it.'

Twenty

Same seat in the same pub. Same card players sitting in the same corner, running through a few hands rather than going home to their loved ones. The only difference was that tonight I had Sawyer with me, so the ache to join in the game wasn't so strong.

We were discussing an article I'd seen in the *Birmingham Post* covering the arrest of Alan Haleson on spying charges. It was of considerable local interest due to his connections with the murdered Tom and Lady Isabelle Barleigh, and with the city's Member of Parliament and Prime Minister, Neville Chamberlain. Haleson had been in custody for well over a week but the news had only just been made public. Doubtless Spencer and Mitchell had needed more time to question him before they'd let the press anywhere near it.

Sawyer still thought there was a possibility that Haleson was our man. He'd clearly become reconciled to it not being Collinge but his inexperience led him to need a quick result.

'He couldn't have done away with the Sharp boy because he was locked up, but he had opportunity for the others. There's no-one who can substantiate his claim he was in the library when the first shooting happened, and on the landing when Jenny was shot. I'm coming to the idea that Billy's death has nothing to do with the others.'

'If that's the case, John, then we have at least two other possible suspects and we're no further forward. You've said yourself Billy's death doesn't look like an accident so it must be associated in some way. Unless we have two murderers, and I can't seriously believe that any more.'

The pub door opened for only the third or fourth time since we arrived and I saw the landlady stiffen when she looked across. I'd warned Sawyer someone might come in who I was looking for in connection with another case and he'd have to follow my lead if they did. I'd left out the details and hoped he wouldn't ask me too much about it for the time being.

'I think they're here,' I whispered, 'get ready to go after them.'

Benito Demma was the first to step inside. He was more than ten years older than the last time I'd seen him but I'd have known him anywhere. He shouted a greeting to the landlady and surveyed the room for other acquaintances. In the couple of seconds it took for me to be sure it was him he'd spotted me. He muttered a word to his brother and the pair took a pace in my direction before they saw Sawyer rise at my side. The two of them turned on their heels and shot out of the pub.

A cheer went up from the card players as we chased out after the Sicilians. The street was dimly lit but their boots rattled on the pavement a hundred yards distant.

'That way, John. You go through the churchyard and try to head them off.'

He was fitter than me. He was bigger too, so if the Demmas ran into him he'd be able to hold onto at least one of them until I got there. He did as he was told and I followed the brothers in the opposite direction.

The road ahead rose steeply up the hill and it was my guess they'd be more likely to veer off than be slowed down by the incline. I wasn't wrong. The sound of their boots disappeared as they turned into a path on the right, with, hopefully, Sawyer waiting for them at the other end.

The path was lined with large poplars and the left side opened out onto a large expanse of greenery known as Abbey

Fields. Beyond the trees on the right were the back walls of the cottages bordering the street we'd left. It was pitch black. I could see hardly anything and automatically slowed down as the darkness enveloped me. Up ahead I sensed a slight movement. It was then I realised Sawyer wouldn't have been able to get through if the church gates were chained.

'Who's there?'

A silhouette stepped from behind a tree and stood full square in front of me.

'Good to meet you again at last, Given. Shame you didn't bring your friend with you.'

A sound behind made me spin round, hoping Sawyer had managed to double back and catch up. Instead, it was Pàulu, Benito's younger brother. He lit a cigarette and in the flare of the match I caught the reflection of the bright steel knuckledusters on each hand.

Twenty-One

Dyer stood at the end of my hospital bed, awkwardly holding a shopping bag which appeared to have been thrust on him by his wife. You can tell those men who are married and never go to the shops themselves; they always seem to hold the basket or bag stiffly and at an angle, rather than relaxed by their side.

He asked me how I felt, and told me how concerned everyone was at the station about me. Then he cut to the chase and wanted to know how I'd ended up in hospital. I told him Sawyer had dragged me in after he'd found me battered and unconscious in the street, and chased off my attackers.

'That much I'm aware of, James — Sawyer gave me the bare bones after he left you here last night. What I want to know is, who did this to you, and why?'

'It's a long story.'

'Well, neither of us is going anywhere so you might as well, as the Red King puts it, begin at the beginning and go on till you come to the end.'

So I told Dyer the relevant bits of my life. The boss listened attentively without interruption as I went through it all, except when he wanted further explanation.

'I was on a boat in the Atlantic. We'd had a good trip, and I'd won a few bob, then the two Sicilians, Benito and Pàulu Demma, muscled in. They'd joined the boat in Naples on the outward trip and had soon showed themselves to be bully boys. I didn't like them one bit, but thought I might be able to take a few shillings off them. I preferred games of skill like crib and gin rummy, but they insisted we play poker. They kept raising the stakes and I was too naive to resist. Before I knew it

I'd lost all my earlier winnings and was heavily into my savings. I couldn't figure out what was going on.'

'Were they cheating?'

'Too right they were. The night before we docked I figured out how they were doing it. They'd devised an elaborate set of signals to give them the advantage they needed. Benito was forever scratching his face and his hands, Pàulu kept massaging his neck and his wrists. What I hadn't seen for days was that there was a pattern.'

'What sort of pattern?'

'Well, I didn't get it all, but every time Pàulu had a good hand, for example, he'd look at his watch and rub his wrist with his thumb. Benito would then fold, or raise the pot and fold next time around. It sounds obvious, but they were very, very good at it.'

'So did you stop playing with them?'

'I wish that was all I'd done but, as I said, I was too young and too rash for my own good. I was losing heavily and accused them of cheating.'

'Never a wise thing to do.'

'Indeed. I threatened to report them to the captain if I didn't get my money back. They huffed and they puffed but knew he'd force them to do it so handed it over. Next morning, as we entered the port, one of my playing companions told me he'd overheard the Sicilians talking about how I'd insulted them and they were going to jump me in Cherbourg to teach me a lesson.'

'But what's all this to do with you being attacked in Kenilworth and ending up in here?'

'I told you it was a long story. I got out of Cherbourg as fast as possible and headed down to Le Havre. A couple of nights later, Benito and Pàulu bashed down the door of my lodgings and I had to jump from a first floor window as they chased up the stairs. I'd moved quickly from village to village through Normandy and Picardy, covering my tracks everywhere, before making a run for the coast and over the Channel to Dover. I'd already decided the New York voyage was going to be my last and I needed to do something else with my life.'

Then came the hard part. I told him about how I'd found Heather murdered by the Demma brothers. Soon after she and I moved north I'd gone into town and heard two foreigners were looking for me. When I got back, Heather had disappeared and one of the fruit pickers told me she'd gone off with two men about an hour earlier. I found her in the undergrowth at the edge of the orchard, naked and covered with blood. I suspected she'd been raped before they stabbed her to death. I went to the police but they took no notice. Why would they? Fights, arguments and worse were rife amongst the pickers and, anyway, who cared? The migrants were the lowest of the low as far as the locals were concerned.

'I've no proof but I know it was them. The police tried to accuse me of doing it but I was able to prove where I'd been at the time. It's why I joined the police. To get justice for Heather.'

I shook as the anger that had waited years to escape took hold. Dyer sipped his tea and let me settle before he went on.

'Why did you think it was the Sicilians? You said you had no proof.'

'I don't. But carved onto Heather's stomach was a message, "*debito non pagato*" — an unpaid debt. And they're still after me to collect that debt.'

He stayed with me for about an hour, going through my story in more and more detail, and getting a clear description of the Demma brothers. I told him they'd stayed in England after killing Heather and become involved in various gangs in London, and how Gerry Costello had told me just before he was murdered they'd moved up to Birmingham. Dyer was interested to hear my theory that they'd now tied in with those carrying out the beatings of Jewish businessmen and said he'd organise a search for the Sicilians.

I was exhausted at the end of it and slept for a while before I was woken again by more visitors. Two pairs of heels clattered down the ward and two hands waved with a "Bye, James" as they left. The WPCs were the last of the stream of visitors I'd had all morning and Elizabeth eyed up the prettiest when they crossed in the doorway.

'Thanks for coming to see me, Elizabeth.'

She continued to stand until I asked her to pull up a seat and waved over to a nurse to bring a vase for the flowers Elizabeth was holding.

Elizabeth eyed the bowl on my bedside table.

'I brought some fruit as well, but can see you've already got plenty.'

The look on her face told me she thought it had been brought by one of my female visitors.

'Yes, I have, haven't I? The boss brought some in and John Sawyer did likewise. It's very kind of you though, all the same.' I tried to lift myself into a more comfortable position to talk to her and pain shot through my ribs. I winced.

'That looks painful. They told me you'd been badly beaten up. How are you?'

'I'm all right, considering. The two fellers gave me a good going over. I've a lot of bruising but nothing broken. Hurts like hell but nowhere near as much as when you walked out.'

She blushed and looked around the ward for anything to focus on so that she wouldn't need to look me in the eye.

'It's true, Elizabeth. I thought we were getting on so well together. You know I was only doing my job. I felt awful about it but you have to see Michael was an obvious suspect. You said so yourself.'

I was taking a chance because she might easily take offence again and we'd be back to our argument. My one hope was she'd cared enough to have come to visit me in the hospital. Her first reaction seemed to be to stiffen, then she took a deep breath to settle herself.

'I do know you were only doing your job, James, but it was still hurtful. Michael is my brother and regardless of what he's done in the past, I care for him. I knew he couldn't be guilty of such an awful crime. You should have trusted me.'

I wanted to say I did trust her, that it was her brother I hadn't trusted. But I thought it better to leave it where it was. There were some bigger issues we'd be facing before too long.

'How did it happen, then? Who did this to you, James?'

So I gave her the whole lot as I'd told it to Dyer and Sawyer before she arrived. Some of it she already knew, most of it she didn't. By the time I'd finished I saw she was shaking.

'That's just ... just awful. Why didn't you tell me before, James?'

She didn't need any more surprises but I said a quick prayer and drew a deep breath.

'Actually, there's two important bits I've missed out. I'm Jewish and my name isn't James Given.'

I filled Elizabeth in on the parts of my life I'd never had the courage to tell her — or anyone — before. How I'd constantly argued with my father about his religion and his abhorrence of Russia. About how I'd believed he should never have left but should have stayed to help build the new state after the revolution. About how I'd run away from home and joined a boat in Grimsby which I fantasised would lead me back to what I thought of as my homeland.

On board I met a Russian sailor who laughed at my naivety.

'Don't you know things are far worse there for Jews now than ever they were under the Tsar?' he'd said.

I later found he was right, up to 150,000 Jews had been killed in 1919 in pogroms and the country was on its knees. Soon after, he started to make repeated taunts of 'Jew-boy' and even spitting at my feet whenever I walked by. He was a great brute of a man and more than a physical match for my skinny frame so I had to take it. Soon he'd pulled his friends into his game and my life became hell on board. I left the ship in Bremerhaven in northern Germany.

I visited my Uncle Gideon at that time, who lived in nearby Bremen. He told me of a man named Adolf Hitler who'd just been released from prison and who was whipping up hatred against the Jews. His ideas on how they were controlling the economy through their ownership of the banks and businesses were attracting a lot of popular support amongst the people. Uncle Gideon thought, even then, he might be forced to move away to safety, like he'd done to escape persecution in Russia. For my part, this convinced me even more that openly admitting to being a Jew was not a good idea.

Shortly afterwards, I abandoned both my ideas of going to help establish the newly declared Soviet Union, and my name, changing it to something less recognisably Jewish. Bremerhaven was always a cauldron of nationalities and it was no problem at all to get papers to give me a new identity. Much more difficult was obtaining the documents to legitimise it when I returned home. The wheels of English bureaucracy grind exceeding slow and it took over six months to obtain the right credentials after I decided I wanted to join the police.

It was as if the cork had finally been pulled from the bottle. All of this poured out of me for what seemed like an age, again with no interruption from Elizabeth. Eventually she spoke.

'But you don't look Jewish.'

I laughed. 'There's the problem, Elizabeth, no one *looks* Jewish. What you have in your head is the demonic picture that's put around about Jews. Shakespeare's Shylock. If you met my father on a Friday night, you'd see his beard, his yarmulke, his dark suit and his prayer shawl and you'd recognise him as Jewish. Take away those trappings and he'd look much like half the elderly men in Birmingham.'

'I don't know what to say, James. When I heard you'd been hurt and were in hospital I suddenly realised again how much I loved you. I was prepared to forget about our argument and see it as just that, an argument, not a nail in the coffin. But this is a lot to take in.'

Elizabeth stayed for over an hour after I revealed my secret, firstly quizzing me about Judaism, then in greater detail as to why I felt the need to deny my heritage. She spent the remainder of the time pressing me to return to my faith, which caused me considerable confusion. Here she was, telling me openly she'd have difficulty coping with me as a Jew but then remonstrating with me for trying to ignore this part of me.

She'd been employed by a clergyman and I thought her own faith must have been quite strong, albeit as a Christian. Perhaps this was why she found it so hard to understand why someone would reject their religion. I tried to tell her I hadn't fully rejected it, only hidden it for a while. Even to me it sounded as hollow as when I'd had a similar discussion with my father a couple of weeks earlier. Who was I trying to fool? Elizabeth, my father or myself?

We'd gone on in this way until Elizabeth had to leave and her final words were still making my head spin.

'You … *we* need to work this out, James. I want us to remain friends, I know we can, though I'm not sure it will now ever be any more than just friendship. I'll not see you again for a while.'

With this, she kissed me on the forehead, her fingers lingering for a second too long on my cheek, then left. I watched her making her way out of the ward, the men in the other beds looking at her appreciatively. I don't think I'd ever felt so alone in my whole life as her heels faded away down the corridor; except perhaps when I saw Heather after the Demma brothers had finished with her.

Twenty-Two

My heart was beating so hard in my chest when I grabbed the handle of the cell door that I had to pull away. I stood with my back and head pressed hard against the cold brick wall, taking in great gulping breaths until some semblance of calm descended. I'd dreamt many times about this moment, about finally having the Demma brothers where I wanted them, locked up and under my control. Now I was there.

Whilst I was in hospital, Superintendent Dyer had set up a search all over the county to pull in the Sicilians, calling in favours from wherever he could. But he hadn't needed to call in many, coppers always respond when it's one of their own. It's part of self-preservation.

In the end, it hadn't been too difficult. Thugs like the Demmas may have long memories but they're not very bright. Thankfully, the criminal masterminds encountered by Sherlock Holmes are few and far between in real life. And the Demma brothers didn't come close. They'd not even bothered trying to leave Kenilworth and had returned a couple of nights later to the same pub, the Blue Pig. Jessie Phipps knew she needed to stay on the good side of the police if she wanted to keep her licence so didn't hesitate to phone the station as soon as she got the opportunity. Within fifteen minutes my attackers had been arrested and thrown in the back of the Black Maria.

Benito Demma sat on a plain wooden chair, his cuffed hands on the table in front of him, a resigned look in his dark eyes. Sawyer had joined me and was leaning nonchalantly against the door, making it clear Benito wasn't going anywhere soon.

'Where's my brother? What have you done with him?'

248

'He's fine, Benito, he's next door. It's yourself you should be worrying about, not Pàulu. Actually, when I say he's fine, he's not entirely fine, he'll be going to prison like you for assaulting a police officer, but apart from that he's well. For the time being.'

I rubbed my ribs and counted to ten.

'Let's talk about you instead. You're not going to deny the pair of you gave me a beating, are you?'

It didn't really matter because his younger brother had already admitted it. He'd also confessed they'd been harassing Jewish businesses in London and Birmingham. In fact, he'd gloated over it so much I'd wanted to smack him. Benito was more restrained.

'It would be stupid to try to say we didn't do it, wouldn't it? It would be our word against yours, and who would believe us? Two wops or two English policemen? Now just lock me up and leave me alone.'

'I'm afraid we can't do that yet, Benito, we have a little catching up to do. There's the slight matter of rape and murder.'

His face hardened and he fixed his eyes on mine.

'Murder? Rape? What evidence you got?'

'It might have sounded more convincing if you'd asked me whose murder and rape I was accusing you of. Have you committed so many it doesn't matter? Or was it just the one? We both know I'm talking about Heather Termon, don't we?'

'Never heard of her.'

He was right, of course, he wouldn't have known her name. She was just a girl who was friendly with me and who he could use to teach me a lesson. This thought punched me in the guts much harder than he and his brother had managed a few nights earlier. In all of the years since it had happened it had never struck me that Heather was only an innocent, and to them nameless, bystander. She was simply the bringer of a few minutes of brutal gratification and the bearer of a message. If they'd found me first then Heather would still be alive.

'It was the name of the young woman you felt you had to butcher eight years ago. You ought to try to remember her name, you're going to hang for her killing.'

He turned and spat on the floor.

'As I said, Inspector, I have no knowledge of this woman. Have you witnesses? Fingerprints? Anything at all to connect me to such a terrible crime? I don't think so.' Benito Demma leaned over the table and lowered his voice so Sawyer couldn't hear. 'So why don't you charge me with the assault and get it over? Pàulu and I will be out in a few months, a year at most, and we can continue where we left off. You still owe us a debt of honour, Given, and you're going to repay it with your life. Be very sure of that.'

I grabbed his hair and cracked his face onto the table. Sawyer was onto me in a second and pulled me away. I struggled but he was too strong for me, even in my rage.

The door opened and Dyer walked in, clearly unable to comprehend the scene playing out before him. I didn't even know he was in the building.

'What the hell's going on here, Inspector? Calm down and get outside. You, Sawyer, stay and keep this toerag company while Mr Given and I have a word upstairs.'

'James, what on earth has got into you?'

My rage had subsided as we climbed the stairs, though I was still trembling when we found an empty office.

'Eight years I've been bottling that up, sir. Eight years of nightmares and sleepless nights. Always on the watch to catch those bastards and I don't have a scrap of evidence to be able to get them put away. Then, calm as you like, he threatens me. What would you have done?'

'You told me you'd joined the police because of them, James, don't get kicked out because of them as well. I understand your frustration but you still have to go by the book. You're ready to charge them with the assault?'

'I am but I'd rather not.'

'How so?'

'A second before I lost my temper, Benito Demma said to me they'd be out of prison in less than a year and he's right. I've no desire to go for half measures so what's the point? If we can let them stew in the cells for a couple of days it might loosen their tongues a bit, or I might think of some way of doing it for them without resorting to violence.'

Dyer agreed to this and then dropped one final comment.

'We'll sort something out with these two, James, don't you worry. I've put a couple of calls out and we'll see where they lead.'

Sawyer and I had another couple of hours with the Demma brothers, first with one, then the other. We were hoping one of them would drop a vital piece of information which might tie them into Heather's murder, but neither was giving anything away. Eventually I sent Sawyer home and left the Demmas locked away, with a warning we'd carry on the next day.

Back in my office the phone rang. It was Sid Miller from the front desk. He told me a note had been left for me by Sir Arthur's driver and should he send it up? I was about ready to head off home myself, so said I'd collect it on my way out.

Sid lifted the faint blue envelope from his desk and theatrically wafted it under his nose, pretending to inhale a strong scent.

'Smells sweet,' he ventured, 'anyone I know?'

I still wasn't in the best of moods but I managed a smile.

'Mind your own business, Sergeant, and I'll mind mine.'

He gave me the note and I thought he seriously expected me to open it in front of him. Instead, I tucked it into my jacket pocket and made my exit. This was more to irritate Sid than any lack of interest on my part so as soon as I was outside I found a streetlamp and read it.

My dear James,

I'm sorry to have delivered this news to you in such a way but I really had no choice. Events have moved along so quickly since we were last together. I've been offered a position at a country house in Devon, far away from the horrible events at Grovestock, and I've decided to take it. My new employers are leaving for a tour of the continent shortly so want me to move in within the next few days. By the time you read this note I expect I'll already be on the train. I will drop it in when Sir Arthur's driver takes me to the station.

I want us to remain friends and to keep in touch but please don't expect any more from me. At least for the time being. I'll write soon with my new address when I'm settled in.

Look after yourself.

Elizabeth

So she was running away. Again.

The next ten minutes blurred as I ran headlong towards the railway station, praying I'd get there before Elizabeth's train disappeared. I heard the whistle when it made its way across the bridge at Mill End and knew it would be touch and go.

Smoke billowed out as I arrived at the station approach so I knew the train was still there and I might be in time to catch her.

Another whistle, this time of the station master, shrilled above the sound of the giant engine, and the platform filled with steam. Tons of steel heaved slowly out as I stood helplessly scanning every passing carriage window. I finally spotted Elizabeth towards the middle of the train, in a second class compartment. She started when she caught sight of me, holding my gaze for the briefest of moments before turning away.

The last carriage trundled past and the steam cleared. It was then I saw Spencer watching me from the opposite platform.

That night I fell off the wagon for the first time in eight years. Not so much fell, as dived. Headlong into a sea of alcohol. Elizabeth had gone, the Demmas would soon be released and the Grovestock House case was going nowhere. I'd sat at my desk staring at Tom Barleigh's photographs for over an hour, drinking endless cups of tea and turning the pictures in every direction to try to glimpse what he'd seen and what I couldn't.

By eight, I'd cleared all of my papers onto the floor and was dealing hand after hand of patience, increasingly frustrated with my lack of success until I grabbed the deck and hurled it across the room. Almost before I knew what was happening I was out of my front door and occupying a stool at the bar of the Queen, the landlord pulling me a second pint. After a third I moved on into town. Another pub, another pint, then a rum chaser. Then it was just the rum. Doubles. With each glass I told myself I'd have one more and stop. Like it used to be.

I vaguely remember borrowing a car from some low-life who owed me a favour and within half an hour was stumbling down the drive of Grovestock House, the car in a ditch somewhere nearby. Blood seeping from my forehead kept running into my eye no matter how many times I brushed it away. I took another swig from the half bottle I'd picked up along the way and collapsed onto my knees on the damp grass. The stucco frontage of the stately home shone bright even under the waning moon, but there were no lights to be seen in any windows as I threw back my head and roared at the house. A stream of obscenities poured out, venting all of my frustrations until I was left gulping for breath. I wanted to storm across the grass, beat on the front door and demand to know what had happened in there. Instead, finally beaten, I turned away down the hill to the lake, a silver blade of moonlight aiming across the water at Grovestock House. I shivered and took a gulp of rum. Then I passed out.

I dreamt I was in a police car, hurtling down a country road alongside a railway line. Elizabeth and Sir Arthur waved from the train, and the engine driver was Benito Demma. Lady Isabelle, with half of her head missing, stood at a door scattering rose petals from an open window. I bellowed at the policewoman behind the wheel to go faster but she turned and laughed; it was Trudi Collinge. The car somehow passed the train and swung onto a level crossing, stopping dead. The engine thundered towards us. For some reason the police bells were still ringing.

Twenty-Three

The first thing I saw when I opened my eyes was a fabulous pagoda rising out of the mist on the hillside beyond the lake. A giant duck stood in its entrance. I closed my eyes again and shook my head to make sure I wasn't still dreaming. As I gained focus I could see it was merely the duck-house, not on the far shore but only a few feet from where I lay on the grass. An illusion, like everything else here, not what it seemed.

Then one image from my dream came rushing back into my head.

It was six o'clock, I was freezing cold and I felt sick.

Two aspirin and a strong cup of tea later the nausea was still with me but my head felt like it might now manage to avoid exploding. Back on my desk lay the photos I'd been examining the night before. I didn't need the magnifying glass to see the difference between Miss Leeming's nephew, Graham Cox, and his two friends. He was short, blond and overweight. The others were almost peas in a pod and if I'd been told they were brothers I'd not have been surprised. Dark haired, slim and very good looking, they were smiling out at the world with not a hint of the horrors of war they were soon to face.

The lens magnified the bare forearm of one of the young men and I whistled as I finally saw what Tom Barleigh had discovered. What I'd thought was an imperfection in the print was now clearly a tattoo, a stylised rose with a single word across its middle. In my dream I'd unscrambled the picture to make me see that the teardrops on Tom's drawing were, in fact, rose petals.

It was well after nine o'clock before I could get over to Priors Allenford. I was beside myself with anticipation as I pounded on Barbara Leeming's door. It was an age before she slid back the lock and cautiously peered out wearing her dressing gown.

'Why, Inspector, whatever's the matter?'

I quickly explained I needed her help in identifying the men in the photograph.

'I told you before, Inspector, they're Graham Cox, Harry Stenson and Sir Arthur Barleigh. But it's written here on the back, did you not see it?'

'No, no, Miss Leeming, I need to know which is which. Who's the one with the tattoo?'

She pushed her glasses further up the bridge of her nose and peered at the photograph again.

'It's been such a long time, Inspector, but I'm fairly certain that would be Harry Stenson.'

Miss Leeming filled me in on everything she knew about Harry Stenson and his two friends and, luckily, was able to dig out the negative of the photos she'd passed on to Tom Barleigh. I returned for my file in the car then waited for Sawyer to come over and join me. He brought some interesting news.

'The fingerprint results on the two weapons are finally back, sir. They're only what we might have expected. The shotgun has those of Perkins and Billy Sharp and the revolver has Tom's, Jenny's and Sir Arthur's. We already know all of these would have handled the guns at one time or another, but why aren't Lady Isabelle's on the shotgun?'

'And why isn't there at least one set of prints the same on each gun? It can only mean, in at least one case, the killer wore gloves and we know Isabelle wasn't wearing any by the time you arrived because they're not in your photographs.'

I shared my own findings of the morning with Sawyer and asked him to pop back home with a little job for me.

The retired teacher and I shared a breakfast of boiled eggs, toast and tea until Sawyer arrived back with the enlargement I'd asked him to make. I took one look at it and laughed at the name now so clear on Harry Stenson's skin. Sawyer nodded.

'I think we need to go up to Grovestock House, John, don't you?'

'What in hell's name...?'

Sir Arthur's eyes narrowed as Sawyer and I walked through his study door. Jervis had let us into the house but we'd instructed him not to try to warn his boss we'd arrived.

'Morning, Sir Arthur, please don't get up on our account.'

The man settled back into his chair and, in a clear attempt to gain some control over his situation, beckoned for us to be seated as well. I gestured to Sawyer to take up a position standing beside Sir Arthur and I sat across the desk from them. I'd hoped the constable at his full height and in police uniform would provide sufficient intimidation to loosen Sir Arthur's tongue.

'What's this all about, Inspector? Why do you feel you have the right to force yourself into my private rooms without the decency of being announced? As soon as this is over I'll be telephoning your superiors.'

'There'll be no need for that, Sir Arthur. If this interview goes the way I want it to, you'll be seeing my superiors before too long at the police station. So, for the time being, just sit quietly and answer our questions, rather than trying to be so high and mighty.'

His scarred features hid his expression well and he might be terrified or might be laughing at us, it was impossible to tell. A flush at his neck, and his knuckles tightening momentarily on the handle of his chair were the only indication I got of his anger.

'How dare you speak to me in such a tone! Do you know who I am?'

'I think I'd need to ask if anyone, other than yourself, knows who you are? Who you *really* are, I mean.'

'What are you talking about, man?'

'I believe you're no more Sir Arthur Barleigh than I am. Your real name is Harry Stenson and you stole Sir Arthur Barleigh's identity when he was killed on the Western Front.'

Barleigh forced a laugh and turned to Sawyer.

'Is your inspector all right, Constable? He seems to be under the impression I'm someone else.'

Sawyer maintained a stony silence.

'I've never heard such nonsense, Inspector, but, for the sake of argument, if it was true, what would it have to do with you?'

'Oh, I'm sure I could charge you with a number of crimes on that count alone. Fraud and theft being two of the most obvious ones, but you're right, they'd not interest me at all. What *do* interest me are the murders you committed to keep your secret. Firstly your wife, then Tom and Jenny, and finally the unfortunate Billy Sharp.'

'My, my, Inspector, you do seem to have fabricated some strange ideas about me, don't you? Why on earth would I do all of this? Why would you suspect me of killing my own son, let alone the others?'

'For a long time I'd asked myself the same question but that's the crux of what this matter is all about. Tom Barleigh wasn't your son, he was Sir Arthur Barleigh's and Tom discovered your charade so you had to silence him. The rest all follows on from there. Tom was carrying out research into the family and came upon a few discrepancies when he started looking at documents concerning you.'

'This is totally preposterous! What do you imagine he could possibly have found?'

'Only minor things. The colour of your eyes, for example. Blue on some of the papers but really they're brown. Signatures on certificates, dissimilar enough to indicate they might belong to different people. Your interest in archaeology. Not much on its own but one you hadn't displayed before you joined the army, although your friend Harry had. This also implied something wasn't quite as it seemed.

'The sad thing in this entire affair is Tom hadn't any concrete proof of your deception, only a series of inconsistencies which led him down a particular path. But when he confronted you with his suspicions you knew you had to take some action. You waited for your opportunity, stole the gardener's shotgun, then waited until the time you thought Tom would be alone in the side garden where you'd have no chance of being observed.'

'I've had enough of this, Inspector. If all you've got are some vague ideas that an incompetent clerk somewhere recorded my eye colour incorrectly and I picked up a hobby from my friend then I think you'd better leave now.'

He made as if to rise from his seat and Sawyer gently but firmly placed his hand on the man's shoulder to force him back down.

'We'll be leaving soon enough, hopefully with you under arrest in the back of a police car, but for now you'll sit and listen. As I said, all of the small points come together to make a bigger picture. Like those paintings by George Seurat. You're an educated man, you must know them. Up close all you see are lots of individual dots but step back and the whole scene emerges. It's what Tom did, and it's what I do all the time. He was given some photographs and then spotted the crucial detail, just as I did. All his life he may have felt deep down there was something different about you when you came back from the War, and not merely your injuries. Even if he'd mentioned it to anyone he would have been laughed at. After all, children have these kinds of fantasies all the time, don't they?'

'But if I wanted to get rid of Tom's accusations why would I murder Isabelle? And Jenny?'

'Come along, Sir Arthur, or should I call you Stenson now? It's no secret you and Isabelle weren't in a happy marriage. I suspect Isabelle knew all the time you weren't who you were pretending to be. After all, she and Harry Stenson had been going out together for a while and she'd also had a fling with Arthur Barleigh before you both joined the army. That's where Jenny came from. Isabelle would have seen any minor differences straight away. I think she saw it as a path to a better lifestyle than she might otherwise expect and blackmailed Stenson — you — into marrying her.'

There are some murderers who crumble when faced with the facts. Unfortunately, Harry Stenson didn't appear to be one. He'd kept up the facade for too many years to be broken down by unsubstantiated allegations.

'That's all very interesting, Inspector Given, but surely it's evidence you need. And the evidence indicates Isabelle shot Tom whilst her mind was deranged, then she shot herself. The coroner, and even your own constable here, confirmed as much.'

This time I did see the flicker of a smile cross his face and knew, right away, he was guilty. It was now coming down to the final game of cat and mouse.

'The coroner's a friend of yours, isn't he? Not that he'd divert the truth for you, but he might err on the side of caution where an acquaintance and respected member of the community is concerned. And it looked much like you've described it. You staged the scene well, stealing Perkin's shotgun rather than using one of your own, then sending Mrs Veasey out to buy fish. Extremely clever.'

The man I believed to be Harry Stenson now said nothing. He stared at me, unblinking.

'What you didn't expect when you hid in the shrubs to attack Tom was Isabelle storming in with her final bit of evidence to stop the wedding. I think you had to grab her and, to keep her quiet, you had to put the barrel under her chin. Tom couldn't get up to prevent you and whether by accident or intent, you shot your wife. I believe you intended to kill her to put an end to all the years of bad feeling between you. I can see it's possible she could have struggled and you pulled the trigger by accident. But what happened next was entirely intentional and will see you with a noose round your neck.

'With Lady Isabelle dead on the ground you had no option now other than to despatch Tom. In a final misguided attempt to stop you, he said your secret was already out because he'd confided in Jenny, little knowing you'd go after her next. You turned the shotgun on the poor man and blasted a hole in his chest. It was no problem at all to slip back through the shrubs to the back wall of the house where you wouldn't be seen, then through the kitchen and up the side stairs to your room to clean yourself and wait for Jenny to return.'

'So now you're saying I sat there, biding my time, and when Jenny came back I somehow enticed her into Tom's room, finished her off with his revolver and made the whole thing look like suicide? You are quite unbelievable, Inspector, with

261

this fanciful story you've concocted. You've not provided one shred of evidence so far, only theory and conjecture. And what about the young gardener, Billy Sharp? Do you think I simply got a taste for blood and roamed the countryside looking for new victims?'

'Oh, the evidence was all there, Stenson, I only had to look for it and piece it together. I think that, with Jenny, you did exactly as you've described it. As for Billy, he was just an unlucky young lad who happened to be in the wrong place at the wrong time. He was weeding alongside the hedge which borders the side garden when he heard raised voices and shots, panicked and ran away. Through the gate he saw a figure disappear into the kitchen and you saw him from the landing window when you were half-way up the stairs. You went looking for him later in the day, and several days afterwards, but couldn't find him. One of the staff must have told you he was hiding over by Pardow's farm and you went there to get him. Again, it might have been another accident when your horse reared up and kicked the boy but, either way, you had planned on killing Billy if you caught him.'

Stenson simply shook his head and smiled to himself. It was beginning to unnerve me that he was reacting so calmly in the face of the accusations. After a few moments he looked up.

'I think I'd like you to leave now, Inspector. If you can't come up with any more than your wild fantasies you'd best go and look for someone else to suspect.' He glanced round at Sawyer. 'And take your pet poodle away with you.'

Sawyer flushed but, to his credit, didn't react.

'I will go now, but I already have enough to convince my superiors to give me more officers to examine this place with a fine tooth comb. I'll be back with them later. And, don't worry; I'll continue digging until we have enough on you to see you hang. In the meantime, my "pet poodle", as you put it, will stay around, just to make sure you don't try to make a run for it. I think you might find he'll turn out to be more of a bulldog than a lapdog if you do.' I thought I'd make one last effort to unsettle him, to throw something on the ground and gauge his response. 'You may also want to know that this morning I've made a formal request for the army records of Harry Stenson and Arthur Barleigh. Those should provide us with evidence of who you really are. Now, could you please roll up your sleeve?'

'What?'

'You heard me. Roll it up or I'll get the constable to do it for you.'

Even though his arm was badly scarred the remains of a tattoo were still evident. What was left resembled the drawing I'd found on Tom Barleigh's desk, just two letters, 'B' and 'E', followed by three teardrops. Most of the design had been burnt away with the rest of his skin but from close up it was obvious the other letters had been removed later. I'd have little problem showing in court that the name had been Isabelle, not Beatrice, and the teardrops were actually the petals of the rose in Harry Stenson's tattoo.

I finally got the reaction I was hoping for. It was only a small thing, a slight intake of breath, but I'd hit the mark and he knew it was all over. He tried to continue with his bravado by ringing his bell for Jervis to show me out. As I left the room and turned back to look at him he fixed me with a glare mixing hatred and fear in equal measure. I couldn't wait to report back to Superintendent Dyer.

Twenty-Four

Faced with the material I'd gathered, Dyer had no hesitation in sending a group of men over to make a detailed search of Grovestock House. Stenson was either extraordinarily arrogant or simply very careless, because they soon found proof guaranteed to put him away.

The charred remnants of his blood-spattered clothing still lay in the garden incinerator where he'd tried to burn them. Stenson must have thought further fires would get rid of anything he'd left but, luckily for us, the season and the weather meant there'd been nothing burnt recently. With the cook's testimony, I'd be able to put together a pretty good case that he'd done this when he returned from killing Billy Sharp. The rain-drenched clothes hadn't burned well and their protection had preserved the contents of Stenson's pockets. One of the items in there was a screwed up letter addressed to Gerald Bamford. The top corner was missing and it matched with the fragment recovered by Sawyer from Lady Isabelle's hand. Stenson had ripped it from her grasp and stuffed it into his jacket when he stepped out from behind the rhododendron. This, without a shadow of doubt, tied him to the scene of the crime.

Harry Stenson's trial lasted a month and attracted wide coverage in the newspapers and on the wireless. It had everything they could want: upper class scandal, spies, tragic lovers and several murders. Every revelation and scrap of evidence was greeted by gasps in the courtroom and headlines in the papers.

I was called to the stand twice. The first time lasted a day and a half whilst I was questioned by both sides on every aspect of my investigations. Ten days later I was called again to contradict a version, proposed by the defence, of Stenson's movements at the time of Billy's death. Everyone knew it was just a last ditch attempt to salvage something from the trial but I was able to link the severed fingers, Stenson's muddy return to the house and his bloody, burned clothing in the garden. My testimony on this point was clear, well-reasoned and, I believe, put the final nail in his coffin.

Sawyer was called once, to confirm the early part of the case and I must say that for a young officer he acquitted himself well in the courtroom.

Throughout the trial, Harry Stenson remained true to his story he was innocent of the killings. He admitted his guilt regarding his long fraud, pleading it had started unintentionally and, in the confusion of a battlefield hospital, he'd been mistaken for Arthur Barleigh because he'd picked up his dead friend's identity tags. He'd been badly injured and shell-shocked so let the mistake continue after he returned home. With Arthur's parents and closest friends out of the picture, Isabelle was the only one who knew Barleigh and Stenson well enough to spot the deception. She blackmailed him into marrying her, fulfilling her desire to find an affluent husband, and he was trapped. The "charade" referred to by Alice Brown had started, sowing the seeds of hatred which were to bloom in late September, twenty years later.

Now he was waiting to be hanged, convicted of the murders of his wife, Tom Barleigh and Jenny Bamford. The jury found him guilty of manslaughter in the case of Billy Sharp because the evidence of premeditation wasn't adequate to secure a murder conviction. But the killing of the others was sufficient to attract the death sentence.

When he was sent down I couldn't tell if he was surprised or relieved. Living a lie for so many years takes its toll. As he was being led out of the courtroom he looked in my direction and gave me the briefest of nods, acknowledging that I'd beaten him.

The evening I'd watched Elizabeth leave, I'd chased over the footbridge to find Spencer but he'd disappeared into the night when I reached the other platform. Due to the arrest of Stenson, it was the middle of the next afternoon before I managed to speak to the Special Branch man on the phone. I demanded to know why he was still following me but he was dismissive, saying he couldn't leave any ends untied while a case was still open. It was tedious but still had to be done. I have to say this struck a chord with me.

I asked him where he was with Haleson's prosecution but he didn't add much more than was in the newspaper reports. Here was a man who was certainly adept at playing his cards close to his chest and he continued to rise in my estimation.

'I've a little news for you about your uncle, old man. Mitchell seems to have come up trumps.'

'Where is he? Is he safe?'

'I understand he's still in Bremen. As for being safe, that's a whole other question. Mitchell's boys found him and his family still living over his shop, surviving but very frightened. All the Jews in the area have been told they should be making plans to move back to the country from which they came. And I don't think Hitler's just giving them friendly advice. All the signs are they're going to be forced out, whether they want to go or not.'

'Can you help get him out? Get the family over to England, I mean?'

'No can do, old boy. Mitchell's top priority is to keep his own chaps secure. They're all undercover and would be in deep trouble if detected. Best he can do is to transmit messages in or out. We've managed to inform your uncle you're anxious about him, but that's as far as we can go.'

I thanked Spencer and asked he passed my gratitude on to Mitchell. He said he'd let me have any further news he received.

My father was ecstatic to hear Gideon was still in relative safety but was alarmed when I explained my informant had suggested it may not last too long. I tried to comfort him, saying I was sure everything would be all right. These reassurances sounded hollow, even to me. He was no fool and, from first-hand experience, he understood how these things might end when the whole might of the State was focused against the Jewish community.

He asked me about how I was getting on with the young woman I'd mentioned when I'd last seen him. I lied to him, telling him everything was fine, and he returned to our earlier conversation.

'You'll need to decide where you're going with your faith if this becomes more serious, Jacob. Marriages between Jews and Gentiles can only work when husband and wife are secure in their own religion, and understanding of their partner's. If either of you is unsure then a wedge will come between you, especially when children arrive.'

I told him I didn't really want to discuss it, that I didn't know what the future held for me with Elizabeth, that I was giving thought to what he'd said before but still hadn't worked it out.

He continued to press and I became tetchy. We parted politely although not on the best of terms. He was worried about my well-being and, as far as he was concerned, I could only be really happy if I acknowledged my faith and returned to the fold. I also knew this wouldn't be an easy path to follow even if I did decide to try.

Two weeks later, in early November, a letter arrived for my father from Uncle Gideon. Hitler's gangs of thugs were everywhere in Germany and Jews were being regularly abused on the street but the family was safe for now. The letter ended with the hope that they would make their way to Switzerland or England in the near future.

Dyer asked me over to his office for a celebratory drink on the day Stenson was sentenced. He offered me whisky from the desk drawer but I stuck with the tea I'd brought in with me. We chatted for a while and he spoke of his plans for retirement, saying I should think about going for Superintendent when he left. I laughed it off, telling him I was too young and, anyway, I still preferred investigating crimes to a desk job. Though I was laughing I was certain I couldn't stay in this mire of death and deceit forever. Sometime, perhaps in the not too distant future, I'd come to welcome Dyer's suggestion.

On the way out of the building I bumped into Terry Gleeson.

'Lucky result there, Given.'

'Thanks, nice of you to say so.'

'Not bad for a Jew-boy.'

They tell me it will be some time before his nose mends.

Epilogue

Extract from *The Daily Telegraph*, 11th November 1938: Krystallnacht

An officially countenanced pogrom of unparalleled brutality and ferocity swept Germany today. Beginning in the early hours of this morning and continuing far into tonight, it puts the final seal to the outlawry of German Jewry.

Mob law ruled in Berlin throughout this afternoon and evening and hordes of hooligans indulged in an orgy of destruction. I have seen several anti-Jewish outbreaks in Germany during the last five years, but never anything as nauseating as this.

Racial hatred and hysteria seemed to have taken complete hold of otherwise decent people. I saw fashionably dressed women clapping their hands and screaming with glee, while respectable middle-class mothers held up their babies to see the "fun."

Women who remonstrated with children who were running away with toys from a wrecked Jewish shop were spat on and attacked by the mob.

The fashionable shopping centre of the capital has been reduced to a shambles, with the streets littered with the wreckage of sacked Jewish shops and offices. No attempt was made by the police to restrain the rioters.

HISTORICAL NOTES

In April 1938 a young British army officer, William McClintock, fell from his horse and fractured his neck, resulting in serious paralysis. Later he returned to his parents' home in Donegal, Ireland, and a new date in September was set for his marriage to a Devonshire girl, Helen Macworth. His mother strongly disapproved of the marriage.

The day before the wedding, William was left out in the garden writing a letter to his aunt. His mother arrived in the garden, armed, and shot him in the head. She was discovered later near a tool shed, where she'd shot herself, also in the head. His bride-to-be distraught at finding her fiancé was dead, shot herself with his rifle, dying an hour later of her injury.

A very quick inquest was held on the night of the deaths and the bodies were laid to rest on the day the wedding would have taken place. Helen was buried in her wedding dress along with her bridal bouquet and her pet dog, which was put to sleep.

You can read about the tragedy here:

http://www.stjohnstonandcarrigans.com/carriganstrag edy.html

Krystallnacht (Night of Broken Glass) was a night of violence against Jews on 9-10 November 1938. It was orchestrated by German paramilitary troops.

The Spanish Civil War was fought between 1936 and 1939. Republicans supporting the elected Government resisted a revolt by Nationalists. It is often seen as a precursor to the Second World War and both sides received support from other countries sympathetic to their cause. Tens of thousands of soldiers from outside Spain participated in the conflict, primarily on the Republican side.

Edward Frederick Lindley Wood, 1st Earl of Halifax, was styled Viscount Halifax from 1934 until 1944. He was UK Foreign Secretary between 1938 and 1940, and one of the architects of the policy of appeasement of Adolf Hitler in 1936–38, working closely with Neville Chamberlain.

Robert Dudley, 1st Earl of Leicester, was a favourite of Queen Elizabeth I with a seat at Kenilworth Castle, Warwickshire. He organised a spectacular three week festival for her visit to the castle in 1575.

Vimto is a soft drink sold in the UK, originally marketed as a health drink then later as a cordial.

A NOTE TO THE READER

Dear Reader,

If you've got this far I suspect you've actually finished the book, unless you've inadvertently landed on this page whilst searching for how the story ended. If the former, I hope you enjoyed it, if the latter then you'll perhaps come back later when you have finished.

It's odd where inspiration for characters and plots come from. Inspector James Given began life as an 18th century Coroner's clerk and only leapt forward 150 years when a plot emerged from an unlikely source. James was conceived in a creative writing group and I liked his voice so had written a few scenes, though hadn't a clue where he was going. When I took a visit to a garden in the West of Ireland and was told the true story of suicide and murder at the heart of this novel I asked: 'what if it didn't happen that way?' The ideas developed from there. More than one reader has expressed the view that the story is far-fetched, and then been shocked to learn the true facts (see the Historical Notes below).

Although I lived in Ireland at the time of writing the novel I had previously lived in Warwickshire much longer so it was more natural for me to set it there. The real deaths took place in September 1938 and this provided a historical backdrop where James Given's heritage became particularly relevant.

I love to hear from readers, so please contact me through my **Facebook page** or send me a message through **Twitter**. You can also see my latest news on **my website** and sign up for notifications.

Reviews are so important to authors, and if you enjoyed the novel I would be grateful if you could spare a few minutes to post a review on **Amazon** and/or **Goodreads**.

Thanks for reading!

Charlie Garratt

Sapere Books is an exciting new publisher of brilliant fiction and popular history.

To find out more about our latest releases and our monthly bargain books visit our website:
saperebooks.com

Made in the USA
Monee, IL
11 June 2022

97860345R00163